The Making of Us

Diane Hawley Nagatomo

Black Rose Writing | Texas

ISBN: 978-1-68513-645-1
LIBRARY OF CONGRESS CONTROL NUMBER: 2025933748
PUBLISHED BY BLACK ROSE WRITING
www.blackrosewriting.com

Printed in the United States of America
Suggested Retail Price (SRP) $21.95

The Making of Us is printed in Chaparral Pro

*As a planet-friendly publisher, Black Rose Writing does its best to eliminate unnecessary waste to reduce paper usage and energy costs, while never compromising the reading experience. As a result, the final word count vs. page count may not meet common expectations.

Praise for
The Making of Us

"Nagatomo's finest work! Perfectly paced, romantic to the core, and culturally authentic, *The Making of Us* will make you laugh, bring you to tears, and tug your heart!"
–Cam Torrens, bestselling author of the *Tyler Zahn suspense mystery series*

"Diane Nagatomo's devoted following will be eager to get their hands on the latest offering of this prolific, talented author. *The Making of Us* is another tale of the twists and turns of fate that bring both love and disaster, happiness and despair, to the characters she so ably describes and whose lives enthrall us in this page-turner."
–Lea O'Harra, author of *Sayonara, My Sweet* and *Dead Reckoning*

"Nagatomo's many fans will be delighted, as I am, with this latest offering, a warm and tender story about love in Japan that leaps over seemingly insurmountable obstacles and crosses cultures. A+"
–Suzanne Kamata, author of *Cinnamon Beach* and *River of Dolls and Other Stories*

"Diane Nagatomo has given us an emotional ride as we follow Rose in major cultural changes as well as love, loss and friendships. *The Making of Us* is one of those books you'll want to read more than once."
–LeeAnne James, award-winning author of *The Thin Blue Line Series*

"Nagatomo's story of unconventional family, friendship, and love in unexpected places has all the feels."
–Lena Gibson, award-winning author of the *Train Hoppers Trilogy* and the *Love and Survival* series*

"Nagatomo's writing is vivid and compulsive, abounding with both elation and tear-jerking episodes. The true to life characters feel as if they should be real people. I couldn't put this down."
–**Thomas Lockley, author of *African Samurai: The True Story of Yasuke, a Legendary Black Warrior in Feudal Japan* and *A Gentleman from Japan: The Untold Story of an Incredible Journey from Asia to Queen Elizabeth's Court***

"Readers like myself who call Japan home, will enjoy a nostalgic trip down memory lane in *The Making of Us*, while readers who have never set foot in Japan will equally enjoy this fascinating glimpse into a foreign world and immediately be absorbed in this heart wrenching and gripping love story."
–**John Rucynski, editor of *A Passion for Japan: A Collection of Personal Narratives***

List of Main Characters

Rose Millstone	English Teacher at FECC (Friendly English Conversation College), commonly referred to as "Friendly" by the people who work there.
Michael Weston	English Teacher at FECC and Rose's best friend
Kenny Watanabe	Office Manager at FECC
Keiko Suzuki	Rose's student at FECC.
Tomo Watanabe	Rose's student at FECC.
Kana Sato	Rose's student at FECC.
Naoko Nagai	Rose's student at FECC.
Daisuke Murayama	Rose's student at FECC.
Akira Kato	Rose's student at FECC.
Emi Kato	Akira's three-year-old daughter
Yuka Kato	Akira's five-year-old daughter
Michie Kato	Akira's mother. She is also called Baba (Granny).
Sumiko Kato	Akira's deceased wife
Saburo Kato	Akira's father, who has Alzheimer's
Fumiyo Ito	Akira's mother-in-law and Sumiko's mother. She is also called Obaachan (Grandma)
Toshiro Ito	Fumiyo's deceased husband
Osamu Ito	Fumiyo's son and Sumiko's brother
Yoko Ito	Osamu's wife
Kazumi Kitamura	Rose's friend
Chris Peters	Kazumi's boyfriend and college English teacher
Steve Dillinger	Chris's friend and college English teacher

Mrs. Hayashi	Leader of the International Culture Thinking Housewives Circle.
Professor Hayashi	Mrs. Hayashi's husband and professor at Yamanote University

For my AFWJ sisters—
especially those who were here in the 1980s

The Making of Us

Chapter One

Tokyo, January 1985

Rose Millstone burst through the door of Friendly English Conversation College, also known as FECC, breathless and flushed from her mad dash through Shinjuku Station. She shoved her timecard into the slot with seconds to spare.

"You gonna be late, you gonna get a salary cut," said Kenny, the Japanese office manager. A cigarette dangled from his lips, and his eyes were fixed on the time clock waiting for any more latecomers.

"Almost late doesn't count," Rose shot back, waving the smoke away from her face. When Kenny turned around, she stuck her tongue out at him.

"Mature, Rose. Very mature," Michael said as she tossed her bag on her desk next to his.

She removed her muffler and coat and slung them over the back of her chair. "I missed the express and had to take the local, getting me into Shinjuku at ten to five. I looked like some kind of crazy *gaijin* running through the station. And when I got here, the stupid elevator was on the eighth floor, so I had to run up the stairs. Four flights in three minutes. I sure hope my deodorant is doing its job today," she added, sniffing at her armpits. "What do you think?"

Michael gave a theatrical shudder. "Where's a gas mask when you need one?"

"Ha. Ha. Ha."

"So, how were things with your class at the Stepford Wives Club?" he asked.

"Don't call them that. Their official name is the 'International Culture Thinking Housewives Circle,'" Rose said with air quotes as she named one of the places she taught at on the sly. Strictly speaking, FECC prohibited any moonlighting, but of course, everyone did. The money Japanese people were willing to pay for private English lessons was just too good to say no to.

"But," continued Michael, "do they ever learn any English? Or international culture? Or even do any thinking, for that matter? But the real question is, did you bring me anything?" He knew all the members of that class came with a wide array of homemade sweets and never let Rose go home empty-handed.

"So, you insult my class and expect me to turn over their goodies?"

"Pretty please?"

"Well, you know the tradeoff. You go first."

Michael pulled a VHS tape from his desk. "Just what you asked for."

Rose saw the label and cracked up. "I'm not sure I specifically asked for *I Love Lucy*, but I'll take it."

"Hey, you get what you get. Whatever my mom happens to record from the TV, commercials and all."

"You're lucky," she said. "My mom would never splurge on the airmail. And besides, the commercials are the best part. They make me homesick in a really bizarre sort of way."

She set a medium-sized plastic container full of confectionary in front of Michael. He opened it, and after studying the contents, he selected a chocolate chip cookie and popped it into his mouth. Then he nodded toward the other side of the staff room. "Hey, check out the new person."

Rose glanced in that direction and saw a woman in her mid-twenties with big hair and a slinky dress sit at one of the desks, and she smoothed down her own wispy blonde hair that hadn't seen a comb since that morning. Unlike the new woman's fashionable outfit, her black slacks and comfortable red sweater looked like they'd come straight from a church's rummage sale. Her shoes (which were, if one scrutinized, black sneakers and against the FECC dress code) were what got her through a hectic day like today. No way would she be able to function in high heels like those that new person was wearing.

"Rose-sensei," Kenny called from his desk by the front door. "Come here."

She rolled her eyes at Michael and groaned. Most conversations with Kenny did not go well, even if he did respectfully call all the teachers *sensei*. "I'll be right back," she whispered.

"So," said Kenny, peering up at her from his desk. His beady eyes shifted between her and the group of Brits having a good laugh over by the vending machine. "You have new class tonight at 7:30. Six people are gonna start tonight and you're gonna be their sensei—"

"But what about my regular class?"

"Well, I'm gonna give that class to Chad-sensei. You gonna take new one."

"Oh, come on, Kenny. I *liked* that class." She knew she sounded whiny, but the thought of losing that class of smart college girls made her want to whack Kenny on the side of his head with the umbrella leaning against his desk.

"Well, Chad-sensei is gonna teach it now. It's all fixed. They wanna study with man."

"Did they tell you that?"

"I can tell that's what they want. I know these things." He waved a dismissive hand, indicating it was already a done deal.

Kenny had probably gone out drinking with Chad, who, of course, would manage to finagle the switch with flattery and a pretense of friendship. A group of six cute college girls he could flirt with was much better than an unknown class, probably filled with boring middle-aged salarymen.

"You good teacher," Kenny said, as if he was offering her a compliment. "So you gonna get new students. They want American woman. So that's gonna be you."

"What about that new teacher?" Rose didn't feel guilty in the least for suggesting that.

"Oh, she gonna teach private lesson tonight. Important private lesson."

Realization hit. "Are you telling me you're giving her Creepy Kaneda?"

"Mr. Kaneda is very important student."

"I don't care what he is. He's gross!"

Rumor had it that Creepy Kaneda's family sold their tofu shop on Shinjuku Avenue to a developer for millions and millions of dollars. And one way he liked to spend some of that money was to take private English lessons with foreign women. FECC wouldn't kick him out, no matter how many complaints there'd been about him. Just last month, a teacher quit on her very first day because the creep had reportedly licked his lips, leaned across the table, and whispered into her ear that he wanted to drink her breast milk. Apparently, the poor woman headed straight back to Utah before she'd even unpacked her suitcase.

Rose returned to her desk in a huff and stashed the flash cards she'd made for her lost class in a drawer. Let Chad come up with his own materials, although she was pretty sure he'd just "wing it" like he did all his other classes. She turned to complain to Michael about that sneaky switcheroo when her attention shifted back to Kenny's desk.

"Welcome to Friendly English Conversation College," Kenny was saying to another new teacher. "You American? Sure you are. So tall. Nice blond hair, too."

Michael and Rose exchanged glances. Oh, this was going to be good.

"Actually, I'm from the UK," the man corrected, ice in his voice. "I'm Kenny Hollingsworth."

"That's great. Nice to meet you. Anyway, I was wondering if you could pick different name. I'm already using Kenny. My name's Kenji, but in America, everyone calls me Kenny. Get it? So, you pick different name, okay? You use middle name or something else, right?"

"You want me to pick a different name because you're already using it?"

Every single person in the staffroom was watching the show now.

"That's right. Okay, good. So that's settled then."

Before Kenny could scuttle off to annoy more people, the new guy pulled himself up to his full height. His quiet voice resonated throughout the room. "Actually, *Kenny*, I don't care if you're already using the name. Kenny's my *real* name and not a made up one. So, no. I'm not changing my name to suit you."

"But, but—"

"I'm sure you know, *Kenny*," he said, exaggerating the name, "it's not all that unusual for two people to have the same name. It happens all the time. So it's fine with *me* if you want to keep on using Kenny. But I'll certainly understand if *you* want to change yours to something else, seeing how you're the one who feels uncomfortable with two Kennys in the office." Then he slapped the Japanese Kenny on the shoulder and headed toward an empty desk.

The teachers stifled their snickers. Everyone knew, from that moment on, those two would forever be referred to as Big Kenny and Little Kenny. And the best part was Little Kenny would definitely hate it.

It's the little triumphs, Rose thought as she trudged off to her first class of the evening that made this job tolerable.

Chapter Two

Rose's first class that night was with a mother and her two elementary school children who would soon follow their father to New Jersey, where he'd been transferred by his company. She figured the kids would assimilate right away, but the mom would probably stick like glue to the other Japanese moms in the community. So she focused on vocabulary that might come in handy for dealing with teachers at the elementary school and while shopping.

Afterwards was an hour with a guy who only wanted Rose to correct the business letters he was planning to send to his company's overseas branch. He wasn't interested in practicing his spoken English—he just didn't want to look foolish at work. So they generally spent that hour in silence while Rose revised the documents that he'd get full credit for writing.

Before her new class started at 7:30, she stopped in the bathroom. She knew she shouldn't compare herself to that new teacher who looked like she'd assembled her outfit from a fashion magazine with her perfect clothes, perfect hair, and perfect makeup. But it was kind of hard not to. She studied her reflection in the mirror while washing her hands, and even though she'd never be mistaken for a fashion model, she thought she didn't look all that bad. Her hair wasn't fashionably styled—just a simple shoulder-length bob that could be put up in a ponytail on busy days. But at least it was healthy and shiny.

She generally didn't wear much makeup—just mascara to frame her blue eyes and blush to give life to her pale cheeks. And whenever she remembered, lipstick. She smeared on a fresh coat from a tube she had in her pocket, smiled into the mirror to make sure she didn't get any on her teeth, and hurried to her classroom.

It was always stressful starting a new group because what if the people didn't like her? What if they wouldn't talk? What if they expected her to entertain them for the entire ninety minutes? All Kenny—correction *Little Kenny*—had told her about this new group of students was that it was a seven-month course for advanced learners. But knowing Kenny's usual approach, it could be a group of random people who had stumbled through FECC's doors on the same day. He probably saw it as a good way to use that empty room at the end of the hall.

Pushing open the door, Rose let her eyes roam around the room before she greeted the five people seated around the horseshoe-shaped table. "Before we begin," she said with an enormous fake smile, "I want you to know that we'll be very friendly in this class, like the name of this school suggests. We'll call each other by our first names. That's how we do it in America."

That was a lie, of course. Rose had never called a teacher by their first name in her life. Even her second graders back home called her Ms. Millstone. But it was FECC's policy that teachers and students use first names with each other. A large part of Rose's job was to perpetuate cultural myths surrounding America and English.

"So," she continued, "my name's Roselyn Millstone, but most people call me Rose. And I'd like you to do that, too. Now, who would like to introduce themselves? Tell us your name and a little about what you do."

Rose scanned their faces and wondered who'd take the plunge. The tanned woman with false eyelashes and long, red fingernails tugging at the hem of her black miniskirt? The young balding guy that woman was leaning toward? The perspiring man fidgeting with a stack of dictionaries in front of him? She guessed it'd be a toss between the nice-looking guy in a dark gray suit or the middle-aged woman who was calmly gazing at Rose.

The middle-aged woman took a deep breath. In soft but fairly fluent English, she said, "I'm Keiko Suzuki. I'm a housewife, but I want to get a job using English because my son is growing up. I haven't worked since marriage, so I'm here to brush up on my skills. I studied economics in college, and I'm interested in business."

"Thank you." It'd taken a while for Rose to get used to hearing Japanese women refer to themselves as housewives. It seemed so 1950s. Like a mom in an old television series. "I'm really glad you're here." Rose gestured toward the man in the gray suit sitting next to her. "And how about you?"

"My name's Akira Kato. I work for Tominaga Corporation." He sounded like he'd spent quite some time in the United States. "It's about ten minutes from here. I have two daughters. And...well... that's all."

Rose's eyes turned to the young balding guy who had scooted his chair a little away from Ms. Make-up. "What about you?"

"My name is Tomohiro Watanabe. I work for the Ministry of Finance. I need English for my job. I will someday have to deal with foreigners."

"Oh, how nice," Rose lied. Somehow, the guy made *foreigners* sound like they were a pesky problem that just wouldn't go away.

Ms. Make-up was nodding as he spoke. "And what about you?" Rose asked.

The woman seemed about as surprised as if Rose had told her to go change a flat tire. She giggled and said in heavily accented English, "I pleased to meet you. I study with fiancé, Tomo-chan."

Tomo-chan, the fiancé, now had his nose buried in his daily planner.

"Yes, but what's *your* name?"

She giggled again. "I Kana Sato."

"What do you do, Kana?"

She glanced over at Tomo, who still wasn't paying attention to her. "I'm fine, thank you."

"No. What do you do for a living? What's your job?"

"Job?"

"Yes, job."

"I work tanning salon."

"Well, that's interesting," Rose said.

"Yes. It important be beautiful," Kana said with increasing confidence.

What Rose really meant was that it was interesting to see a tanning salon girl engaged to someone from the Ministry of Finance. Especially one like this guy, who seemed rather huffed up with self-importance.

Rose smiled at the last person to go. "What about you? Can you introduce yourself?"

He mopped the sweat off his forehead with his handkerchief. "I'm uh, uh…" He cleared his throat and began again. "I'm Daisuke Murayama, and uh…"

Rose silently rooted for him. "What do you do Daisuke?"

"I'm uh…" He took a deep breath. "I'm an English teacher."

"You're an English teacher?" Rose hoped her question conveyed curiosity and not disbelief.

Daisuke's face was now purple. "I teach at Kamamomo Junior High School. I love English. But I get so nervous when I have to speak it. I want to be a good teacher, so I came here to get confidence." His relief at getting all that out morphed into a tentative smile, and everyone smiled back at him.

"Well, your pronunciation is certainly very good. I'm sure you're a wonderful teacher." Rose believed her words because he did seem gentle and sincere. He reminded her of that Kimpachi-sensei on TV, who could always solve his students' problems.

A pretty woman in a tailored navy pantsuit pushed open the door and hurried to the empty seat on the other side of Tomo-chan. That didn't seem to sit very well with Kana, who inched a little closer toward her fiancé.

"I'm so sorry to be late," the woman said, quite out of breath. She shrugged off her black wool coat and laid it across her lap.

"Hello and welcome," said Rose. "Everyone has just finished introducing themselves. Can you do that, or do you need a few minutes to catch your breath?"

"Oh no. I'm fine. My name is Naoko Nagai." She smiled at her new classmates and spoke in flawless English with a slight British accent. "I work for a securities company, and I'm hoping for an international transfer some day."

"Welcome." Rose was thinking this was definitely not your average tea-making, photocopying kind of office lady—OLs, as they were called.

She cast her eyes around the room and smiled. "Before we go any further, do you have any questions you'd like to ask me?"

"Where do you come from?" asked Daisuke, who sounded a bit more confident now.

"I'm from Felix, Nebraska, a small town with a little more than seven hundred people. I've been on trains here in Tokyo that had more people than that in one car."

Everyone laughed at that tried-and-true joke.

"Do you have a middle name?" asked Keiko.

"As a matter-of-fact, I do. It's Marie. I'm named after both my grandmothers. One was Roselyn and the other was Marie."

"Roselyn Marie," said Akira. "That's a beautiful name."

Rose looked over at him and was taken aback by the intense way he was studying her. "Thanks," she said, surprised but pleased at the compliment.

The class continued like this—asking each other and answering a variety of questions. Rose watched how everyone was interacting, and her gut told her that this was going to be a good class. Maybe Chad

had done her a favor after all when he snatched her class of college students away from her.

After deciding the next week's discussion topic was going to be everyone's favorite movies, Rose hurried them all out the door at 9:00. It was Friday night, after all, and the weekend was just starting.

Chapter Three

Rose and Michael headed straight to a popular *izakaya* not too far from their school right after they clocked out of Friendly. It looked like they might have to go elsewhere because the place was crowded with revelers who also seemed to be eager to celebrate Friday. Luckily, a group of tipsy college students was calling it quits, and a table opened up. Michael ordered two beers from a rather frazzled server before they even got their coats off. The server came back a couple of minutes later with their beers, an appetizer plate of edamame, and hot *oshibori* towels for them to wipe their hands with. They ordered a few dishes, and the server hurried over to a different group that was frantically trying to get his attention by waving empty beer pitchers in the air.

"How do you think that new teacher did with Creepy Kaneda?" Michael asked as they clinked their glasses to toast another week behind them.

"You won't believe it," Rose said, "but I saw her giving him a piece of her mind, wagging her finger like a scolding mother, and ordering him not to forget the textbook next time. His head was bobbing up and down like one of those little bobble-head dogs they have in the back of cars."

"Seriously?" he said, cracking up. "What do you think she did to tame that beast?"

"I have no idea," she said, squeezing some of the edamame beans out of a pod and into her mouth, "but I'm dying to find out."

A couple of women in their twenties sitting a few tables away were staring at them, and Rose sighed. That wasn't really all that unusual, because people always stared at her in Japan. But when she was with Michael, it was a different kind of stare. It wasn't just the "oh-my-god-there's-a-*gaijin*" kind of stare, but more of a "who is-*that*-guy?" kind of stare. She imagined the two women watching them were trying to place where they'd seen Michael before. Because, with his good looks, he did look like someone who should be in the movies. He had perfect white teeth that he flashed at everyone and was always impeccably dressed. Sometimes people even asked for his autograph, and being the nice guy that he was, he always complied. Once, when he and Rose were in Harajuku, a so-called fan approached and asked him to hold her baby for a picture. He agreed and held the baby, who was screaming at the top of its lungs after being handed over to a total stranger. Later, they nearly died laughing at the absurdity of it all.

The server came back with a platter of assorted yakitori sticks, and Michael asked for two more beers. "What?" he asked innocently in response to Rose's raised eyebrows. "Teaching's thirsty work."

"Cheers to that," she agreed, taking a hefty swig of her own beer.

"So," Michael asked, "have you decided?"

"About what?" Rose picked up the grilled chicken and leek yakitori stick, sprinkled it with *shichimi,* and bit into it.

"About renewing your teaching contract."

"Oh, that. I'm definitely not."

Michael rolled his eyes. "You said that last year."

"Yeah, but this time I mean it. I only planned on staying in Japan for a year. Now it's coming up on three. I don't know how much longer I can take."

"Japan's not the problem. It's the job. It's FECC."

Most of the teachers who worked at Friendly English Conversation College referred to the place as the "Feces School" or often, something even worse. Rose and Michael decided early on they'd try not to do that because who'd want to admit to working in such a place? They tried to stick with the official name or with the unofficially approved name of "Friendly." For the most part, they were successful, but sometimes it *was* hard. Because at times, the management polices really were full of... feces.

"I know," Rose agreed, "but—"

"You can get a better job anytime. You already have your MA. I have two semesters to go, but as soon as I finish, I'm getting out of there."

"Yeah, but my visa's connected to Friendly and—"

"Forget the visa. You could get someone else to sponsor you. And don't give me that nonsense that your graduate degree is in child development and not language teaching. Blah blah blah. I know of someone who got an MA in pumpkin research, and now he's a professor at some college out in Chiba. Teaching English, of course, but still." Michael gulped down the last three inches of his beer before handing the mug to the server who had just delivered their second round. "You're afraid of change. You've got to move out of your comfort zone."

"Hey, I got myself all the way over here, didn't I? How much more out of my comfort zone could I possibly get?" Rose was only halfway through her first beer, but the second one was keeping it company.

"Nebraska country girl goes all the way to Tokyo," Michael air quoted as if he was reading a news headline. "Granted, you only got this far because that scumbag dumped you at the altar."

"It wasn't at the altar. It was five days before the wedding."

"Details, details." Michael gestured toward the red-faced salarymen at the table next to theirs. "The point is, you'd be missing all this if that hadn't happened."

Rose snickered and waved away some of the cigarette smoke wafting over from that table. "Lucky me."

"Tell me honestly, Rose. Don't you wake up every single day thankful you dodged a bullet by not marrying that two-timing jerk?"

"I suppose. And thankful for being in the right place at the right time." Rose had hauled herself to the job placement office at the University of Nebraska on what was supposed to have been her wedding day to see if there was an opening for a grade school teacher *anywhere* but Felix. Even her second graders would've heard all about Rose Millstone getting jilted by Brad Billford. She couldn't stand knowing the entire town was gossiping about every aspect of her humiliation and wanted to get as far away as possible. As it happened, an agency was at the university that day, recruiting for English schools in Japan. She filled out an application on a whim, thinking you couldn't get any further away from Felix than Japan. When they learned that she'd just finished her master's degree, they hired her on the spot.

"You're right," she said to Michael. "I *am* glad I'm here. But I don't want to become one of those losers who've stayed so long they can't ever go home. How depressing would that be?"

"Not as depressing as going back and watching Reagan screw things up for another four years."

Rose rolled her eyes, thinking Michael was about to get going on politics again. But for once, he didn't. Thank goodness because she tended to disagree with him on that half the time.

"And what about all that Japanese you've been studying?" he asked. "What are you going to do with *that* in Nebraska?"

"I don't know, but I don't want to go back and say I lived in Japan for years and can't speak a word of the language. But," she said, dipping a piece of tuna sashimi into the soy sauce, "you know, the real reason why I need to get out of here and go home is I want to find someone and settle down. I want to have a family before it's too late."

"It's the 1980s, not the 1950s. What's the rush? You should just have fun now."

"I am. Look at me here tonight."

"I mean with a guy."

"You're a guy."

"I don't count. Not in *your* grand scheme of things, anyway."

"Most of the foreign men I know are only into Japanese girls."

"So what about a Japanese guy? You always say you don't have enough opportunity to speak Japanese. Sex and a language exchange. You could scratch two itches at once."

Rose snorted out a laugh. "I'll just go ahead and ignore that sage piece of advice, thank you."

They finished eating, divided the bill, and stepped out into the cold winter night. "Want to go to 69?" Michael asked, winding his muffler a little more securely around his neck, "and see what's happening over there?"

"I'm too tired tonight, but I'll walk that way with you."

They headed toward West Shinjuku by going under the train tracks and past small cubby-hole drinking establishments that looked like they'd been there since the war ended. They came out on Shinjuku Avenue, where all the buildings were lit with colorful neon signs and wove through the crowd milling about under the Studio Alta TV screen. Once they passed Isetan Department Store, things became a little quieter.

"Sure you don't want to come in for a bit? Listen to some music?"

"Oh, all right. Just one drink, though." Two years ago, Rose had never even heard of reggae music. Now she was a huge Bob Marley fan, and 69 was one of her favorite hangouts.

"Maybe you'll meet Mr. Right tonight," Michael said.

"Maybe it's *your* night to meet Mr. Right," Rose replied.

"One could dream," Michael said with an exaggerated, wistful sigh, making Rose laugh.

The thrum of the music could be heard from the street. They went down the steps, pushed open the door, and found the place packed with *gaijin* and Japanese, both straight and gay. They ordered bottles of Corona from Keisuke, the owner and DJ, and leaned against the wall, scanning the crowd. Rose recognized a few familiar faces but no one she wanted to talk to. Michael spotted some of his friends, so they went over to their table. The cigarette smoke was giving Rose a headache, and after "Buffalo Soldier" finished playing, she slid her half-drunk beer across the table to Michael. "I think I'll call it a night."

It was a relief to be back outside, even though the air was icy and snowflakes were drifting down from the sky. Few pedestrians were going in her direction, but Shinjuku Avenue was packed with taxis, ferrying people about now that the trains had stopped operating for the night. Ten minutes later, Rose turned into her quiet residential area of Daikyo-cho.

She wondered if Michael would ever meet the man of his dreams in the bars of the Ni-chome neighborhood. They'd become such good friends over the past couple of years, and she couldn't imagine life in Japan without him. He was one of the few teachers at Friendly who didn't ridicule her when she confessed that her first time on an airplane was when she got herself over to Tokyo. Or that she'd never eaten Japanese food before. He didn't make her feel like a country bumpkin, which she clearly was, compared to those who'd come to Japan via an adventure-packed overland trip through Asia or who'd spent their junior year abroad in some other exotic locale. Rose's desk was next to his in the teacher's room, and they helped each other get used to a job they had no prior experience doing or no knowledge about. Rose had taught in an elementary school before coming to Japan, and Michael had worked as a waiter at Sambo's Pancake House while majoring in marketing at college. Neither were prepared for *eikaiwa* teaching, and they were way out of their league. But they somehow muddled through those first weeks together. About two months into their contract, Michael noticed something was bothering Rose and suggested dinner after work.

"What's wrong?" he asked after they placed their order.

"I'm in trouble," she said, deciding to be honest. "You know, the old-fashioned kind of trouble? I'm such an idiot," she choked out when she saw Michael's face register understanding. A teardrop slid from her eye, and he handed her a paper napkin from the table. She wiped it away and continued, "Remember that Australian guy, Malcolm?"

"The guy who had that big going-away party a few weeks after we got here? The one where everyone got totally smashed?"

"And the one where I stupidly ended up going home with him."

"Oh crap."

"Oh crap is right. And now, he's somewhere in India meditating on a mountain top, and here I am, stuck in Japan, with a bun in the oven."

"It's not the end of the world," Michael said quietly, but Rose thought it pretty much was.

They stayed in the restaurant, with Michael handing her one tissue after another to dry her eyes, until it was too late for him to get a train back to his apartment. They found a little park in Shinjuku, sat on a bench, and discussed Rose's options until the sun came up. By then, Rose knew what she had to do. She called the Tokyo English Lifeline that morning, and they gave her the name of a clinic in Roppongi that had a female English-speaking doctor. Michael went with her for the preliminary examination and again for the procedure. Afterward, he took care of her in her little apartment while she cried buckets of guilty tears. But what cemented their friendship forever was when he put his name on the documents as the baby's father. Unless Rose could track Malcolm down and get permission to terminate the pregnancy, she would have had to list the father as *unknown*. Everything was terrible enough as it was.

Those were the worst days of her life—far worse than the day her fiancé had informed her he had gotten another woman pregnant. Having that abortion was the hardest thing she ever had to do, and the guilt just wouldn't go away. She reminded herself as she unlocked the door to her apartment and stepped in, that it had been the right thing to do. The *only* thing to do.

And yet, she still couldn't overcome her grief.

Chapter Four

Akira Kato hurried home as soon as his English class finished, wanting to get back before his daughters went to sleep. Screaming with delight at having their father home, Yuka and Emi demanded he join them in the bath. Like families all over Japan do together as a nightly ritual, they stripped down in a little cold washroom. With a small towel covering his private parts, they stepped into the bathroom where the bathtub was filled with steaming hot water. Sitting on little wooden stools in front of the tub, they shampooed their hair, scrubbed themselves from head to toe with scratchy washcloths, and doused themselves with buckets of water from the bath. When all three were squeaky clean, they climbed into the large tub, and with the water up to their chins, the girls chattered about their day. What they did at daycare. Who they played with. Visiting his parents, Baba and Jiji, that afternoon while Obaachan, their other grandmother, went to her poetry-writing class.

"We helped Baba make a cake," said three-year-old Emi. "And then we helped Jiji eat it!"

"What kind of cake was it?" Akira asked with a smile.

"Chocolate!" said five-year-old Yuka. "It was yummy, but Jiji kept spitting it out. Today," she added in a voice that sounded very much like his mother's, "was a bad day. He made a bigger mess than a baby."

"Well, he can't help that."

Yuka nodded in agreement. "That's what Baba said, but he's a lot bigger than a baby. And sometimes he smells bad, too. Today he was stinky twice."

Akira sighed. He needed to have another talk with his mother. This was getting to be too much for her to handle.

"Papa," said Yuka. "Did you go to school today? Obaachan said you were going to learn English."

"What's English?" asked Emi.

"That's what the foreigners speak, silly."

"Don't call your sister silly. And that's not what *all* foreigners speak—there are other languages as well."

"Say something in English," Yuka demanded.

"Like what?"

Yuka listed words in Japanese: doll, crocodile, chocolate, TV, cat, tomato, pumpkin. The girls repeated their father's English and rolled the strange sounds around on their tongues, giggling as if English was the funniest thing in the world.

"Can we learn English, too?" Yuka asked.

Akira chuckled. "Why not?"

After the girls brushed their teeth, they went upstairs and nestled in the bottom bunk in their room while he read *Everyone Poops*, the book all the kids in daycare were crazy about. When he thought they'd fallen asleep, he eased out of the bed and turned off the light.

Yuka's whisper broke the silence as he was tiptoeing out of their room. "Papa, why did Mama have to die?"

Akira's heart twisted a little, and he went back and sat on the edge of their bed. "Mama got very sick. And she just couldn't get better."

"I don't remember her anymore. I try and try and try, but I just can't. When I think of her, all I can see is one of her pictures."

"You were only three." Akira rubbed his forehead, and his voice was quiet and full of sadness when he said, "Of course you wouldn't be able to remember her clearly."

"My friend Ayumi told me that if you can't remember a person, you don't love them anymore."

"What! That's not true. You can still love your mother, even if you don't remember her. She'll always be a part of you. She'll always watch over you."

"Does she watch us all the time?" asked Emi, who had only been one when her mother passed away.

"Yeah, I'm pretty sure she does."

"Will she watch me sing at the winter festival?"

"Yeah, I'm sure she'll be cheering you on."

"Does she watch me when I poop?"

"Um…"

"Does she watch *you*?" Yuka interrupted.

"I suppose she does."

"Is that why you don't get a girlfriend and you don't get married? Because Mama's watching you all the time?"

Akira hadn't seen that question coming.

"Because," Yuka continued, "Ayumi told me you have to go on a date and then you have to get married and then you kiss and then you make a baby."

"I want a baby," Emi chimed in.

"Don't be silly," said Yuka. "We can't have one if Papa's not married."

"Oh. How come Papa isn't married?"

"Because Mama's watching him. If he gets a girlfriend, Mama's ghost will be angry and scare him. That's what Ayumi says."

"Huh?" said Akira, thoroughly confused.

"So, are you going to marry a picture-lady?" Yuka asked.

"A what?" Akira had no idea what she was talking about.

"You know, one of the ladies in the pictures. I saw Baba looking at them, and she said one of them could become your wife."

Akira was stunned into silence, knowing they were referring to the *omiai* portraits of marriageable women his mother sometimes dragged out for him to look at. The last thing he wanted, he kept telling her, was an arranged marriage.

"Anyway," Yuka continued, "Ayumi said that if you marry a picture lady, she'll be our new mama. And then Emi and I'll have to clean the house all day long. And we'll have mean and ugly sisters who will take our toys and sleep in our beds. She said we'd have to sleep in the *genkan*—"

"Papa," whined Emi. "I don't want an ugly girl to take my toys and sleep in my bed."

"Girls, don't listen to Ayumi. She's telling you the Cinderella story. You know, that's just a fairy tale. It's not real."

"You're not gonna marry a picture-lady?"

"I'm not going to marry a picture-lady."

"We're not getting a new mama?" Emi somehow seemed disappointed.

It was a lot easier answering their earlier questions about where poop goes after the toilet flushes.

"Do you want a new mama?" he asked.

Emi was silent for a moment. "I don't want a mean one who'll take away my toys."

Akira smiled. "Don't worry. That'd never happen."

"But how are you going to get us a new mama if you don't marry a picture lady?" Yuka asked.

"Don't you think things are fine the way they are?"

"But Ayumi said that Papas always need Mamas to help out and—"

"Well, Obaachan always helps us out, doesn't she?"

"But what about the kissing and making a baby and—"

Akira jumped in. "For now, everything is just fine. No new mama. And especially not a picture-lady new mama."

Akira slipped out of the room after the girls began snoring softly and headed downstairs. He needed to talk to his mother and warn her to watch what she said in front of the girls. He was also going to have to find out who that little troublemaker Ayumi was.

"Have you eaten?" His mother-in-law was at the kitchen sink washing the dinner dishes when he came in.

"I had something around six," Akira replied, settling down under the quilt at the low *kotatsu* table and warming his legs. The kerosene heater in the corner was glowing and steam from the teakettle set on top of it was wafting into the air. "But I wouldn't mind some *ochazuke* if there's any rice left."

She opened the rice cooker, scooped some into a little blue ceramic bowl, sprinkled a flavored packet of seasoning on top, added a pickled plum, and poured hot water over it. She handed it to Akira and sat down across from him.

"*Itadakimasu*," he said, bowing his head slightly in a gesture of thanks. He ate it in comfortable silence while they watched a variety program on TV where comedians competed, doing silly and seemingly dangerous challenges. When he finished, he carried the bowl to the sink and washed it.

"Do you want tea?"

"No, thanks. I think I'll just go upstairs and read."

And as he did nearly every night, he left Obaachan downstairs so she could enjoy her television programs in peace.

Akira's study was across the hall from his daughters' room and next to his bedroom. It was only the size of four and a half tatami mats, so there wasn't space for much else other than a bookcase, a desk, and an easy chair. It didn't take long for the small electric heater to warm up the room. While he didn't make a regular habit of it anymore, he decided to have a nightcap. He poured an inch of whiskey into the crystal glass he kept in his desk drawer and had it neat. One shot went down smoothly, and he poured himself another. Like he did whenever he drank on his own, he found himself staring at the bookcase. The bottom shelf, to be precise. The shelf that held the photo albums documenting the five years he'd had with Sumiko.

In the weeks and months after she died, he saw her face every time he closed his eyes. Sometimes he could even hear her voice. But what Yuka said earlier really hit home because the only images he could conjure up of Sumiko now were those from the photo albums. The time they dated. Their wedding. When Yuka was born. And then Emi.

Their entire life together was contained in just four albums.

He remembered why he stopped drinking alone and why he shouldn't have had that second shot. Alcohol always brought out the regrets.

If he had known that the morning of October 15, 1982 would be the last time he'd have a normal conversation with his wife, he would've paid a lot more attention. But no, he was too busy thinking about a meeting that day with clients from the Kansai area and the company report that was overdue. He barely listened when Sumiko said she was planning to go to the hospital to have her breast infection checked out. He didn't think it was such a big deal, so instead of showing concern, he'd gotten angry when Yuka spilled her milk on him. He remembered yelling at her before stomping upstairs to change his trousers. By the time he went back downstairs, he felt bad for having lost his temper, but he didn't apologize. He was just too stressed out from work. Too stressed out by the kids.

Excuses, excuses.

But at least he hadn't forgotten that day was Sumiko's birthday. At least there was that. As he was leaving the house, he promised to take her out on the weekend. They'd go to Isetan Department Store so she could pick out a new muffler or hat for the winter, and then they'd have dinner at that tempura place they both liked.

He was five minutes into his presentation for the clients when one of the office ladies slipped in and whispered in his ear that there was a telephone call from his wife. And no, the woman insisted, he could not call her back later. It was *urgent*. He handed his notes to his section chief and bowed an apology. He'd be in for it later, no doubt about it.

"Why are you calling me at work?" Akira demanded. "Don't you know how busy I am?"

"Come to the hospital right now." Sumiko's voice was full of fear. "The doctors say it's an emergency and they won't let me leave. I can't reach your mother and the girls need to be picked up."

Akira scribbled a memo for the office lady to deliver to the section chief, explaining why he wouldn't be returning to the meeting. He hurried out of the building, flagged a taxi, and rushed to Keio Hospital. He found his daughters at the nurse's station and took them to his parents' house, just a block away.

When he returned to the hospital, the doctor, a young balding man in his mid-thirties, explained that a nurse in the OBGYN department had been alarmed by what she'd seen and called him for further consultation. He decided to admit Sumiko to the hospital after a preliminary examination.

"Of course the results aren't in," he said, "but it looks like Triple Negative Breast Cancer. It's very unusual in a woman her age."

"Is she going to be all right? Will she need to have a…" Akira couldn't think straight and couldn't remember the word for mastectomy.

The doctor shook his head. "I'm sorry, but TNBC is the most aggressive form of breast cancer. My fear is the tests will show that the cancer has spread elsewhere in her body."

"Why wasn't it caught earlier? During her pregnancy?"

The doctor shook his head and lit a Seven Stars cigarette. After inhaling deeply, he tossed the match into an ashtray perched on a stack of files. "Sometimes these things happen. Now I've told your wife that it's just a severe breast infection."

Akira nodded. When his grandfather had cancer, he wasn't told either. He barely heard the doctor's words as he explained that Sumiko's treatment would be tough, painful, and probably unsuccessful. But he agreed to everything and signed all the papers.

That evening, Akira slumped over his parents' kitchen table as his mother told him his daughters, who'd never been separated from their mother before, both cried themselves to sleep.

"Call Fumiyo," she said, sterilizing the baby bottles she had to run to the store to get for Emi. "Sumiko's mother needs to know. And maybe she could help."

Akira's head moved up and down in a nod. His brain had pretty much stopped working after having that consultation with the doctor, but he did know he wouldn't be able to rely on his mother for much. Not since his father had been diagnosed with Alzheimer's.

Sumiko died a few weeks later. It happened so quickly that most people thought she'd been killed in a car accident. It seemed that one week she was perfectly fine, and the next she was gone. Gone!

The funeral was a blur, but he somehow got through it all. Sumiko's mother stayed on afterward because there was no way he could've handled a baby and a toddler on his own. And even though his daughters were bigger now, he still wouldn't be able to manage without her. Obaachan was, and still is, an important and permanent part of their lives.

He finished his whiskey, washed and dried the cup in the upstairs bathroom, and put it back in the drawer next to the bottle. Two was his limit. From the other room, he heard Emi muttering something in her sleep, and his heart twisted with love for his daughters. When Sumiko died, it felt like the world had ended. But he still had those girls, and they were everything to him.

Chapter Five

Fumiyo made her way to Akira's mother's house after dropping their granddaughters, Yuka and Emi, off at the day care center near Shinanomachi Station. Since she lived just a block away, she made a point of visiting Michie as often as she could. Today, the dark circles under Michie's eyes spoke volumes, and Fumiyo wondered how much longer she'd be able to handle her husband on her own.

"Bad night?" Fumiyo asked as she sat down at her usual spot at the kitchen table. After two years, she was as comfortable in this kitchen as she was in Akira's, and she didn't bother to take off her apron, which today was geometrically patterned with bursts of purple, pink, and black.

Michie sighed and nodded. "Around midnight, I thought Saburo was asleep, so I decided to take a bath. But then I heard the front door open."

"Oh, no!"

"Thank goodness Akira had that bell installed, or I'd have never known he'd left the house. I threw something on and caught up with him in the park at the end of the road."

"At least he didn't get all the way to the main street this time."

"Yeah, but I lost my temper and yelled at him. And can you believe it? A young couple came over and asked *him* if he needed any help with *me*! Somehow he'd gotten dressed—properly, mind you. And I,"

Michie said with a mirthless laugh, "looked like a complete lunatic with wet hair and a jacket over my pajamas!"

Fumiyo glanced over at Saburo, who was watching a video recording of *Oshin*—NHK's wildly popular morning drama. From the way he stared at the screen, she couldn't tell if any of it was making its way into the poor man's head or not. But that drama did seem to be one of his favorites, and he could sit still and watch it for hours.

Michie reached for a tangerine in the dark red lacquered bowl in the middle of the table, peeled it, and handed it to Saburo. As he ate the tangerine, she tenderly adjusted the blanket covering his knees, and Fumiyo wondered if she'd be doing the same if it was her husband who had become debilitated like this. Probably. Duty was duty, after all. But because of the heart attack that killed him nearly twenty years earlier, she was never put to the test. Fumiyo helped herself to one of the tangerines, thinking that dying was the only considerate thing Toshiro had ever done for her in his life.

Fumiyo refilled their teacups, frowning at the blue veins that had recently become prominent on her hands. They looked like they belonged to someone else—a much, much older person.

"Thanks," Michie said, sinking back into her chair and cradling the warm teacup in her hands. "I don't know what I'd do if you didn't come by every day. I'd never see anyone except the visiting nurses."

They both turned their eyes toward the long-suffering Oshin on the television and sipped their tea in silence. Seven years ago, Fumiyo had been so worried about meeting her daughter's fiancé's family. After all, she was just a country housewife from Kyushu, but the Katos were sophisticated people. Akira's father had held an impressive position in the Ministry of Foreign Affairs. He spoke English fluently and could get by in German. Fumiyo had also seen him on NHK as a regular guest commentator on news shows because of some influential book he'd written in the 1960s.

Akira's mother was also a housewife, but compared to Fumiyo, she was so accomplished. A college graduate, she could speak English and French. When Fumiyo met her for the first time, she felt she looked ten years older, even though they were actually the same age. She never should've let that snooty sales clerk at the Fukuoka Mitsukoshi Department Store bully her into buying such an outrageously expensive and dowdy suit.

But Michie and Saburo had never been anything but gracious and kind to her. And to each other, as well. At the first dinner they all had together in some fancy Ginza restaurant, Michie had come right out and contradicted Saburo over some small thing. Fumiyo waited for an explosion, but Saburo simply guffawed and admitted he was wrong. That would've never happened in her house. Not the contradiction and certainly not the ensuing laughter. Fumiyo's husband rarely talked to her about anything—not even routine household matters.

There was no denying the fact Toshiro was much better as a dead husband than a living one. That he had left her financially secure wasn't because of any great concern for her welfare—he just hadn't planned on keeling over in the middle of a lecture on the reproduction of frogs and dying in front of 100 first year biology students several days after he'd moved all of his assets into her name.

But that's exactly what had happened.

She was just as stunned as Toshiro's two brothers, who had insisted on accompanying her to the lawyer's office after the funeral, pretending to support her in her time of grief. When the lawyer informed them the ownership of the patents Toshiro Ito had gotten early in his career now belonged to his wife, they were speechless. And not only the patents but also his other assets as well, which included several pieces of property and the contents of bank accounts she had no idea existed. In addition, his will named her the sole beneficiary and the lawyer as the executor. After the brothers stormed out of the office, Mr. Kanno leaned back in his chair and explained the situation to Fumiyo. Apparently, her husband was about to be sued by his most current mistress, and he wanted to move everything out of her reach. The lawyer didn't go into too much detail, but he assured Fumiyo the mistress had good reason to sue. He also assured her she had no reason to worry because everything had been done legally, fair and square. The will was airtight, and neither the mistress nor the brothers could get their hands on a single yen of Fumiyo's new fortune.

Right then and there, she asked the lawyer to draw up her own airtight will, making her children her heirs. She figured Toshiro wouldn't have hired anyone but the best, so she stuck with this guy. After Sumiko died, she had Mr. Kanno make another will, dividing Sumiko's share between her granddaughters. She hated to admit it, but she didn't trust her son to do the right thing any more than she did her husband's brothers.

"When the homecare people come by later today to help with Saburo's bath," Michie announced, bringing Fumiyo back to the here and now of this cozy kitchen, "I'm going to ask them to help me find a place for him."

"Maybe that's a good idea," Fumiyo replied.

"But I don't have to rush into anything, right?"

"It wouldn't hurt to start looking into it." Considering how fast Saburo was deteriorating, Fumiyo was thinking the sooner the better.

"By the way," said Michie. "I had a chance to meet Watanabe-san's granddaughter."

Fumiyo arranged an interested expression on her face and ignored the discomfort gathering in her gut. "And?"

"She didn't look a thing like her picture. And can you believe she admitted she didn't know a thing about children?"

"Okay. So she's probably out then," confirmed Fumiyo, hiding her relief.

"Especially after she came right out and admitted she didn't particularly like them."

"Definitely out," Fumiyo said firmly.

"If Akira can find anyone half as good as Sumiko," Michie said, like she always did whenever they discussed Akira's marital future, "he'd be lucky."

Fumiyo remembered the day when her daughter called to tell her she had found the boy she was going to marry. Sumiko's voice was full of excitement and hope for the future. Such a contrast from the day her father came home and announced over dinner she'd be marrying his junior colleague. As Fumiyo watched Michie open another package of rice crackers, she thought how lucky Sumiko had been to have had such a nice husband and such a nice mother-in-law. Yes, Sumiko was lucky, all right. Until she got that cancer that killed her.

It was hard for Fumiyo to accept the possibility of some other woman coming in and taking her daughter's place in the Kato family, but she knew Akira shouldn't be alone forever. The girls needed a mother and not just their two grandmothers. So she asked, with pretend interest, "What about the matchmaking service?"

"He refused to even look at the pictures of the candidates they sent. It'd be different if he made some sort of effort, but how can he find someone if he never goes anywhere?"

"Well, he went somewhere yesterday."

"Oh? Where?"

"Some kind of English class. He said he's taking the class so he can talk to foreigners when they visit the company."

Michie looked rather surprised. "Really? Akira's English is already good enough for that. But," she added, "I suppose it could be something fun for him to do."

"Studying English is fun?" Fumiyo asked, confused.

Later that evening, the girls were watching cartoons and Fumiyo was ironing Akira's shirts. It'd been two years since she'd moved in with Sumiko's husband and daughters. It was supposed to be just a temporary measure until Akira got his life back on track or until the girls were old enough to fend for themselves. He certainly couldn't depend on Michie for much help when Saburo was becoming more and more of a handful. The solution was for Akira to find a wife, but a prickle of pain pierced her chest as it always did, whenever she thought about Sumiko's replacement moving into her house, sleeping with her husband, and raising her daughters.

People at the supermarket, the post office, or her poetry-writing club have started mentioning a granddaughter, a niece, or a friend who was looking for a husband. They all thought they were being helpful by offering up prospective brides, but they seemed to have forgotten she was *not* Akira's mother—she was the mother of the woman they were so eager to replace. That was a pretty hard pill to swallow, but she kept a smile plastered on her face and always agreed to pass on the information.

The phone rang and Fumiyo turned off the iron before answering it. Ikeda-san and Yamazaki-san from her poetry writing group were planning on having lunch together in Ginza the next day, and they wanted to know if she'd like to join them. She penciled that into her daily planner, something she actually needed to go out and buy after moving to Tokyo. Her days were not only filled with her granddaughters' activities but her own as well. Here, she never had to wait for someone to feel like driving her somewhere. All she had to do was get on a subway or a bus. She could stroll around Ginza or Shinjuku whenever the mood struck. Or spend a weekend at a hot springs hotel with her poetry-writing club.

She didn't like to admit it, but Akira's family had always been a lot nicer to her than her own family. Osamu says he misses her and wants her to come home, but she suspected what he really missed were the clean clothes, the orderly house, and the tasty meals she provided. It'd been quite a shock to find her Kyushu home in such a neglected state on her last visit. Her daughter-in-law may be fond of going on and on about how she's a college graduate and all that, but Yoko didn't know a thing about managing a home. Fumiyo would've never been able to get away with that around her own mother-in-law. Not to speak ill of the dead, but that woman was as mean as a wild boar.

She didn't like to play favorites with her children's spouses, but it was impossible not to like Akira far more than that Miss Smarty Pants daughter-in-law of hers. For one thing, he (and his mother) never made her feel small. But Yoko went around acting as if she knew everything about everything and Fumiyo knew nothing about nothing. Despite majoring in English literature, she had never heard that girl utter a single word of English, and as far as she could tell, she had never picked up a book in *any* language, either.

No, Fumiyo did *not* want to go back to Kyushu and live with her daughter-in-law, who was always concocting all sorts of rules and stipulations for her, even though the house was technically still hers. But she couldn't stay with Akira forever. A mother-in-law was bad enough, unless you hit it lucky, like Sumiko did in that department. But the first wife's mother? No, she couldn't stay here, no matter how much she loved her granddaughters.

As she was folding up the ironing board, a radical thought popped right into her head. If she liked Tokyo so much, why couldn't she just stay? Why couldn't she get an apartment here? She didn't *have* to go back to Kyushu. She was a free and independent woman, and she could do whatever she wanted. She gathered up the folded and ironed laundry and carried it upstairs, feeling quite pleased with herself for having come up with the perfect solution for everyone.

But when she reached the top of the stairs, it occurred to her that even though she was a woman in her sixties, she'd never spent even one night alone in her entire life. She felt crestfallen when she realized becoming completely independent might not be such an easy thing to do after all.

Chapter Six

Akira decided to write the report of his earlier meeting with clients in Nihombashi in Doutor Coffee near FECC instead of going back to his office and doing it there. He knew that when five o'clock rolled around and the office ladies began distributing cups of tea, people started relaxing. An hour or two could easily pass, and he didn't want to be late for his English class. Or worse, end up missing it altogether.

When he told Obaachan he was going to go to an English conversation school, she'd acted as astonished as if he'd said he was taking up hula dancing. And when he told his section chief at Tominaga Corporation that he'd have to leave the office early most Fridays because he was going to take English lessons, the guy slapped him on the shoulder and congratulated him. He seemed to think Akira's step toward professional development was a sign he was getting himself back on the corporate track after a much too long period of mourning. No one had said much when he turned down international business trips like the one that would've involved a nine-week stay in India. Or when he missed all but the most important after-work drinking parties. But it'd been two years since his wife had died, and Akira knew they were all thinking that enough was enough.

Akira had stopped by FECC after seeing their classes advertised in the newspaper. He almost walked out after the strange office manager, a guy more likely to scare prospective students away than to inspire confidence in their programs, tested his English ability by firing a series of unrelated questions at him. But determined to make a change in his life, he purchased the six-month package with a bonus month thrown in. He just wanted to go somewhere where people didn't know him. Where they weren't trying to fix him up with Fujioka's single daughter, Yamada's single niece, or Kawakita's single sister. He knew his colleagues were wondering why he just didn't get it over with and pick one of the office ladies who didn't have a boyfriend or a husband in sight.

But he's got two kids. He's the oldest son with filial obligations. And not to mention, there's that unusual relationship with his mother-in-law. But he also knew plenty of women were out there who'd probably overlook all those cons because of the pros. He worked for a good company, earned a decent salary, and owned a home in central Tokyo. But he'd rather be alone than be with someone who wanted him just because the material advantages outweighed the family complications.

Akira pushed his sandwich to the side of the table and spread out his papers. After jotting down a few figures in his notebook, he realized the report wouldn't take long to do at all. Ten minutes later, he put it away and started making notes for tonight's discussion on movies. It'd been a long time since he'd been inside a theater that wasn't showing children's movies. In fact, the last time he saw a regular movie was a few weeks before Emi was born. His mother watched Yuka while he and Sumiko went to see *Raiders of the Lost Ark*. They enjoyed it so much they sat through it twice, even though Sumiko's bladder forced her to go to the bathroom every ten minutes.

He remembered how hungry they were when they left the theater and how they headed straight to McDonald's and ate two Big Macs each. "Double the fun," Sumiko had joked. "Two movies and two Big Macs all in one day."

He had pretty much forgotten about that day, but now it all came back—he could even remember the pink floral maternity dress

Sumiko was wearing. Memories like this used to hurt, but now they didn't. Not so much, anyway.

He wondered what the others would say about movies tonight. It felt kind of odd having classmates at his age, but he didn't know what else to call them. They weren't friends. Or colleagues. They were just people who were different from those he normally associated with. And that was a good thing.

"Hi," said a voice.

Akira glanced up and saw Rose, his English teacher, standing right in front of him and flashing a smile that went all the way to her blue eyes.

"Remember me? From FECC? I'm Rose."

"Of course I do," Akira said. "Would you like to sit down?" In the process of moving his briefcase from the chair across from him, he almost knocked over his iced coffee.

"I don't want to disturb you if you're working, but all the other seats are taken."

"You aren't disturbing me. I'm just killing time before our class."

"You've got *three* hours to kill?" she said as she set her tray on the table and slid into the seat.

"Well, I had an appointment in Nihombashi and it was getting a bit late, so I…"

Rose smiled at his embarrassment for having been caught playing hooky from work while she took off her coat. "I totally get it," she said with a wink. "Your secret's safe with me."

"Whew," he replied, pretending to wipe the worry away from his forehead. "What a relief to know you won't be reporting back to my boss that I'm shirking my duties."

"Well, the day's still young," she said seriously. "I may change my mind and call your boss later." And then they both laughed.

"Will I have to bribe you to keep quiet with another pastry?" he asked, pointing at the one on her tray.

"Not right this moment. But I might have some future demands for my ongoing silence."

Akira laughed again, but an unfamiliar sensation hit his belly when Rose said the word *future*. It'd been a long, long time since he'd felt anything even remotely like that, and he fumbled around in his head for what to say next. Luckily, he was saved when Rose changed the subject.

"I'm curious. You're not the usual type who goes to FECC. Your English is so good I don't see why you need lessons at all. So," she said as if she was asking him to reveal some deep, dark secret, "why are you *really* there?"

Akira didn't want to go into his real reasons, so he kept it simple. "I spent a year in California when I was in high school. That was almost fifteen years ago. I rarely have a chance to speak English these days, so I thought going to some kind of class would be fun. And useful."

"California? I've never been. What was it like?"

"It's certainly different from here, that's for sure."

Rose put her elbows on the table and leaned forward. "How?"

"Hmm, let me see…" He pushed aside the jumble of thoughts concerning Rose's hair, eyes, smile, and an ever so faint scent of a floral perfume that had penetrated his senses. "It wasn't what I'd expected at all. And…" He went on to describe the family he'd lived with in San Marino, their five-bedroom house, their pool, their gardener, and their maid.

Rose shook her head, half in half awe and half in disbelief. "I thought only movie stars lived like that."

"Me, too. So when they picked me up at the airport, I thought we'd stopped at some sort of hotel to have lunch first."

"Wow. I can't imagine such a life. It must've been a fantastic experience."

A rather cynical expression fell across his face. "You'd think so, right? At first, I thought it was pretty great, but it turned out the family was—what do you call it? Dysfunctional? Yeah, that's it. Dysfunctional. My host father was hardly ever home. My host mother drank a lot. *A lot*. Usually starting around noon and going on till about midnight. My host brother mostly stayed in his room and smoked marijuana. The only person who talked to me was the maid, but she was from Guatemala and couldn't speak much English either."

"So then, how did you learn to speak the way you do?"

"Volleyball."

Rose's eyes widened with surprise. "Did you say *volleyball*?"

"Yeah," Akira said with a nostalgic smile. "Volleyball. I showed up at the gym a few weeks after school started with my dictionary and asked the coach if I could join the team. At first, he treated me like some short, dorky Asian guy who couldn't do anything."

"That's terrible! You're not short at all. You're really tall!"

Akira kind of liked the flash of indignation he saw in Rose's eyes when she came to his defense. "Well, it's true that I was a lot shorter than everyone else. But I could jump pretty high. And I was a good setter. When the coach realized that, he made me a regular team member. That was the year they went to the state championships and came in second. So I guess you could say I learned English by hanging around all the jocks. But later," he chuckled, "I had to unlearn all the swear words. I got in trouble with one of my college professors because of that. It seems there's a time and a place for that kind of language."

Rose sputtered a laugh. "I can just imagine. I've heard all kinds of things from my students—things you'd never say to a teacher." She took another bite of her pastry and said, "You know, there was a Japanese exchange student in my town, too. He wasn't an athlete like you, but we were in the chorus club together. I didn't think about it at the time, but I bet that's how he learned most of his English. By hanging out with us. He was a really good singer, so they gave him a lot of solos. But me? They made me stand in the back and told me not to get too loud."

"I'm sure you're exaggerating," Akira said, thinking her voice sounded lovely.

"Believe me," she replied, "I'm not. But I kept in touch with Kazuo after he came back to Japan, and now I live with his grandmother."

"With his grandmother?" Akira was unable to hide his surprise.

"Well, not exactly *with* her, but in a little studio apartment that was built onto her house for her grandchildren to live in when they went to college. You know, with a separate entrance and bathroom. It was empty for a while because all the grandkids had grown up. They didn't want strangers living there, but when Kazuo found out I was coming to Japan, he asked if I wanted to move in. I wasn't crazy about that idea at first. I mean," she said wryly, "who wants to live with some old person you don't know? But it's in a convenient location, and I didn't have to pay a deposit, buy furniture, or get a telephone installed. It even came with an air conditioner."

"Sounds really ideal."

"It is. She's very nice and we get along pretty well. Even though in the beginning we had a real hard time communicating."

"Does your friend live nearby? To help out and all that stuff?"

"No, he got a job in Atlanta, and he and his wife are living there now."

"Oh, I see." Akira felt weirdly relieved to learn the Japanese guy seemed to be just her friend.

Rose glanced down at her watch and pushed back her chair. Before she stood, she asked, "Did you ever go back to California?"

"Well, I visited California on my...um... honeymoon. So that was, I guess, around six years ago."

"Did you get to see your host family again?"

"I went by their house but found out they'd moved. When I saw my old coach, he told me there'd been some sort of embezzlement scandal and my host parents had gotten divorced and moved away somewhere. He also told me that my host brother had gone to law school and became a defense attorney. Now that was the biggest surprise of all. Back in high school, I never would've pictured him on *that* side of the law."

They shared another laugh while Rose slipped on her coat. "I wish I could stay and hear more, but I've got to go. I'll see you in a couple of hours. Thanks for sharing your table with me." She carried her tray to the counter, and as she went out the door, she turned around and waved.

Akira waved back and gazed out the window, watching Rose until she turned the corner. He was surprised by how much he didn't want her to think he was still married.

As Rose hurried to get to Friendly on time, she thought about bumping into Akira in Doutor Coffee. She usually avoided the café on the first floor of Friendly's building, having learned the hard way that many of the students go there before class. And if they see their teachers, they understandably want to talk to them. But that makes the teachers feel like they're giving out free English lessons off the clock. Everyone at Friendly quickly learned it was better to get their caffeine fixes elsewhere.

But today, for some reason, when she saw Akira bent over his notebook at the café down the street, she didn't hesitate in going over to him. For one thing, she remembered his English was quite fluent. He also seemed a much better alternative than sharing a table with a random salaryman and his overflowing ashtray, who *also* might consider Rose's presence as a golden opportunity for a spontaneous English lesson.

Nothing about that hour with Akira felt like an English lesson, though. The time passed so quickly it was almost like hanging out with a friend. Sure, a *married* friend with kids. And one of her students. But still, it was nice to be able to sit back and talk like that with someone.

"What did you bring me today?" Michael asked after she clocked in and sat at her desk.

"Sorry, you're out of luck. The International Thinking Housewives Circle canceled this week because they all went to Kyoto. So you'll just have to suffer through the weekend without their goodies."

"Oh, darn," Michael said, reaching into his desk and pulling out a Meiji chocolate bar. "Good thing I have backup supplies."

"Oh, you and your sweet tooth," Rose said indulgently before heading over to the photocopier. She greeted the guys milling around the vending machine and ignored Kenny, who made a comment about how her top looked an awful lot like a T-shirt (which would be a Friendly dress code violation). Feeling somewhat magnanimous, she asked Chad how he liked his new class, and from his sheepish response, she could tell he was indeed the one who'd engineered that switch. She knew those girls would bat their eyes and flirt with him, thinking he was as cool as John Travolta. As far as she was concerned, though, Chad had the personality of a sea slug.

Rose got through her first two classes and stepped into the last one of the day to find the students already chatting with each other. Her instincts were right—this *was* going to be a good group. She smiled at Akira, acknowledging their earlier encounter at the café.

After a bit of warm-up chit chat, Rose began the class. "So last week we decided our topic for discussion would be movies. Are you ready?"

Daisuke, the nervous English teacher who could barely speak last week, put up his hand and opened a notebook, revealing detailed notes. He'd clearly done his homework—it almost looked like he'd prepared a scrapbook. Compared to the previous week, he spoke with confidence. He learned English, he explained to everyone, by going to the movies. And later, from recording *Little House on the Prairie* on NHK every day and imitating the characters' speech.

"That explains why your pronunciation is so good." Rose enjoyed watching Daisuke beam as she spoke.

"What's your favorite movie?" Naoko asked Daisuke.

"*Alien*," he replied.

"Mine, too!" she said.

Rose wrote a list of movie genres on the board, and everyone called out the names of various movies that fit into the categories: *Roman Holiday, Ghostbusters, Godfather, Dirty Harry, Kramer vs. Kramer, The Blues Brothers, The Shining*. They could've gone on listing movies until the class ended, but she sat down and asked a different question.

"What movie changed your life? For example, as for me, I saw a movie when I was a child that was about a teacher and his students.

I'm pretty sure that movie made me want to become a teacher. Has any movie ever had a big impact on you?"

"I'm not sure if it changed my life," said Naoko. "But I really liked *9 to 5*. I loved how those women got the best of their boss in the end."

"I saw! I saw!" exclaimed Kana. "Bad boss! Funny!"

"But that would never happen in Japan," said Naoko.

"Why not?" asked Rose.

"Japanese women wouldn't come out ahead at the end like the women did in that movie. Nothing would change because the boss would still be the boss. He'd just get new women to work for him. He'd be exactly the same person but with different women. And, they'd be young because there aren't many older women in the workforce because they quit working when they get married."

"Why do they quit?" Rose knew the answer to that already. This was a common topic among all the women in her English classes. But asking questions like this was one way to keep students speaking.

"It's expected," replied Naoko.

"But why is it expected?" pressed Rose. She found herself giving Akira a quick peek, wanting to know what his thoughts were about this. He looked like he was about to say something, but then Tomo spoke up.

"Men are supposed to work," he said, as if he was clearing everything up. "And women are supposed to stay home and support them. That's the way it's always been."

"That's what your mother says," Kana muttered in Japanese, flashing him a dirty look.

"Many teachers," interjected Daisuke, "continue working even after they get married. Maybe education is different from business."

"But how many of those women are principals? Or in positions of power?" asked Naoko.

Daisuke paused. "Not many. I guess it'd be too hard to do that work *and* take care of a family."

"It *is* hard to do both," agreed Akira. "And—"

"That's why men have to start doing more at home," Keiko interrupted, a touch of anger in her voice. "Because it isn't fair."

"You husband no do homework?" asked Kana, surprising Rose by how well she was following what had become an active discussion, even if she did get the word for housework and homework mixed up.

"No," admitted Keiko. "He doesn't."

"What happen when you do job?"

"He'll come around. He says he is a modern thinker. He says women should have equal rights. When I get a job, he'll change."

"What does he think about you studying English now and your future career plans?" asked Rose.

Keiko's face indicated her husband didn't know a thing about any of that.

"It secret?" asked Kana.

"Not a secret," said Keiko. "A surprise."

Rose saw everyone's skeptical faces and decided to move on. "Is there a movie you've seen over and over? That you don't mind watching again and again?"

"*Blues Brothers*," said Akira. "It's not the story so much, but I love the music."

"*Karate Kid*," said Daisuke. "I like karate." When quizzed by the group, he admitted not only did he *like* karate, he had a black belt of the highest level.

"If I go to America, I'll take you to fight off all the criminals," said Tomo, who was a fan of *Beverly Hills Cop*.

"America's not all about guns and crime. But," Rose quickly added, "it's not all *Little House on the Prairie* either. Just like Japan isn't all geisha or yakuza."

The class continued like this until nine. As they were getting ready to leave, Naoko suggested going out somewhere together.

"Sorry, but I can't this time," said Akira.

"Neither can I," said Keiko.

Kana, Tomo, Daisuke, and Naoko all looked at Rose.

"I'll take a rain check," she said. "That means 'maybe another time.'"

Rose tidied up after they all left and hurried to the teacher's room to meet up with Michael.

Chapter Seven

Rose stayed up late reading the Sydney Sheldon novel she'd picked up yesterday on the giveaway table at Friendly and had just fallen asleep when the phone rang. *"Moshi-moshi?"* she said groggily into the receiver.

"And mushy-mushy to you, too, dear."

"Mom! What's wrong?"

"Wrong? Why, nothing's wrong. I just called to say hi."

"It's two in the morning." Even though she'd sent her mother a chart illustrating the time difference between Nebraska and Japan, she still couldn't quite grasp the concept of calling Rose at a normal hour.

"Did I wake you?"

"It's the middle of the night. What do you think?"

"Well, anyway, this is expensive, so I'll be quick. Now, I don't want you to get upset, but—"

"Something *is* wrong! Is it Dad?"

"Nothing's wrong! Well, nothing like *that*, anyway. I just wanted to let you know Denise is getting married."

"Well, that's nice, and I'm happy for her," Rose said automatically, wondering why this information about her cousin wasn't sent by airmail in a much cheaper aerogram. She also wondered why Denise hadn't contacted her directly, considering how close they'd been as kids.

"You know how easily your nerves get frayed," her mom continued. "And—"

"My nerves are fine." Just because Rose had totally lost it when Brad dumped her, her mother now thought she was a permanent mental case.

"I didn't want you to hear it from anyone else."

"What are you talking about, Mom? Who's Denise marrying?"

"Brian."

"Brian who?"

"Brian Billford."

The information that her cousin was engaged to the brother of her cheating ex-fiancé sunk in, and she felt a swirl of emotions.

"Your Aunt Eunice," her mom continued in a somewhat bitter and jealous tone, "is running around and telling anyone who'll listen how her daughter's gone and snagged herself one of the Billford boys."

Rose knew that she shouldn't care about any of that, but she did.

"Now, honey. I know you feel you can't hold your head up after what happened with you and Brad. Everyone knows that's why you ran off all the way to the Orient. But Denise wants you to be her maid of honor at her wedding next summer and—"

"Oh, Mom, I don't know about that. I don't think I want to—"

"Now you listen," her mother said sharply, "I won't have the town whispering that you're full of sour grapes because she's got one of the Billford diamonds on her finger and you don't. You're going to say yes and hold your head up high. Do you hear me?"

Rose's mother's kitchen timer beeped, indicating the call was reaching the three-minute limit. "Oh, honey, just because you let Brad slip through your fingers doesn't mean you'll end up an old maid. Come home for the wedding and put on a brave face." Right before disconnecting, she added, "Besides, people hardly talk about any of that now."

Rose seriously doubted that was true because a scandal of that magnitude could fuel the town gossips for decades. Her mother and aunt had never graduated from the 1950s, where the ultimate goal in life for a woman was to marry the most eligible bachelor around. And in Felix, it was one of the Billford boys. When she was with Brad, her mom ran around acting like her daughter had snagged Prince Charming. So when Brad dumped her for that snippy cheerleader from Riley, her mother was absolutely convinced that Rose must've done something to make him stray away from her like that.

Her cousin could have the whole Billford clan as far as she was concerned. But she was still upset at her for not telling her about the rumors going around. So much humiliation could've been avoided if only she'd known about Brad's cheating a lot earlier.

Rose was wide awake now, so she turned on the kerosene heater to warm up the room, made a cup of hot chocolate, and settled under the lap quilts of her *kotatsu* table. At least tomorrow was Saturday and she could sleep in.

She opened her book but couldn't get back into it. She *knew* she was way better off without Brad. Common sense told her that if he'd been cheating on her when they were engaged, he'd cheat on her after they were married. It was everyone's sideways glances, filled with pity that she wanted to avoid. Especially now that Kimberly was pregnant. Again. But Rose knew she'd have to go to that stupid wedding, smile at Brad and Kimberly and their growing passel of kids, and pretend all was well between them.

Well, it wasn't.

But then a brilliant idea popped into her head out of nowhere. A masterminded idea. She'd get Michael to come with her to Denise's wedding. He might be gay, but she knew he'd be the best wedding date ever.

Chapter Eight

Rose woke with a stiff neck from having fallen asleep at the *kotatsu,* and her head felt thick and heavy from a lack of sleep. The clatter in the garden just outside her window was impossible to ignore, so she turned on the heater, put on the padded house jacket her landlady had given to her the first winter she lived there, and opened the sliding glass door facing the garden.

"*Ohayo gozaimasu,*" she called out to Mrs. Fukuda. They exchanged pleasantries, providing a daily dose of Japanese conversation practice. After two and a half years of this, Rose was pretty fluent in most discussions concerning weather or laundry. It was all the other gazillion topics she needed to work on.

Still thinking about last night's phone call from her mother, Rose slipped on a pair of garden clogs and carried her laundry basket out to the washing machine that stood in the garden's lean-to. Since her landlady had gotten a fully automatic washer a few weeks earlier, she no longer needed to move freezing wet laundry from the washer tub into the spinner and then back into the tub again for rinsing. Now all she had to do was turn it on and wait for the load to finish. It felt like she was living in the 20th century again!

She went back inside and switched on the radio to listen to Casey Kasem and *American Top 40* and tackled her weekly chores. FEN's DJ came on every ten minutes or so to give announcements about things happening on the military bases, reminding Rose of how different her life in Japan was. There were no all-you-can-eat Mexican food buffets or waffle breakfasts in her immediate future. No special bargains at the PX and no dollar movies at the theater. But at least there was music. She tidied her apartment and hung her wet laundry in the garden while listening to Cyndi Lauper, Bruce Springsteen, and Stevie Wonder. As soon as Madonna's "Like a Virgin" finished at number one for the week, Rose set her kerosene containers out by her landlady's front door for today's kerosene delivery. Last time she forgot and nearly froze to death before having to go to the local gas station on her bicycle to get some fuel for her heater.

Then Rose biked to the supermarket for her weekly supplies and parked in a space next to a woman who had a baby strapped on her back, a toddler in the seat attached to the front handlebars, and a preschool-aged child in the backseat. With a package of toilet paper in the front basket, and two bags of groceries dangling from the handlebars, the woman zipped off down the crowded sidewalk.

Rose was about to go inside the supermarket when she practically bumped right into Akira, looking every bit as handsome as he did the night before in their class. He was clean shaven and wearing slim-fitting jeans, which suggested he still had the athlete's body of his youth. Rose wished she was wearing anything but her baggy sweatpants and down jacket. She wished she had put on some makeup.

"Oh," she said with surprise. "Hi."

"Hi," he replied with equal surprise.

"Do you live around here?" they asked at the same time, making them both laugh.

"And who do we have here?" Rose asked, looking down at the two little girls holding his hands. They were wearing identical pink jackets and black leggings. If it weren't for the difference in their size, she might've thought they were twins.

"These are my daughters, Yuka and Emi."

"Hello, Yuka. Hello, Emi." Rose squatted to be down on their level, just like she did when talking to her students back in Felix. "Are you out shopping with your daddy today?"

"Papa, she speaks Japanese," the smaller one said, looking up at her father.

"Of course she does. This is Rose-sensei. She's my English teacher."

"I have a teacher, too," the bigger one announced.

"You do, do you?" said Rose. "What's her name?"

"Sato-sensei.

After a few minutes of standing there and chatting, the littler one tugged on her father's arm. "Papa, I'm hungry."

"Would you like to join us for lunch? It's just at Denny's," he said with some hesitation. "That's their favorite place, and I promised. But if you have other plans…"

"Will your wife be coming along, too?" Rose asked nonchalantly as she glanced over his shoulder, expecting to see a well-dressed grownup version of Akira's pretty daughters appear at any second.

Akira scratched his head the way Japanese men often do when they aren't sure what to say. "Actually, I'm not married. I'm a widower."

"Oh. That's uh…" She caught herself before saying a generic, but disastrous, *that's nice*. "Lunch sounds great. I'm pretty hungry."

They asked to sit in the non-smoking section but were seated at a table right next to it. Judging from the overflowing ashtrays in front of a group of construction workers, they'd been killing quite a bit of time there. Rose caught a glimpse one of her neighbors, who was sitting two booths away, watching her. Because *gaijin* news in the neighborhood traveled at the speed of light, her landlady would probably hear about this before she even got home. Considering the way everyone had gotten involved when she accidentally threw away non-burnable garbage on burnable garbage day, imagine how much more entertaining *this* would be.

"Papa," Yuka whispered, pointing at a different table. "Those ladies are staring at us."

"I'm sorry," Rose said uncomfortably. "I tend to get stared at a lot. It used to make me feel like a movie star, but now—"

"But you do look like a movie star," interrupted Yuka. "Doesn't she, Papa?"

Akira looked a little flustered. "I guess—"

"Well, are you one?" demanded Emi.

"Hardly," said Rose with a laugh, thinking that today of all days, she looked least like one. "Although I was once in a Japanese TV commercial."

"Really?" asked Akira.

"Yeah," Rose said, grinning. "Well, kind of. You see, I was just walking down the street in Shibuya one day, and they were filming a commercial for some kind of potato chips. The guy in charge stopped me and asked if I wanted to be in the background. You know, to add some kind of international feel to it. So, I said yes." Rose shrugged with pretend modesty. "And that's my claim to fame."

Akira translated for the girls, who now looked at Rose with awe. In their minds, she was famous—she'd been on television!

The server came over with some crayons and mini coloring books for the girls, and after they got down to business with that, Akira said, "I didn't know you could speak Japanese so well."

Rose let out a sigh. "I wish I was a lot better. I take lessons, but other than talking to my teacher, the shopkeepers, or to my landlady, I rarely get a chance to practice."

Akira looked rather surprised. "No chance to practice speaking Japanese *in* Japan?"

"As hard as it might be to believe, it's true. I teach English all the time, right? It's against the rules to speak Japanese at Friendly, even if students can't understand a word of English."

"What about with your friends?"

Rose couldn't very well tell him most of the Japanese people she knew *paid* her to teach them English. They were kind of like friends, but not really. Not when they were charged for the pleasure of her time. "Most of my friends speak English. Like you do. So, we tend to slip into English." Then she added, "I think it's pretty different for people who go to the States. You probably didn't have that many people in California dying to practice their Japanese with you."

"That's so true! Some people actually thought Japan and China were the same country." They laughed together, and Rose felt like an unspoken connection was beginning to form between them. "We could speak Japanese if you like," Akira offered.

The food came, and they did indeed spend the next hour speaking in Japanese, with English thrown in when Rose couldn't find the right words or when she needed Akira to translate what Yuka or Emi were saying. Rose enjoyed talking to the girls because they didn't have trouble understanding her broken Japanese the way adults often did.

When the server removed their plates, the girls returned to their coloring books, and Rose said with a wry smile, "How about we switch back to English? That pretty much drained me."

"All right." Akira leaned forward and encircled his coffee mug in his hands. "Tell me. How do you like living in Japan so far?"

"Hmm." Rose felt somewhat discombobulated by how Akira's eyes crinkled in the most perfect way when he smiled at her. "Sometimes I get tired of being stared at and asked the same silly questions over and over again. 'Can you use chopsticks?' 'Can you eat Japanese food?' 'Do you know about Mt Fuji?' That sort of thing." She picked up her own mug and added, "But to be honest, I *do* like it here. It's really, *really* different from where I come from, though. That's for sure."

"Felix, Nebraska, right?"

Rose was pleased he'd remembered. "Back home, for example, there's *one* neon sign. Just one. A small one. A Budweiser Beer sign in front of the town bar. There aren't any traffic lights—just a couple of stop signs. You have to drive for thirty minutes before you hit a traffic light. And Tokyo? Well, it just never sleeps, right?" A wave of homesickness for Nebraska washed over her. The good-hearted neighbors. The smell of freshly cut grass. The county fair. Her family.

"Of course," she continued, trying to keep her voice from wobbling, "there are lots of things I do miss."

"I'm sure there are. After all, home is home," Akira said warmly, "even when you're far away."

"True. I'm pretty comfortable here now, even though it took quite a bit of getting used to. Tokyo's even beginning to feel a bit like home," she said with a little shrug. "So, I guess you could say it's possible to feel at home in more than one place."

Rose was in no hurry to leave, so she was glad when Akira ordered chocolate sundaes for everyone. She'd had more than enough caffeine in her system but accepted a third refill from the server, leaving it mostly untouched.

"Before I came to Japan," she said, eating a spoonful of her cornflakes-sprinkled sundae, "I thought Chinese food and Japanese food were the same. Remember, I'm from rural Nebraska, and I'd never eaten Japanese food before I got here. The first time I ate tofu I thought it was some kind of weird yogurt. And sashimi? Well, I'd heard that Japanese people ate raw fish, but I thought they ate an entire uncooked fish!"

Akira burst out laughing. "It must've been quite an experience for you the first few months."

"That's for sure. Believe it or not, I'd never even been on an airplane until the day I left Nebraska." She smiled, remembering how terrified she had been that day. Now it all seemed funny, but back then, it certainly wasn't. "It's a wonder I didn't end up in Brazil or Australia after changing planes in Chicago. Although it did take a little while for my luggage to get here. Apparently, it went to Hong Kong for a little mini vacation first."

"Well, I hope it had a good time there," Akira deadpanned.

"It said it did. Until it got food poisoning and needed to be medevacked to Japan ASAP."

Yuka and Emi demanded to know what was making their father laugh so hard, so he translated for them. The girls giggled wildly at the absurdity of a suitcase taking a holiday on its own.

"So," continued Rose, "when I finally got to Japan, I was never so happy to see anyone in my whole life as I was when I saw my friend at the airport. If Kazuo hadn't been waiting to take me to his grandmother's house, I'd *still* be trying to find my way to Daikyo-cho. But that first night I was so homesick. I debated if it was too late to change my mind and go home."

"But you stayed."

"Yeah. I stayed."

"So how much longer do you think you'll be here?"

"I don't know," Rose answered truthfully.

Chapter Nine

After lunch, Rose finished her weekly shopping, and as she put her groceries away, she mused over her afternoon with Akira and his daughters. It'd been so nice to feel part of a family, even if only temporarily. Sometimes she'd watch families who were having fun doing ordinary things out of the corner of her eye and feel a bit sad. Because if things had gone the way they were supposed to, she'd probably have a toddler by now. Maybe even a baby as well.

"But then," she said aloud to herself. "You'd also be stuck with that idiot, Brad." Thank goodness that wasn't the case. Looking back, he had always been a jerk. She'd just been too good at ignoring all the warning signs.

Now Akira, she mused, seemed different. She barely knew him, of course, but something about him made her think he wasn't a thing like Brad. Not only was he much nicer looking, he didn't have that bragging swagger about him. He seemed like someone she could trust.

Rose whacked her palm against her forehead to chase such crazy thoughts away before they took hold. She had trusted Brad just fine at first and look where that got her. Besides, what did trusting Akira have to do with *anything*? He was just one of her students. Possibly a new friend.

Before she could consider that any further, the phone rang. "So," Kazumi said as soon as Rose picked it up. "We'll meet you at 6:00 in front of Almond Coffee Shop in Roppongi."

Kazumi, who'd never been one of Rose's students, was her closest girlfriend in Japan. She was smart, savvy, and fashionable. They met at 69, the reggae bar in Shinjuku, shortly after Rose had arrived in Japan. She was fluent in English, namely because of her love of reading English books, her passion for anything and everything Clint Eastwood, and an ongoing parade of foreign boyfriends. She was also funny and kind, so it didn't take long for the two of them to become fast friends.

Rose had no idea what Kazumi was going on about before remembering they'd talked about getting together with Kazumi's new boyfriend, Chris, this weekend. And now it seemed one of his friends was coming along as well. "Listen, I'm not so sure I want to go out tonight. It's cold and—"

"Oh, come on! It'll be fun!"

Rose heard Kazumi drop another coin into a pay phone. "All right," she sighed. It wasn't like she had anything better to do tonight. "I guess I'll go."

Later that evening, Rose stood at Roppongi Crossing, her cheeks red from the icy wind, wishing she was home with her book and a nice hot cup of tea. When she left the house in her wool coat, black jeans, and flat pumps, she thought she looked just fine. But most of the women walking past her were in short skirts and high heels. Even if she wanted to wear fancier footwear, it wasn't like size 8.5 shoes were sold on every street corner in Japan. Or on *any* street corner, for that matter.

"Rose! Sorry we're late," Kazumi said, rushing toward her from the subway exit.

"Nice to meet you," said a guy who was nearly six feet tall and with dark blond hair. He stuck out his hand in a friendly manner. "I'm Chris Peters. And this is Steve Dillinger."

There was no mistaking the disappointment on Steve's face when he said hello, making her realize he must've assumed Kazumi's friend was a much more fashionable and petite Japanese woman and not a *gaijin* in her comfy flat shoes. Steve wasn't as tall as Chris, and he already had a slight paunch to his belly.

"So, where are you from?" Steve asked as they walked toward the restaurant.

"Nebraska. And you?"

"California. Never met anyone from Nebraska before," he said, looking down his rather prominent nose at her. "What's it like? Cowboys? Corn? Cows?"

"Yeah. Pretty much so. And California? Surfers? Movie stars? Drugs?"

Steve laughed. "Yeah. Pretty much so. Or at least, that's what they tell me. So, have you been here long?"

Foreigners always liked to know where they stood with each other in the Who's-Been-Here-the-Longest-Game.

"About two and a half years. And you?"

"Seven. Came in '78. But those first two years," he said knowingly, "they're the longest."

"Do you speak Japanese?" asked Rose.

"Sure. Enough to get by, anyway."

She knew that could mean just about anything. She didn't mention the Japanese classes she'd been taking for two years and he didn't ask.

Ten minutes later, the four of them were sipping beer and trying to talk over the blaring music in the Hard Rock Cafe.

"Oh, I got out of *that* loser business right away," he said when she told him she worked for an *eikaiwa* school.

That rude comment, regardless of how many elements of truth it might contain, rendered Rose momentarily speechless. Besides, his schedule of twenty classes in six different universities all over Tokyo seemed like an awful lot of work to her. When she probed him about his visa status, though, he admitted he *did* work for a small *eikaiwa* school. In exchange for a few occasional Saturday classes with senior citizens, the owner, a friend of his, sponsored his visa.

Curious about the world outside of teaching in a place like FECC, Rose asked lots of questions. It was kind of like getting a student to talk about himself, but actually a lot easier because it turned out Steve really did like talking about himself.

"Yeah, and so another good gig I've got going here," he continued, "is voice narration. There's a ton of work out there, and it's better than the modeling. It's a lot more regular. But of course, modeling pays more."

Rose could understand the narration work because Steve did have a nice, clear voice. But modeling? Granted, for Japan, he was tall. And he did have lightish-colored hair and blue eyes. That was always a plus here. But his nose! Japanese people would probably see it as such a nice *high nose*, but back in Nebraska it would just be called a great big honker.

"But that Prince Charming thing," he was saying, "didn't work out."

Rose cracked up, thinking he'd made a joke, but it turned out he was dead serious. Tokyo Disneyland was just about to open, and there'd been a call for auditions. "That would have been a great gig, right? I thought I had a pretty good shot at it, but I guess they already had someone lined up. You know how it is with connections here. Knowing someone at the top counts for everything."

Even though Rose was pretending to show interest in his words, she couldn't imagine a less likely Prince Charming. In fact, the more Steve talked, the less charming he became. Especially when he flagged the server over and ordered another beer for himself. The woman glanced at Rose, but she shook her head. She still had most of hers left. Kazumi and Chris were huddled together over their menu, and Steve flipped through theirs. When the server came back to take their order, Rose hadn't even had a chance to glance at the menu yet. Steve ordered the California Cheeseburger, so she simply asked for the same.

"So Rose, where do you live?" Steve asked.

"In Shinjuku. Kind of near Yotsuya."

"Oh. You share with someone?"

"No, I'm by myself." He may have been in Japan a lot longer than her, but she figured she lived in a far better place than he did.

"Shinjuku," he said. "Cool area, but I need space. I wouldn't want to live in one of those old, rundown wooden apartments. Or have to go to a public bath."

"Me either," agreed Rose. "But what I really like about my place is having a garden. It's so nice to be able to chill out under one of the cherry trees. Until it gets too hot in the summer, of course. Then having an air conditioner's really nice." Let him wonder how she was swinging all that as an *eikaiwa* teacher.

Rose decided to try to get to know Chris better, since Kazumi seemed crazy about him. She knew he was also an English teacher but didn't know where he worked. It turned out he taught at some universities, too, but he didn't brag about it the way Steve did. In fact, Chris admitted he'd gotten his start in *eikaiwa* and had a few lucky breaks along the way.

"And I just started an MA program at Temple University," Chris said with a slightly embarrassed smile. "I like teaching and I wanted to learn more about it."

"You didn't have one before you started?" Rose asked.

"Who does?" interjected Steve. "A waste of time and money, if you ask me." He stopped the server as she was going to another table to ask for another beer before continuing. "Schools don't care. Besides, they never check. All they want is some *gaijin* on display to show how cosmopolitan their program is."

"Maybe an MA is a waste of time and money," conceded Chris. "But who knows? It could come in handy some day."

Rose didn't say anything about having one herself, because it certainly hadn't helped her get ahead in this country.

The conversation went back and forth across the table, and Rose realized she was actually having a pretty good time. Chris seemed like a decent guy, but she wondered if he knew Kazumi's number one goal in life was to snag an American husband, live abroad, and have a freezer full of big containers of different flavors of ice cream. When the food arrived, they dug in, and Rose was glad she ordered the hamburger—she hadn't had a decent one like that in forever.

She didn't mean to monitor Steve's alcohol consumption, but he had six beers to everyone else's two. And beer by beer, he inched closer to her. He must've have recovered from his initial disappointment in her being a *gaijin*, because with every beer he drank, Rose felt like she looked better and better to him. By the time they were finished eating, their legs were touching. He breathed into her face, giving her a whiff of the onion from his burger on top of all that beer, and she almost gagged.

They divided the bill up four ways, which was okay with her because she didn't want Steve to think this was really any sort of date. But it was kind of cheap of him to not offer to pay more, especially since it was all his beers that ran up the bill.

In the bathroom, while washing their hands, Kazumi turned to Rose. "Steve seems to like you."

"That's because he's drunk."

Kazumi laughed. "No, *really*."

"It was fun, but I think I'll go home now."

"You can't," Kazumi said while applying a shade of deep-red lipstick to her mouth. "You promised you'd go to that piano bar to hear my cousin perform! If you back out now, Chris and Steve will probably just go home."

"Oh, all right," Rose said, even though she didn't remember agreeing to any such thing.

The guys were waiting for them outside the restaurant. Steve tossed his cigarette into the gutter, slung his arm across Rose's shoulder, and pulled her close to him. She shot Kazumi a *rescue me* look, but she was too busy with Chris to notice.

Rose smiled through her teeth at Steve, but now there was something else to worry about. It'd been so long since she'd been out with a guy, so long since a guy had touched her. And that terrified her. What if she didn't have the willpower to resist Steve's sudden boozy charm? Look at all the trouble she'd gotten herself into the last time that happened! Once that thought made its way to her brain, it started bouncing back and forth like a bull on steroids.

"Rose-sensei!"

She turned toward the voice, and when she saw a couple standing there, her mind went blank when she couldn't quite place them. "Oh, hi!" she exclaimed when she realized it was Kana and Tomo from her Friday night class. "What're you guys doing here?"

"We just had dinner and thought we'd go somewhere to listen to music," Kana said in Japanese, shifting her weight in her high-heeled suede boots.

"Do you want to come with us?" Rose asked impulsively. "We're going to a piano bar near here."

Tomo looked over at Kana, who nodded.

"Who are these people?" Steve whispered when he realized their party had suddenly expanded.

"My students."

"You invited your *students* to come with us?"

"Sure. You'll like them. They're lots of fun."

Rose didn't believe a word of that, but with Chris and Kazumi getting friendlier by the minute, Rose needed a buffer to prevent Steve from getting any ideas about the two of them. And that buffer just happened magically to appear in the form of Tomo and Kana.

Rose smiled sweetly up at him and then turned to her students. "So, where did you have dinner?"

"Spagos," Kana answered.

"We were at the Hard Rock Cafe next door. Isn't Spagos awfully expensive?"

"Yes, very, very expensive," Tomo said.

"Expensive," Kana echoed.

"Well, I guess you members of the Ministry of Finance are so rich you can afford to eat at all the ritzy places."

Tomo looked pleased that Rose remembered where he worked.

At the piano bar, they got a booth for six, and Rose scooted in next to Tomo and Kana, forcing Steve to sit next to Kazumi and Chris.

Although Rose didn't like whiskey, they ordered a bottle and everyone had it mixed with water, *mizuwari* style, and a few snacks, including raisin butter. "Now, back in Nebraska," Rose explained to Tomo and Kana, "people eat butter. People eat raisins. But usually in a cookie or cake. Not like this." She stabbed a slab of the raisin studded butter with a toothpick and popped it into her mouth. For some reason, this was the bizarre go-to snack in Japan when one had whiskey.

By the time Kazumi's cousin had played two sets on the piano, it was getting close to midnight. A decision would have to be made to hurry for the last train or to stay out and party all night. Rose wasn't constrained by the late night availability of public transportation because she didn't live too far away. But honestly? She just wanted to go home.

Kazumi cast hopeful eyes at Chris. But when it was clear Steve was in pretty bad shape, especially after he vomited in the gutter, Chris said he'd better make sure Steve got home okay. Rose went with Kazumi and Chris and waved goodbye as they helped Steve down the steps to Roppongi Station. She crossed the street to get a taxi going in the direction of her neighborhood, and by the time she reached home, she could barely remember what Steve looked like.

Except, of course, his great, big honker of a nose.

Chapter Ten

Yuka and Emi were playing make-believe in their room. Papa was in his study across the hall reading, and their Obaachan had gone to her Sunday afternoon poetry-writing meeting. It was too cold and icy to go to the park, so they dragged their blankets over their bunk bed and made a house for themselves and their dolls. And inside their cozy little house, they discussed their papa's marital future. The adults would have been shocked to know how often this was a topic of their conversation, especially after their friend Ayumi had wisely informed them that a new wife for a papa also meant a new mama for them.

Now, having a new mama was something they agreed with in principle. But they also agreed that Papa should not have just any old wife—he needed one that met their approval.

But what characteristics should a new wife and a new mama have? Unsure, they considered all the ladies they knew that might qualify.

Their preschool teacher, Hara-sensei, was one they had briefly considered, but Emi didn't like the scary mole on her forehead.

The next-door neighbor, who left for college every morning at 7:00 with a tennis racket slung over her shoulder, was quite pretty, but they suspected she might be a bit on the young side.

The lady at the supermarket checkout counter was one they had heard their grandmothers say was single, but they didn't approve of her gloomy appearance at all.

Once, Emi snuck an envelope back to their room that had some snapshots of one of Baba's picture-ladies in it. That one, they both agreed, they did *not* like at all. She looked too much like Popeye's girlfriend, knobby knees and all. And all that makeup made her look spooky!

For lack of candidates, they studied the models in their grandmothers' magazines. They especially liked one woman standing in front of an array of homemade cakes. Now that kind of mama could be really handy to have, but they couldn't figure out how to get their papa to meet her.

But now, for the first time, a real person fueled their imaginations: Rose.

"Do you think Papa will marry *her*?" Emi asked as she was arranging the toy dishes on a plastic box they used for the table in their little house.

"He might," said Yuka, the older and wiser sister.

"Next week?" asked Emi. "Will she be our mama before the spring festival?"

"No, silly. It takes a long time for that to happen." Yuka wasn't sure of the logistics, but she suspected a wedding probably wouldn't take place that quickly. "They have to do a lot of stuff first."

"Like what?"

Yuka thought carefully as she tucked her hair behind her ears. "They have to go on a date."

"What's that?"

"They go to a restaurant and eat something. There have to be candles."

"Like on a birthday cake?"

"Yeah, like that."

"I like cake," said Emi.

"Well, it'd be a grown-up cake."

"Don't we get to have any?"

"Forget the cake," said Yuka. "There's a diamond ring, too. Papa needs to give her a ring. Like in the movies."

"Where can he get a ring?"

"I don't know. But I think he can get one at a store."

"Rose is nice," said Emi.

"Pretty, too," added Yuka.

And then they held a Barbie and Ken wedding, with Akira and Rose as the bride and groom.

Later that evening, Fumiyo unlocked the door to the house, and stepped into silence because Akira and the girls were having dinner with the other grandparents. She was full from that Korean barbecue in Okubo with the members of her poetry-writing club and a little tipsy from the beer they all had. She'd just switched on the television and settled in her chair to watch the Saturday night programs when the phone rang.

She hoisted herself up to go answer it. "*Moshi-moshi?*"

"Kaa-chan." Her son still called her mommy even though he was in his forties. "I've been trying to reach you."

"Osamu? Is anything wrong?"

"Just wanted to say hi and see how you're doing."

"Well, I'm fine. Everything's fine." Fumiyo could hear Yoko saying something to him in the background, and she wondered what they wanted now. They never called just to say hi and see how she was doing.

"Have you've given any thought to what we talked about?"

"What was that again?" she asked, even though she clearly remembered their last conversation.

"Don't you think you've stayed there long enough? We feel Akira can get along without you now that the girls are so big."

"Big? Why, they're not even in elementary school yet."

"Surely there are other people around who can help. Your home is with us."

"How are those new kitchen cabinets?" Fumiyo asked, changing the subject. "Did that give you enough storage space?" Her son and his wife not only lived rent-free in her house, they badgered her for money for endless home improvements.

"They're looking pretty good, although we're thinking about changing the hot water heater so we could run hot water directly into the bath rather than using gas to heat up the cold water in the tub."

"How much would that cost?"

"I'll look into it. But Kaa-chan, we want you to come home. We need you."

Fumiyo knew what that meant. They wanted her to come back and cook and clean for them. They also probably thought a closer proximity would grant them easier access to her money—something she was not going to let happen. Good thing she had that fancy lawyer of her dead husband handling her financial affairs. "I can't do anything until things get more settled here," she said firmly.

"It's time Akira found a woman and you leave them to it. It's not like they're your real family."

"How can you say such things about your own sister's children? Your nieces?"

"But Yoko and I feel that—"

"Yoko doesn't have a job. Surely she can manage the house on her own. After all—" Fumiyo stopped herself before saying something about her daughter-in-law she couldn't take back. Before Osamu had a chance to reply, she added, "And maybe *you* could help out more."

"Me?"

"Who else?"

Osamu snorted as if she'd made a joke. "I'm much too busy for women's work."

"Is that so?" Osamu was her son and Fumiyo loved him, of course. But sometimes he was so much like his father. "Anyway," she blurted out before considering her words. "I've decided to stay in Tokyo."

Osamu groaned with impatience. "For how long?"

"Forever."

"What!"

"That's right. I think I'll buy a small apartment near here." In the silence that followed, she added, "Not for a while, of course. But I like Tokyo. I like city life. I think I'll stay here."

"Oh," Osamu said with a dismissive laugh. "That's impossible."

Fumiyo was thinking the impossible would be moving back in with him and his wife, who always tried to put her down.

On Monday morning, Fumiyo dropped the girls off at their kindergarten and headed straight to Michie's house. "Did you know Akira has a foreign girlfriend?" she asked before she even got her shoes off.

"Did Akira tell you that?"

"Of course not. I just found out from the girls."

"The girls!" Michie said with amusement. "Well, get in here and tell me all about it."

Fumiyo followed Michie into the kitchen. She took off her quilted jacket, but underneath, she was still wearing her apron. Today it was lilac with a tulip design. "It's his English teacher from that *eikaiwa* school," she said. "They had lunch together at Denny's. Can you believe that? Lunch with the girls?"

"I hardly think that means she's Akira's girlfriend." Michie said, as she made a pot of tea.

"What else could it possibly mean?"

"That they were hungry and had lunch together."

"I don't know, Michie. I don't like the idea of some foreigner putting who knows what kinds of ideas into Yuka and Emi's heads."

"Oh, Fumiyo—"

"The girls told me all about it this morning on the way to the daycare center. They went on and on about how pretty she was. About how she can speak Japanese. About how their father can speak English. Akira never said a thing about it at all this weekend. It's like it's some big secret." She scoffed and repeated, "A *foreigner*."

Michie poured the steeped tea into the cups. "You're probably reading more into it than necessary. After all, you said she's his

English teacher. Maybe he just wanted to have more English practice. Or maybe they're just friends."

"Friends? With a *foreigner*?" Fumiyo looked as shocked as if Michie said Akira was joining the Buddhist priesthood and about to shave his head.

"It has been known to happen.

"Well, I—"

"Fumiyo, have you ever met a foreigner?"

"I've seen them on TV—"

"That doesn't count. I know you wouldn't have had much opportunity when you were in Kyushu, but what about since you've been living in Tokyo?"

Fumiyo thought a moment before speaking. "There was the time at the Renoir Coffee Shop in Ginza when a foreigner sat down at the table next to me and asked if he could have the cream pitcher."

"What did you say?"

"Nothing. But I gave it to him. I was too scared not to."

"Dear brave, Fumiyo," Michie said. "But getting back to the matter at hand. I think you're jumping ahead of yourself."

"But what if it's serious?" Fumiyo asked, her brows knitted together. "What if he wants to *marry* her?"

"Would that be so terrible?"

"Of course it would be!"

"Why?"

"Why? Well, because..." Fumiyo had to think for a moment. "Because she's not Japanese."

"Yes, well, that's true. If she's a foreigner, she wouldn't be Japanese. You didn't say anything to Akira about this, did you?"

"Of course I didn't."

"Because maybe the girls are just imagining things."

A hopeful look crossed Fumiyo's face. "Do you think so?"

"I don't know, but if I were you, I wouldn't get too worried about it."

Fumiyo couldn't let the matter drop. "But what would people say?"

Michie frowned. "I hate to tell you this, but just now, you sounded like your son."

Fumiyo swallowed an angry retort before she realized that *did* sound like something Osamu would say.

"Do you really care what people say?"

Come to think of it, she didn't.

"Would a foreigner be all that bad?" asked Michie softly. "If Akira found someone he really wanted—would it matter?" She reached across the table and patted Fumiyo's hand. "None of us will ever forget Sumiko. She lives in our hearts—*all* our hearts—forever. Even if Akira got married again, Sumiko would always be a part of him. A part of all of us. No matter what."

Fumiyo blinked back the tears that were behind her eyeballs. She knew what Michie was saying was true, but the pain of losing her daughter was always lodged in her chest.

"And have you thought perhaps it'd be easier with a foreigner? Someone so different from Sumiko?"

Fumiyo took a sip of the tea and considered what Michie had just said. She was right. In a way, comparing Sumiko with a foreign woman would be like comparing apples and cauliflower.

"So, we have two choices," Michie continued. "We can go along with him, or we can go against him. But I know Akira, and either way, he'll do what he wants to do."

"How can he know what's best for him?"

"If he doesn't know at his age, he'll never know."

Sometimes, Fumiyo got confused by Michie's big city ideas. "But what about Yuka and Emi? What'd be best for them?"

"A happy couple is always the best thing for children."

"But what if she doesn't want to be a mother? I don't even know if she's old enough to be one."

"Well, how old is she?"

"You can never tell with foreigners. They all look the same with their blond hair and big noses."

Michie turned away to hide her smile. "Well, I'm sure she's old enough, or she wouldn't be working here in Japan. But before you get too wound up about it, the whole thing could fizzle out. It's best if we just forget about it for now. Akira will tell us when he's ready. If it ever comes to that."

Chapter Eleven

"Rose-sensei," said Mrs. Hayashi, the de facto leader of the International Culture Thinking Housewives Circle when their Friday afternoon class ended. "Could you stay a few minutes longer? There's something important I need to talk to you about."

Rose glanced at her watch and figured she had a little time before she had to catch the express train to Shinjuku. She followed Mrs. Hayashi into her living room and hoped this wasn't a polite way of being told they no longer needed her. But if it was, at least she had the good grace to tell her in person. Not like that private student last year who'd left a note on her door, apologizing for not being home and informing her she didn't need any more English lessons. And that was *after* Rose had trekked all the way to Yokohama and spent a couple thousand yen on transportation.

A man the same height as Mrs. Hayashi came into the room. He had a high forehead, indicating he might become bald at some point, and slightly crooked teeth. "As you know," Mrs. Hayashi said when she introduced them, "my husband is a professor at Yamanote University in Tokyo."

Actually, Rose didn't know. Or if she did, she'd forgotten. It was hard enough to keep track of what all her students did, let alone their spouses.

"How do you do, Miss Rose?" the man said, offering a polite bow before shaking her hand. "I am Professor Hayashi." His accent was more British than any of the Brits she'd met in Japan. In fact, he sounded like he'd sprung straight out of a 1930s romantic comedy. She was so distracted by the *by joves* and the *jolly goods* he started to throw into the conversation, she didn't realize when it had become a job interview.

When she told him she had a master's degree (something Mrs. Hayashi didn't even know), he exclaimed, "Oh good heavens! You are not just an English language teacher, you are a scholar!"

She managed to keep a straight face when she told him she didn't have any academic publications or any university teaching experience. But then he began talking about the classes and the teaching schedule. "Excuse me, Professor Hayashi," she interrupted politely, "are you offering me a job?"

"One of our teachers went to England during the spring break, and we have just been informed that he will not be returning to Japan. You see, it is rather urgent for us to settle this matter. We would like you to teach two morning classes on Tuesdays and two morning classes on Wednesdays. Would you mind terribly coming to my office next week? You must meet the dean and there will be some paperwork to take care of."

"Certainly," she said, stunned. "I'd be happy to."

The offer was looking better by the minute, especially when she learned the university was within bicycling distance from her apartment. When Mrs. Hayashi poured cups of green tea and placed colorful Japanese sweets on red lacquered plates, Rose decided to forget about getting to work on time. Who cared if her pay got docked now? She was moving up in the world! While nibbling on those sweets and drinking the tea, she calculated what this new job meant to her financially. Professor Hayashi said she'd get paid every month—even during the twenty-two weeks of the year there were no classes. No wonder Michael was trying so hard to get his foot in that door. And no wonder Steve had been so smug about it all.

She caught a local train to Shinjuku and breezed into FECC twenty minutes late.

"Yeah, yeah, yeah. Sorry," she said to Kenny, tuning out his nagging voice as she punched her card into the time clock. "Something unavoidable came up."

"What's going on?" Michael whispered after she flopped down at her desk.

She opened her bag and handed him the usual assortment of Friday sweets. Shaking her head as if she didn't quite believe it herself, she whispered, "You know how you're always telling me I should quit my International Culture Thinking Housewives Circle class because all it does is make me fat? Well, get this. The leader's husband is a professor at Yamanote University, and he just offered me a job. Twice a week, four classes. Starting from the spring semester."

Michael stared at her for a few seconds. "Are you freaking kidding me?"

"Nope," she said, grinning but keeping her voice down. "Of course, I still have to keep my job here. Those classes are just part time."

"But they're a definite step up."

"Yeah. And they'll give me some time to think about my future. It'll look a lot better to have that on my resume than just this insane asylum."

"That's for sure," Michael said. "And who knows? Maybe you'll meet someone, fall in love, and stay in the Land of the Rising Sun forever."

Rose snorted, but Akira's face flashed before her. She scolded her imagination for running wild and said with more sarcasm than she'd intended, "Like you?"

"Hey, you can't say I don't try. And besides, it doesn't hurt to have a bit of fun while searching for Mr. Right."

Michael was always teasing her for wanting to settle down by the time she was thirty. He was always making fun of couples who could finish each other's sentences and who started to look like each other as they marched toward middle age and beyond. But she also knew that was what he wanted for himself. What *she* wanted for herself. To find someone special.

Chapter Twelve

When Naoko and Daisuke discovered Rose's twenty-seventh birthday was the second week of March, they insisted on celebrating with her after class that week. By nine-thirty, all six class members, including Akira, were gathered around a sunken table in a private tatami-room at a restaurant near the school. From beer, they moved to wine, *sake*, and *shochu*. With alcohol as a social lubricant, everyone's English flowed, and the conversations got louder and louder as the evening progressed. Daisuke's confidence soared, and he ordered another round of *sake* from the teenage server in English. Kana translated that into Japanese, sending them all into hysterical laughter, including the server.

Everyone, except for Keiko, who had switched to oolong tea after one glass of beer, was tipsy. It was the kind of tipsiness where people are having great fun, but one more sip could result in total drunkenness. Rose, who'd been pacing herself since the first *kampai*, was pretty sure some of them had already made that crossover. Naoko had just knocked over a glass of white wine, but Kana mopped it up with an *oshibori* towel. Tomo and Daisuke had their heads together, laughing about something as if they were the best of friends.

Akira cleared his throat and announced they should come up with a better name for themselves than just Friday Night Class.

"How about Rose Power?" suggested Daisuke.

"The English Hunters," said Tomo.

"Or the Magnificent Six," said Keiko.

In the end, they decided on the Super Six, even though Rose joked that it sounded a bit like a cigarette brand.

Akira left the table with Keiko, and they returned with the server carrying a slice of cake with a candle on it. After everyone sang a joyful and drunken happy birthday, Akira reached behind a screen near the door and pulled out an enormous bouquet of roses.

"Happy birthday," said Akira.

As he handed her the flowers, his arm grazed hers, making her feel fluttery on the inside. Their eyes met, and for a moment, Rose forgot the others from the class were even there. "Thank you," she murmured, feeling heat rising from her chest.

"Roses for our Rose," shouted Daisuke.

Rose whipped her head back toward the group. "Thank you so much, everyone!" she said, overwhelmed by their thoughtfulness.

Even though the cake was small, she insisted they all have a bite.

Then Keiko stood. "I'm so sorry, but I must go home now."

"No! No! Let's *karaoke*!" insisted Kana.

"My husband will be worried if I stay any later." She handed her share of the bill to Daisuke and slipped out the door. Cups of hot green tea were brought to the table, signaling the party was over and the table was needed for the next group of revelers. Plans were being made to go to a karaoke bar in Kabukicho.

"Sorry, I'm too tired," said Rose, "but you guys go have fun."

"I'm afraid I can't go either," said Akira.

Before Daisuke, Tomo, Naoko, and Kana set out toward their next destination of the evening, Kana gave Rose a small envelope. "Present for you. Coupon. Tanning salon."

Rose offered an awkward smile. "Thank you, but I can't do tanning—I'd turn as red as a tomato if I did."

"It facial. You get beautiful face. No tan. Promise. Tomorrow. Saturday. 5:30. Okay? You facial."

Students had given Rose all kinds of presents in the past—tickets for baseball games, movies, sumo tournaments. So why not a facial coupon? "That's so sweet of you, Kana. Thank you. I'll see you tomorrow then."

"Do you want to get a taxi?" Akira asked in the awkward silence after the two of them were left alone on the sidewalk.

"I don't know. It's nice out and a walk would be good. Get the alcohol out of the system. Unless you're in a hurry to get back."

"No, walking's great," he said.

Rose held her birthday flowers close to her chest, grateful to have something to do with her hands. Despite the easy conversations they'd had before in the coffee shop and at Denny's, Rose wasn't really sure what to talk about. "So, how are your daughters?" she asked.

"Good. They're probably already asleep, so there's no rush to get back." He slowed his pace a little, and Rose did the same. "What're your plans for the weekend?" he asked. "Besides your trip to Kana's salon, of course."

"Well, Saturday night I'm going out with Michael. I think you know him. His classroom is next to ours."

"Oh," said Akira. "That sounds nice." After a moment, he added, "Is he your boyfriend?"

"My what?" Rose barked out a little laugh. "No, he's not my boyfriend. We're just good friends." Was that relief she saw on Akira's face? Did he actually care if she had a boyfriend or not? They walked a dozen more paces, and Rose decided to tell him about her new job.

"You're quitting FECC?"

The shocked tone in Akira's voice warmed her. "No, it's just a new daytime job. This is between you and me because it's against the rules to work outside of Friendly. For the record, everyone does, though. Anyway, from the middle of April, I'll also be teaching at Yamanote University."

Akira whistled. "That's a really good school."

"Is it? I don't know much about that sort of thing."

"Every person in Japan would know it. It's a pretty big deal."

When they reached Daikyo-cho, where Rose would go her way and Akira would go his. Akira stopped. He looked like he wanted to ask her something, and Rose's chest tightened. She could feel their closeness with every inch of her body, making her both nervous and hopeful.

After a long moment, Akira nodded and said, "Well, goodnight. See you next week."

"Goodnight," she replied, turning quickly in case her face registered disappointment.

Back in her apartment, Rose placed the flowers into a pot full of water since she didn't have a vase, turned on the heater, poured a glass of barley tea, and opened the letters that were in her mailbox. A dozen birthday cards from Felix had arrived today, and she put them on the table with the others that had been coming all week long. She was touched so many people from Felix had remembered her birthday, and she felt homesick. Back home, you couldn't leave the house without running into people and having to stop and make small talk with them. There was the daily ritual of picking up the mail at the post office or of stopping in at the Uptown Café for coffee, pie, or a burger. She saw her students and their parents outside of class every day and knew where every single one of them lived.

What a contrast that was to life in Tokyo. Well, of course, the population here was a gazillion times larger than the 720 people back in Felix. People always said cities were lonely places, but the funny thing was, she really didn't feel that lonely with thirty million people all around her. She didn't really mind the anonymity of Tokyo. At least here, no one looked at her as the jilted bride of Brad Billford.

She removed her makeup, brushed her teeth, and got into her futon, thinking about the nice time she'd had with her students. It was almost as if the people in that particular class had clicked together like pieces of a puzzle. Each person was so different, but all together, they made a complete and interesting picture. Most group lessons didn't work out that way. Sometimes students were like pieces from different puzzles, and no matter what she did as a teacher, they never were able to form a community. Something was certainly different about this group of students, that's for sure. And something was different about Akira, as well.

In her futon, with the lights out, her mind swirled. Akira was someone she actually wanted to spend more time with. Someone she actually wanted to get to know. She hadn't felt like that about anyone for such a long, long time. But he was also a single dad, and she wasn't sure she was ready for anything like that. Not to mention the fact that he was Japanese, Japan was his permanent home, and she was just here for the short-term.

Chapter Thirteen

Late Saturday afternoon, Rose pushed opened the door to Kana's tanning salon, located on the third floor above a chain drugstore in Ikebukuro. When she stepped out of the elevator and into the salon, she saw it took up the entire floor. The waiting room was spacious and soft classical music played in the background. She handed the person behind the reception desk her invitation card, sat in one of the comfortable armchairs, and discretely observed her surroundings. Clearly, some of the clients with their caramel-colored skin were there for the tanning machines, particularly those two guys who looked like body builders. Several teenagers were studying the anti-wrinkle creams on a shelf. Ironically, Rose noted, considering this was also a tanning salon, skin whitening lotions were also on prominent display.

Kana came out a few minutes later wearing a white coat. She issued a string of instructions for the receptionist and then turned to Rose.

"Welcome my salon." A proud look was on Kana's face when she announced, "I boss."

Rose stared at her, utterly flabbergasted. She'd been seeing Kana as the Japanese equivalent of a dumb blond, and certainly not as a young entrepreneur, the owner of what clearly seemed to be a thriving business. "Wow, that's great," Rose said with more enthusiasm than she had intended to cover her shameful stereotyping of the young woman.

"Come. My best girl give best facial now."

Rose, whose skin care rituals were pretty bare-bone basic and involved mostly drugstore-brand face wash and moisturizer, had never experienced anything like that beauty treatment in her entire life. An hour later, her face was glowing from the application of numerous scrubs and creams. When she was asked if she'd like to have her face made up with their new brand of cosmetics, she readily agreed. By the time she joined Kana in her office in a small room at the back of the salon, Rose not only felt like an entirely new person, she looked like one, too.

Kana was typing away on a desktop word processor but stopped and invited Rose to sit in the chair across from her. Unlike the color-coordinated and comfortable decor of the salon, Kana's tiny office screamed practicality with every inch of floor and wall space utilized. Nothing touchy-feely here. Not even any soft music. It was the operation's business center. But even so, it felt comfortable, probably because of the owner's warm and welcoming smile.

The assistant came back with a pot of tea and slivers of cheesecake. Kana poured the tea, and now the proverbial shoe was on the other linguistic foot. Rose spoke broken Japanese by piecing sentences together any way she could, and Kana was the one with the advantage. With the help of a dictionary, though, Rose learned the following:

Kana's grandmother had been, in her very young days, a geisha. Not just any geisha, she explained, like those in some hot springs areas like Atami, but a high-class Akasaka geisha. Akasaka geisha, Rose learned, came second only to those in Kyoto. Her grandmother had several patrons, but one was special and she had a baby with him. He was Kana's grandfather. Before he died, he bought Kana's grandmother a building where she ran an exclusive bar on the top floor and rented out the other units to people running equally exclusive establishments. And when she died, Kana's mother took over.

"But I no want be hostess," Kana said, switching back into English and finishing up her cheesecake. "I like business, but I no like man customers."

Kana had asked her mother to help start a business, and she hit on the idea of a tanning salon after reading about how popular they'd become in the US. With that start-up money, she rented a small space and bought two tanning beds.

"I pay money back and go beauty school." Kana explained she wasn't planning on doing the beauty treatments herself, but she wanted to be sure her future employees did them right. And now, instead of borrowing money from her mother, she gets it straight from the bank.

"Well, it looks like you've got a great business. I'm so impressed." And Rose really was. What Kana had accomplished was admirable. Even enviable. She was so young to be this successful. Changing the subject, Rose asked what she'd been wondering for months. "Tell me. How did you meet Tomo?"

Kana gave a little nostalgic sigh and smiled. "We met in a coffee shop in our neighborhood."

"Was it love at first sight?" Rose wasn't sure how to say that in Japanese, but Kana seemed to understand.

"Actually, I think at first we were both in love with the shop's air conditioner," Kana replied in Japanese.

"What?"

Since neither Kana nor Tomo had air conditioners in their south-facing apartments back then, they both retreated every August afternoon to a little place in their neighborhood called Coffee Paradise, which was owned by two elderly women. With hardly any customers to occupy the tables, they didn't mind a couple of young people spending hours over their one cup of coffee. After a few days of being there at the same time, they struck up a conversation. Soon, they began sitting together. Kana was about to start her business, and Tomo was still in college. "We became lovers," Kana added, "and for Tomo, I was his first."

"Ah, that's sweet," said Rose and meaning it.

"But we will probably never get married," Kana said, quite matter-of-factly.

"Why not?"

"Because," Kana said, her voice hardening a little, her French manicured finger tapping her desk, "Tomo's mother despises me. She would never allow such a match."

"Does she have that kind of power over him?" Rose spoke as if she was shocked by Kana's statement, but in reality, she understood all too well how difficult it was to break free from a domineering parent.

"If it were only that simple," Kana sighed. "You see, Tomo's father died when he was young, and his mother sacrificed her life for him. Well," she added with a snort, "she brought him up to believe she'd sacrificed everything. And in a way, she did, I suppose. She made sure he went to the best school and got the best job. Every step of the way, she drilled into him the fact that their future and their security rested squarely on his shoulders."

"That's an awful lot for a kid to have to deal with." Rose had never met Tomo's mother (nor did she ever want to), but she could easily imagine what kind of woman she was. A few of her students also seemed to have invested themselves heavily in their sons' lives, living vicariously through their achievements while supplying them with home-cooked meals, elaborately assembled *obento* lunches, and perfectly ironed clothing. She pitied those boys' future spouses, because clearly, from those moms' points of view, no woman could ever be good enough for their little darlings.

"Tomo had no freedom," Kana continued. "He never could do what he wanted. He wanted to study psychology, but she made him go for economics. He wanted to work for a private company, but she made him become a bureaucrat. He wanted to marry me, but when he told her, she collapsed and had to go to the hospital in an ambulance."

"Oh my god! What happened?"

Kana gave a mirthless laugh. "She was faking it. She didn't have a heart attack. Or a stroke. The hospital couldn't come up with any explanation for her problem, so they just told her to take it easy. Her solution was to insist Tomo break up with me at once."

"Did he?"

"Of course he did. He does everything she tells him."

Rose shook her head in disbelief. How was it possible in this day and age someone could have *that* much control over their child? Even she drew the line as necessary when it came to her own overbearing mother.

"But," Kana added with something of a smirk, "he couldn't stay away. He came back to me a week later."

"I guess he loves you too much."

"He does," Kana said matter-of-factly. "So for now, our love is a secret."

"But what's going to happen? To both of you?" Part of Rose couldn't help but wonder if Kana would be better off without the guy, because, as far as she was concerned, he certainly was no prize.

"I think he'll marry someone his mother chooses."

The calm way Kana spoke surprised Rose. "What will you do?"

"I don't know." Kana shrugged and added cheerfully in English, "But I strong woman. I okay."

"Who are you and what have you done with my friend?" demanded Michael when Rose slid into the booth across from him at Victoria Station in Shibuya.

"Very funny. I just had my first facial ever. And my first professional make-up job. What do you think?" She turned her face so he could catch it from different angles.

"Did you buy all their products for an unheard of amount of money? Are you planning on a complete image change? Are you going to go around like this from now on?"

Rose threw her head back and laughed. "Of course not. It's just for today."

"Well, in that case," Michael said, letting out an exaggerated sigh of relief, "you look great. I mean, for a bit of fun, that is. For today. But honestly? I don't think that's really you under all that make-up."

"Yeah," Rose admitted. "I agree. I hardly recognized myself when I looked in the mirror. I think that girl must've put on five coats of foundation."

The server came to the table, and they ordered a bottle of the house wine and steak dinners. When they came back from filling up their plates at the salad bar, Michael asked what she had been doing at an esthetics salon, of all places.

"You know my class threw me a birthday party last night, right? I got a gift coupon from one of the women in it. Anyway, she's in way over her head because she can barely string three English words together, but—"

"I hate when they throw students together with mixed levels," said Michael. "It can really mess up a class."

"Yeah, but the funny thing is that she somehow manages to fit in. And I'd completely misjudged her." Rose chuckled as she recounted her afternoon with Kana. "She came right out and said she didn't have time to start learning English at the bottom."

"I suppose that's one way to look at it."

"Right? She said she took some English classes at a cultural center taught by a retired high school teacher, and he just drilled them on grammar from a junior high school textbook."

Michael groaned. "Why am I not the least bit surprised to hear that? Stupid old fart."

"Anyway, when she was telling me that, she grabbed a fistful of pens on her desk and said, 'I already know how to say, *This is a pen!* I need to learn how to talk to customers. I don't have time for all that grammar. I just want to learn how to talk.'"

Michael almost choked on his wine. "Who could blame her? I do like this woman."

"Me, too," Rose said, wiping tears of laughter out of her own eyes. "And get this. All this time, I thought she depended on Tomo-chan, that pompous boyfriend of hers. Remember how I told you I saw them coming out of that super-expensive restaurant in Roppongi? Well, guess who paid for that dinner?

"Ah..."

"And guess who pays for the English lessons? And *everything* else they do together."

"But why—"

"Because his mama controls his purse strings," Rose said before filling him in with the rest of the details. "But to be honest, I can't figure out what she sees in the guy. On a scale from one to ten, I'd say he's a five. Possibly a four. More likely a four minus."

"Sounds like he's no big prize."

"Right? And all this time, I thought she was using him for his money. Or for something. But now I'm wondering if he's using her."

"Maybe it's all about sex," Michael said, waggling his eyebrows and pretending to fan himself with his hand. "Maybe he's a real Adonis in the sack and—"

"Oh, shut up!" Rose set her wineglass down on the table with a clink and reached over and playfully flicked him on the forehead. "That's the last image in the world I need floating in my brain."

"You're just jealous," Michael said, rubbing his forehead as if she'd caused him real pain. "Because she's getting some and you're not."

Chapter Fourteen

Rose hardly slept the night before her first day at Yamanote University. She was worried she wouldn't hear her alarm. Or that she'd get lost on her way to the campus. Or that she'd lose the nerve to stand up in the front of a classroom full of college kids. She got there before the part-time teacher's room was even open, so she had to loiter in the hallway until the staff arrived. She checked her assigned mailbox, made photocopies of the materials she'd prepared for the first day, and headed to the classroom. Because she was hired just before the academic year was to begin, she had to use the textbooks the original teacher had already ordered. So, she spent the past few weeks pouring over those 1970s volumes and devising as many activities as she could think of to supplement what seemed to be only repetition drills.

Students trickled into the large lecture hall and sat way in the back. Rose glanced at the enrollment sheet she had in front of her and did a quick head count. Clearly, there were more than the forty names on the list. A *lot* more. By the time the nine o'clock bell rang, there were sixty-two students in the classroom, many of whom looked like they were settling in for a good, long morning nap. Others were chatting loudly in Japanese.

She cleared her throat and began speaking, but no one paid any attention. Then she discovered the microphone at the podium, turned it on, and started to take roll. But the sleepers still slept and the chatterers still chatted. She couldn't hear any responses and couldn't see those who were acknowledging their presence by lifting a finger. Plus, students continued to slip in through the back door, making her think she'd have to start calling roll all over again.

Only five minutes into her career as a university teacher, and things were not going well.

Then she remembered what Professor Hayashi had told her when she visited the campus for a quick tour. He said she was required to accept those who were officially enrolled in the class, but many more might try to get in. It was, he explained, up to her if she wanted to accept them or not.

She stopped taking roll and set the attendance sheet on the podium. She breathed deeply, closed her eyes, and imagined everyone in the room was a second grader. She projected the teacher voice she used when students were misbehaving and not her friendly *eikaiwa* teacher voice. "My name is Ms. Millstone and I'm the teacher for this class." Dammit, she thought after getting everyone's attention. She should've said professor. It was too late now, so she continued. "Before I go any further, I'm going to tell you how this class will operate. This'll help you decide if you want to stay or leave."

She turned around and began writing on the board.

- *There will be two hours of written homework every week.*
- *Students will also keep a daily diary in English with a half-page entry every day.*
- *Weekly quizzes will be worth 40% of the grade.*
- *Students absent more than three times will fail.*
- *Students who sleep in class will be marked absent.*

Rose paused, thinking about what else she could add to the list that would scare students away. She heard some leaving out the back door and thought her trick was working. She wanted to reduce the class size without drawing names like Professor Hayashi had suggested. She wanted students who *wanted* to take her class and not those who just got the lucky draw.

Next, she wrote: *Students who sit in the first three rows will get five bonus points every week.*

Some of the students made their way to the front, and now, with a much more manageable class size, she called the roll, added the names of the five extra students who were willing to brave her class, and passed out the papers she had photocopied earlier. Everyone seemed relieved to see the real syllabus, which was nowhere near as strict as what she'd written on the board.

Her second period went pretty much the same way, and packing up her books and materials at noon, she was exhausted. She returned to the staff room, where teachers were having lunch, and heard English spoken at one table. To her surprise, one of the people sitting there was Steve from that disastrous Roppongi dinner a while back.

"Oh," she said. "Hi."

Steve frowned at her for a moment before he recognized her. "Oh, hi. Rose, right?"

"Yeah. Steve, right?" If he was going to struggle with her name, she'd do the same with his.

"What're you doing here?"

"Well," Rose replied, thinking that question was rather blunt. "I guess I'm doing the same thing you're doing. Teaching. It's my first day."

She said hello to the other men at the table and exchanged names. After chatting with them for a few minutes, Rose said goodbye, wanting to go home and relax a little before her evening classes at Friendly.

"I never heard of them hiring anyone directly from an *eikaiwa* school before," she overheard Steve say as she put her things onto her allotted shelf space in the cabinet. "Something's kind of fishy, don't you think? That they passed Stewart over for her?"

Idiot, she thought as she walked out the door.

Rose clocked in at Friendly a few minutes before five.

"How'd it go today?" Michael asked.

"Great, but exhausting. I went home and took a two-hour nap. Good thing I set the alarm or I might've slept through to morning. I'll tell you all about it, but let me get some coffee first."

She came back from the vending machine with a can of Georgia Coffee, popped it open, and drank it down like it was a cold beer. "First, you'll never believe who also teaches there. Remember that guy I had dinner with in Roppongi with Kazumi? The one who got so drunk? Can you believe he works there? He actually insinuated I must have friends in high places to have gotten the job because, according to him, no one ever got hired from a conversation school before."

"He's not entirely wrong. You do have friends in high places."

Rose sputtered a laugh. "That's true. But it's also none of his business. I think he was basically upset because the friend he recommended for the job didn't get it."

"What a jerk."

"Believe it or not, he was better drunk." Rose saw Kenny watching them, so she opened her desk, pulled out some papers, and pretended she was using the half hour before classes began like she was supposed to: by preparing for them. "The two other foreigners I met seemed nice enough, though."

"Based on your one-day experience," Michael asked, his books spread out in front of him, "What was it like being a college professor? Different from this zoo?"

"Considering there were over sixty students in each of my classes, I'd say so."

"Sixty! How're you supposed to make that many people have a conversation with each other?"

"That's why I got rid of a lot of them. By scaring them to death."

"Not literally, I hope."

Rose gave him a sly grin that meant neither yes nor no. She looked over at the clock on the wall, sighed, and pushed back her chair. "Well, I guess it's time to get the next show on the road."

Chapter Fifteen

Because Michael was busy working on his MA thesis, he said he needed to stop going out on Friday nights and buckle down. Rose didn't mind too much because she was exhausted from her new teaching schedule and was basically dead by Friday, anyway. Tonight, she was looking forward to going straight home, taking a bath, and getting into bed with her new book. Just a few minutes before the last class was to end, Kenny stuck his head in the door and said there was a phone call for Akira.

All the other students left shortly after that, and while Rose was tidying up, Akira returned, his face ashen.

"What is it?" she asked. "What happened?"

Akira had a little trouble speaking. "That was my mother. My father had a stroke about a half an hour ago and went to the hospital by ambulance."

"Oh, no. I'm so sorry to hear that."

"I need to get to the hospital right away," Akira said, shoving his books and papers into his briefcase, "but I don't know what to do. The girls' other grandmother is away for the night. A neighbor's there, but she needs to leave by 9:20 at the latest."

Rose didn't hesitate. "If you need someone, I could stay with your daughters."

"But—"

"After all, we *are* neighbors."

Akira's eyebrows pinched together as he rubbed his forehead. "I can't ask you to do that. It's too much."

"You didn't ask. I volunteered."

Rose saw relief, tinged with doubt, on Akira's face. As she gathered up her own things, she said, "Don't forget. I used to be an elementary school teacher. And not only that, I used to babysit all the time. In fact, that's how I paid for a good portion of my college. So you could say, I'm something of a professional at this."

"Are you sure? I mean, I don't—"

"I'm sure. Let's go."

Akira flagged down a taxi in front of the building, and in less than fifteen minutes, they arrived at his house. The young woman, who'd been watching the kids, rushed out the door before they'd even removed their shoes.

"That was Shoko," Akira explained as they went into the living room. "She lives next door and helps with the kids sometimes. I promised I'd be back in time for her to make the overnight bus to Kyoto with her college friends." He motioned toward the kitchen at the other end of the living room. "I know there's curry on the stove, so you could eat that if you get hungry. But please feel free to help yourself to anything." He pointed at something on top of the television that looked a bit like a radio. "Our TV's old, but if there's a movie, you can turn that receiver on to hear it in English."

"I'm sure I can figure it out."

In the hallway, he pointed out the toilet, the washroom, and bathroom. Stopping in front of the closed door to the left of the staircase, he said, "That's, um... Obaachan's room... My mother-in-law's room. She lives here."

Rose nodded as if she'd known that all along. But earlier at Friendly, when Akira said the other grandmother was away for the night and couldn't help, she assumed that meant she lived nearby or something.

"Your daughters are upstairs?" she asked, not knowing how to comment about the resident mother-in-law.

"Come on, I'll show you." Rose followed Akira up a rather steep staircase. "These are my rooms," he said, opening the doors to a compact bedroom with a semi-double bed and a free-standing wooden wardrobe up against the wall. The room next to it seemed to be his study, with a desk, bookcase, and easy chair. The door to his daughters' bedroom was open, and a nightlight cast a soft shadow across the room. Both girls were tangled together in the bottom bunk, and Akira stepped in to cover Yuka with the blanket she'd kicked to the floor.

"Papa?" Yuka mumbled. "I have to pee-pee." She didn't notice Rose standing there when her father took her to the bathroom at the end of the hall.

"Emi," Akira explained after tucking Yuka back into bed, "might not wake up, if she has to—you know what I mean?"

"Don't worry," said Rose. "I'll manage if anything happens."

She went downstairs to let Akira change out of his suit, and he came back down a few minutes later in a pair of black jeans and a cotton sweater that looked as if they'd been made-to-order for his body.

"I'm sorry I have to rush off so quickly, but—"

"Don't apologize. I'll be fine here. Just go."

Rose locked up, and from the living room window, she watched him ride off on his bicycle. This certainly wasn't how she had planned to spend her Friday night. She told herself that this was what any good neighbor would do in such a situation. Akira needed help, so she offered it. She was being a good neighbor. That's all it was.

She wasn't hungry, so she put the curry that was on the stovetop in the fridge, fixed a mug of tea, and took it into the living room. Doing her best to ignore the memorial photo prominently displayed on the family altar, she turned on the television. But curiosity finally won out. Feeling like a great big snoop, she went over and studied the picture. How sad, Rose thought, that this pretty woman had died so young. And how sad for Emi and Yuka, who must've been babies when they lost the mother they resembled so strongly. Seeing what Akira's wife actually looked like made her existence feel all the more real to Rose. This was a person who was obviously missed by her family. A person who had left a big hole behind when she died.

A large book on the bottom shelf of the bookcase caught her eye, and she could tell it was Akira's high school yearbook. She took it to the couch and sipped her tea while thumbing through the pages. She found him with the volleyball team, and while he was indeed the shortest guy among those giant gawky teenagers, the shot of him jumping over the net to block a ball was pretty impressive.

After she finished her tea, she put the yearbook back and washed the teacup. She gathered the still-damp bath towels from the back of the dining room chairs and hung them up in the washroom. She put the dirty clothes that were on the floor into the laundry basket. Slipping off her socks so they wouldn't get wet, she stepped into the bathroom and put the plastic cover over the tub. The water was still hot enough for a bath, but she wasn't about to be stripping down and getting into it. She knew, of course, that the girls would've scrubbed themselves thoroughly before taking their bath, but it was far too intimate of a thing to even contemplate doing. Oddly enough, sharing bathwater with strangers never bothered her when she went to hot springs resorts in the countryside. But here? In Akira's house? No thanks.

She went to pee and found rolls of toilet paper stacked behind and above the toilet. The Katos were probably exchanging their old newspapers for toilet paper with the *chirigami-kokan* recycle truck, just like her landlady did. On her way back to the living room, her eyes fell on the door to the grandmother's bedroom. No matter how curious she might be, she told herself that she'd never open that door or cross over that threshold. Luckily, the temptation to do exactly that disappeared the moment the phone rang. Rose froze. How could she explain what she was doing alone in the Kato house on a Friday night?

The caller would probably freak out and get the police to come investigate. She considered ignoring it, but what if it was Akira?

"*Moshi-moshi?*" she whispered into the phone, breathing a huge sigh of relief when the caller did turn out to be him.

"Sorry," he said in a rushed and distracted tone. "Things don't look good here, and I don't think I'll be able to get home any time soon. Maybe not at all tonight."

"I'm so sorry about your father," Rose said automatically. "But don't worry. Everything's under control, and I can stay as long as you need me to."

After hanging up, she climbed the stairs to check on the girls, thinking that this whole crush thing she had going for Akira needed to be expelled from her brain. His life was just too different from hers. And obviously, it was more than a little complicated. Being here tonight was certainly proving that.

From the hallway, she saw a pile of folded clothes on the chair next to Akira's desk, and she decided to see if there was something she could sleep in that'd be better than her work clothes. Surely he wouldn't mind, she told herself, as she changed into a black sweatsuit. It hung big on her and smelled not only of laundry soap and sunshine but also of *him*. Then she retrieved a blanket and pillow from his bed and took them downstairs.

Sitting on the sofa, she flipped through the TV channels and finally settled on a late night drama involving a jealous rivalry between the owners of competing bakeries in a Tokyo suburb. It became background noise while she considered that among all the scenarios fueling her imagination the past few weeks about her and Akira, spending the night alone in his house and babysitting his kids had not been one of them.

Chapter Sixteen

Yuka woke up first at 6:00 a.m. When she saw Rose sleeping on the couch, she ran and got Emi, and the two of them acted as excited as if Santa Claus was making an off-season visit. A bit bleary-eyed from tossing and turning on the sofa all night long, Rose told them that their grandfather was sick and that their papa had gone to the hospital to see him. She was going to stay with them until he got back.

Then they bombarded her with questions:

"How long are you going to stay?"

"What's Papa going to eat for breakfast?"

"When's Obaachan coming back?"

"Can you take us to Disneyland?"

"Will you read us a story?"

"Can we have ice cream for breakfast?"

Rose had a feeling her Japanese was going to improve an awful lot that day. She answered:

"No, we aren't going to Disneyland."

"Yes, I'll read you a story."

"No, you can't have ice cream for breakfast."

"I don't know what your papa is having for breakfast."

"I don't know. No. Maybe. Yes."

Then Rose noticed Emi was wearing wet pajamas. "Did you have an accident?"

The girls exploded with laughter, and they repeated what she'd just said over and over like it was the funniest joke in the world.

"Well, take them off and put on something dry. Is the bed wet, too?"

Emi didn't know, so with the girls following on her heels, Rose went to check. The sheets were soaked. And so was the mattress pad. But at least the futon was dry. She removed the bedding and hung the futon across the upstairs balcony railing to air out. Thank goodness the rain had stopped.

She carried the soiled bedding downstairs, but now Emi was running around naked. "Why don't you go back upstairs to get something to wear?"

"I don't know where my clothes are," Emi said, jumping on the sofa.

Rose grabbed her arm and guided the next jump to lead off of the sofa and to the floor. "You don't?" she said, smiling through her teeth. "Sure you do."

Emi shook her head innocently.

"Well, I certainly don't know," Rose said, trying to hide her exasperation. "Come on. I'll help you pick something out." The girls giggled when she added, "Otherwise you'll be naked all day long and if we go to the park, people will think that's strange."

Rose managed to prevent them from emptying all the closets and drawers while choosing their outfits for the day, and after they got dressed, they went downstairs. In the laundry room, Rose changed back into her own clothes and added everything, including Akira's sweatsuit, to the washing machine.

Next, breakfast. Rose pulled a container of something out of the fridge and sniffed it.

"What's that?" asked Yuka.

"I don't know," Rose admitted.

"How can we eat it if you don't know what it is?" the girl asked.

Rose thought quickly. "I don't know what it's called in Japanese. But in English we call it, um, dingledorf."

"Okay, dingledorf. I'm going to eat dingledorf, dingledorf, dingledorf," Yuka said in a sing-song voice, rolling the exotic word around on her tongue.

"So, how about some eggs to go with the dingledorf?" If only Rose's friends could see her now.

"That's a ramen bowl," Yuka said when Rose cracked the eggs into it.

"That's okay. It'll make the eggs taste better. Chinese style."

The girls eyed her suspiciously.

"Well, that's the only bowl I could find."

The washing machine came to a thunking halt that reverberated all the way to the kitchen. Oh god! Had she somehow managed to break the damn thing? She swallowed her swear words before they escaped from her mouth, because if Emi and Yuka had learned to say dingledorf so quickly, imagine how they'd take to cursing!

Rose went to check and saw she'd simply overloaded the washer. A scream from the kitchen came as she was putting half of the dripping laundry into the sink to separate the load, and she raced back to find an entire carton of milk had been spilled on the floor.

"It's all right," she said to Emi in as normal of a voice she could muster up. "We can clean it up. Not a problem. It was just an accident."

The girls howled with laughter again, and Rose made a mental note to check if she was using the Japanese word for accident—*jiko*—correctly. She reached for a towel to clean up the spill, but when she stepped into the milky puddle, her foot shot out from under her and she fell and banged her head on the chair.

"Are you all right?" asked Yuka, hovering over her.

Seeing stars, Rose raised her hand to her throbbing head, relieved to find no blood. She pulled herself up off the floor and ordered the girls to go into the living room. "Don't do anything until I fix breakfast," she said, blinking back tears of pain.

"Can we talk to each other?"

"Yes, you can do that."

"Can we play with our dolls?"

"Are they in the living room?"

"No."

"Well, then," Rose said, putting on her teacher's voice of authority. "You can't do that. I need you to sit there. Talk to me while I clean up."

Rose wiped the floor, scrambled the eggs, dished up rice that was still in the rice cooker, and called the girls back into the kitchen for breakfast. It was now 7:00 a.m.

"I'm thirsty," said Emi as she took a bite of the dingledorf. "Can I have milk?"

"There isn't any!" Yuka cried. "You spilled it."

Before an argument could break out, Rose promised they'd go shopping after breakfast. The girls ate and Rose sat at the table, rubbing the small lump forming on the back of her head.

"Aren't you going to eat anything?" asked Yuka.

"No. I wish I had some coffee, though."

"Obaachan likes coffee," Emi said.

"Do you know where she keeps it?" Rose asked, not daring to get her hopes up.

Emi shook her head.

"But I know where the coffee pot is." Yuka pointed at the bottom of the cabinet.

Rose almost fainted in relief when she found not only the coffee pot but also a stash of coffee. Salvation. She fixed a large pot, knowing she'd need a triple dose of caffeine to get through the morning. After practically inhaling that first cup, she felt slightly more human.

Hiding her concern that Akira hadn't called since last night, she sipped at her second cup of coffee. "Your papa might have to stay at the hospital longer," she explained, more for herself than for them. "So, what would you like to do this morning?"

"Let's go to Gaien Park," said Yuka.

Rose certainly wasn't confident enough to take them that far. "Let's go to the playground down the street instead."

"We always play there," protested Emi.

"But I've never been. You can show me all the stuff. It'll be fun."

After Rose hung the laundry outside, cleaned up the puddles in the laundry room, retrieved the futon from the garden after it had fallen off the balcony railing, they walked to the playground. It was now 10:00 a.m.

Several of their preschool friends were on the swings, and Emi and Yuka rushed over to join them.

"Are you their English teacher?" one of the mothers asked with suspicion.

Rose could imagine her reporting back to the Kato family that she was shirking her duties by speaking in Japanese to the Kato children. She pretended not to understand and smiled at the women standing together under a late blossoming cherry tree before realizing that probably made things worse. Now she simply looked incompetent. She moved closer to Emi and Yuka because the last thing she needed was for one of them to fall off the monkey bars, making an emergency room stop the next item on the morning's itinerary.

At 11:00, the girls were hungry, so they went to the little neighborhood supermarket and came back with milk, grapes, cookies, and already prepared fried noodles. Rose prayed Akira would come home soon because she couldn't even begin to think as far ahead as dinner. Although, she figured the curry in the fridge would do if absolutely necessary. She prayed again that it wouldn't be.

After lunch, they read books, drew pictures, and played Candy Land. Rose told them what things were in English, and the girls repeated after her, having fun making such exotic sounds. After a while, they fell asleep on the floor, and Rose dozed off shortly after them.

She was in that comfortable, half-asleep state that only daytime napping can bring, when she was jolted awake. Standing over her was an older woman, looking as shocked as if she'd just come across a horrific crime scene.

"*Konnichiwa*," Rose said from her spot on the floor. She pushed the girls away from her and stood. Not sure what to do next, she bowed.

The woman looked rather surprised but bowed back.

So Rose bowed again.

"Obaachan!" Emi and Yuka had also awakened and wanted to know if she had brought them any presents.

"Where's Akira?" The grandmother's eyes darted about the room as if he might be hiding somewhere.

"Papa went to the hospital last night because Jiji's sick," said Yuka. "And Rose came to babysit."

Rose wanted to hug the kid for her quick explanation because she wasn't sure if she would've been able to do that herself. Especially when she realized she didn't know what the word for "stroke" was in Japanese.

"Last night? What about today?" the grandmother demanded.

"I don't know," said Rose uncomfortably. "Akira hasn't called at all today."

A frown covered the older woman's face when she marched over to the telephone and adjusted the receiver so it fit properly on the cradle. Rose inwardly groaned with embarrassment and was about to apologize when the phone rang. The grandmother snatched it up and spoke excitedly for a few minutes before waving the receiver at Rose to come and talk.

"I've been trying to reach you all morning!" exclaimed Akira. "Is everything okay?

"Sorry. I hope I didn't worry you too much. I didn't know the phone was off the hook until just now." Rose felt like a complete idiot. "Everything's fine here. How's your father?"

"Not so good," Akira replied, sounding completely spent. "I'll tell you about it when I get back."

"I was thinking I should head off, now that the girls' grandmother's back." It had been such a long day. Rose's head ached, and she couldn't wait to get out of yesterday's clothes and into a hot bath.

"I'll be home in ten minutes. Could you wait till I get back?"

"All right," Rose replied, hiding her reluctance.

She hung up the phone, and the grandmother, with a navy and yellow apron now tied over her clothes, motioned for her to sit at the dining table. Rose watched in discomfort as the older woman scurried about, arranging cups and saucers and a plate of snacks on a tray.

It looked like tea time was about to begin.

For the past eighteen hours, Akira had been so busy dealing with his father's doctors and comforting his mother at the hospital, he barely had a chance to think about what it meant to leave Rose overnight in his house with his kids.

She had been on his mind constantly the past few weeks, even though he tried not to think about her in any way other than the English teacher for his Friday night class. But her image constantly slid uninvited into his thoughts. He found himself daydreaming about Rose at times he should've been concentrating on work or family.

On the day they walked home together after her birthday party, he had come this close to asking her if she'd like to have coffee or dinner with him sometime. But he lost his nerve. He reminded himself as they stood there on the street corner that she was younger than him. That she was free and single and only in Japan temporarily. He, on the other hand, was not that many years away from forty. He had a family, and his life was cemented to Japan. He walked away from her that night, telling himself it was best to keep things the way they were.

As hard as he tried, though, he couldn't shake off his growing interest in Rose. He wanted to get to know her better, and he imagined having long candlelit dinners where they told each other what was on their minds. He imagined taking her in his arms and kissing her lips, touching her body, and holding her tight. It was a fantasy, he told himself. But one he couldn't stop indulging in.

He never imagined Rose would jump in so quickly with an offer to help when he told her his father had been hospitalized. He never imagined leaving her in his house with his children, alone, for hours and hours. He never imagined coming home after a long night and day at the hospital to find her huddled over his old junior high school English-Japanese dictionary with Obaachan, eating snacks and drinking tea.

"*Tadaima*," he said as he stepped into the room. He hadn't realized how tired he was until he heard the exhaustion in his own voice.

Obaachan jumped up and almost knocked the teapot off the table, but Rose managed to grab it before it fell onto the floor. Akira slumped into the chair next to Rose. Just being that close to her somehow made him feel better. Emi and Yuka climbed into his lap, and feeling their arms around his neck was another tonic that lifted his spirits.

"How is he?" Obaachan demanded.

Akira sighed, and in a mixture of Japanese and English, he updated them on his father's situation. "The worst is over for now, but we have to just wait and see."

"I should go see if Michie needs my help," said Obaachan.

Akira shook his head. "Maybe later. It was a hard night, and I think she's planning to get some sleep."

Rose cleared her throat as she pushed her chair away from the table. "Well, I think I'd better get going."

"*Chotto matte*," Obaachan said, holding her hand up in a stop gesture. She disappeared into the kitchen and came back a minute later with two bags of food containing plastic containers of leftovers, packages of instant ramen, a bunch of bananas, and, of all things, a box of cornflakes.

"Here," Obaachan said, handing it all to Rose. "You can have this for dinner tonight."

Akira wondered how much Obaachan thought foreigners actually ate for dinner. Rose stared at the offering before turning her eyes to him. He nodded. "Please take it. It'll make her happy."

With her best and most formal Japanese, Rose bowed and said thank you.

The girls, sensing presents were being doled out, came to check.

"Oh Papa," Emi said, pointing at one of the food containers, "did you know that's called *dingledorf* in English?"

Akira looked at the *kimpira gobo*—sautéed carrots and burdock root—and smiled. It was the first natural smile he had produced in hours. "Dingledorf?"

"Don't ask," Rose said, her cheeks turning pink. "I'll explain later."

"Since you've got so much to carry, I'll give you a hand. Give me the bag with that dingledorf. It looks a lot heavier than the one with the... spangle-dongers." His hand brushed Rose's shoulder when he pointed at what seemed to be a container of meatballs.

"Yeah, right," Rose said, laughing.

"When they were halfway down the block, he said in all seriousness, "I can't tell you how much I appreciate you stepping in yesterday like you did. You were a real lifesaver." There was so much more he wanted to say, but the words just wouldn't come out.

"It was nothing," Rose replied automatically.

"Nothing? If that was nothing, I hate to see your definition of *something*."

"Well..."

"You can be honest. Was it that bad? Because I do know there's a fine line between being cute and being obnoxious when it comes to kids. Especially mine."

"It was harder than I thought it'd be," Rose admitted. "I was totally exhausted by the time we finished lunch. That's why their grandmother found me sprawled out asleep on the floor. She looked so shocked to see me there. I think I might've traumatized her for life."

"To be honest," Akira said, half smiling and half frowning, "I don't think she's ever talked to a foreigner before."

"That was kind of obvious," Rose said with a wry laugh. "But thanks to your dictionary, we somehow managed."

"What did you two talk about?"

"I'm not sure, but I think it was mostly about you."

Akira groaned a little. "Maybe I shouldn't ask."

Chapter Seventeen

All week long, Rose wondered how Akira's father was doing in the hospital. She thought of calling to find out but realized she didn't have his telephone number. She thought of stopping by his house and leaving a note in his mailbox, but with all the mixed feelings she was having about his complicated life as a single father, she decided it'd be better not to.

She knew from the get-go that allowing her brain to fantasize about one of her students was a bad idea. Maybe last weekend was the wake-up call she needed to rein in her imagination. But she couldn't stop thinking about how Akira's twinkling eyes always showed strength and kindness. About how his voice was so pleasing to her ears she could listen to him speak all day long. About how his slim and muscular body filled out his clothes—even his conservatively cut business suits—in the most perfect way.

When Friday evening rolled around and Kenny told her that Akira Kato had called to say he'd be absent, she realized exactly how much she had been looking forward to seeing him in the class. She hid her disappointment and hoped that didn't mean his father had taken a turn for the worse.

Once she started teaching, though, she had little time to think about any of that. The last class of the week—the "Super Six" they now called themselves—was as pleasant as always, even without Akira.

Daisuke led the discussion, which tonight was on gun control in America. Since that mass shooting at a McDonald's in San Diego last year, guns were always a hot topic for advanced classes. And thanks to shows on Japanese TV like *Columbo* and *Miami Vice*, everyone was convinced that all Americans owned guns. Which, from her personal experience, was pretty much true. Even her father had one, she told them. But when she explained that was only to hunt wild turkeys in the fall with his friends, they looked at her in disbelief. Apparently, hunting for sport was equally unimaginable for them. The class unanimously agreed that living in a society where no one but the police (and an occasional yakuza) had a gun was far better. Rose kept her opinions to herself, but she didn't exactly disagree with that sentiment, either.

By nine, she was exhausted and was more than ready to go home with her brand-new copy of *The Handmaid's Tale* she picked up that morning at Kinokuniya Book Store. But when she saw Akira standing in the shadows of the building's entrance, her tiredness evaporated.

"Sorry I couldn't make it to the class," he said, smiling as he approached her. "Something unavoidable came up at work. And sorry I couldn't contact you during the week. I didn't realize until after we said goodbye that I didn't have your phone number."

"I missed you tonight. I mean," she added quickly, "the *class* missed you. It's always nice when you're there. With your opinions and thoughts and—" Rose bit her tongue before something even more idiotic escaped from her mouth. "How's your father doing?"

"No real change since the weekend," he said. "That's not a bad thing. He's getting the care he needs in the hospital and it's giving my mother a break. But listen, if you aren't in a hurry tonight, there's a place I know about ten minutes from here. I was hoping to take you out to say thanks for watching my kids and—"

"You don't have to thank me," Rose interjected, but still feeling pleased by the offer. "I was glad to help."

"But you're hungry, right?"

Akira looked so hopeful, and she smiled up at him. "Yes, I'm hungry."

"Have you ever been to Golden Gai?"

"Yeah, a couple of times with Michael and his friends. There's a bar there they like to go to. But I don't think I've eaten there. I don't think I'd have a clue where to go."

"Well, let me be your guide," Akira said as they set off toward that part of Shinjuku. When they turned into the six blocks that made up the Golden Gai neighborhood, they passed a group of middle-aged women in pastel suits taking pictures of themselves in front of a three-foot tall pink plastic flamingo guarding the entrance of a bar called The Farky Flamgo. "Not here," he said with a chuckle. "A bit further down."

At the next corner, they turned into a darkened lane and walked through a maze of alleyways. Akira stopped in front of a ramshackle building and said, "It doesn't look like much from the outside, but I think you'll like it."

Rose followed him down a flight of creaky stairs and into a restaurant filled with well-dressed people of all ages. Ribbons of aromatic smoke from meat roasting on the grill drifted toward them. All the staff shouted out *irashaimase* in greeting. A tiny woman, who seemed to be in her late seventies, with permed, jet-black hair, guided them to a table in the back.

"This place is incredible," Rose said, her eyes gleaming in anticipation. "I never would've found it on my own."

"Probably not. My grandfather brought me here when I was a student. He used to hang out a lot in this neighborhood in the '60s."

"I thought Golden Gai was mostly gay bars."

"Yeah, but there are other kinds of places as well. Some you'd definitely want to stay away from because they're notorious for overcharging people. But back in the day, this neighborhood was popular among artists and writers. My grandfather—my mother's father—was a literature professor, so he liked hanging out in the literary bars. He wasn't much of a writer himself," Akira added with a chuckle, "but he associated with them. He even knew Yukio Mishima—you know, the guy who wrote books like—"

"Of course I know who that is. After I came to Japan, I read all his books. He's the one who committed suicide in front of everyone on top of that government building, right?"

"Yeah. That was an enormous shock for my grandfather. Well, for *everyone*, actually."

"What a waste of talent," Rose said. No one back home had ever heard of Yukio Mishima, but it was on all the news when he disemboweled himself in a ritual suicide in front of a shocked public audience. It was one of the few things about Japan she'd actually known before she arrived.

The old woman appeared back at their table and looked at Akira expectantly.

"How about a beer?" he asked Rose. "Or maybe sake?"

"I had a bad experience with sake once, but beer sounds good."

After determining Rose's likes (sashimi okay) and dislikes (slimy things not okay), he ordered.

The woman came back a minute later with their beers and plopped down a small dish, which Rose automatically slid across the table.

"You don't like *shiokara*?" Akira asked.

"Fermented squid guts fall under the category of slimy."

"But they're *good*!" he said in a joking tone.

"Aren't you glad they're all yours, then?" she said, laughing. "I tried them once, and believe me, that was more than enough."

Their table was soon covered with a variety of dishes, including simmered eggplant with shaved bonito fish flakes, deep fried tofu, grilled sardines with grated *daikon* radish, fresh tomato salad, sticks of grilled *yakitori*, marinated mushrooms, and to round it all off, a large plate of hot, crispy french fries.

Rose sighed as she bit into a french fry. Here was a man after her own heart.

Akira's face turned somewhat serious as he set his beer mug down on the table. "Actually, I didn't bring you here just to say thanks. I guess I wanted to…"   With a little laugh, he said, "I guess I'm pretty nervous. It's been a long time since I've been on… a date." His intonation rose slightly at the word *date*, making it sound almost like he was asking Rose a question.

"Is this a date?" she whispered.

"Well, no. Um, yes. Um, maybe." He picked up his beer and sipped it. "It can be a date if you want it to be."

Rose felt heat rising out of her belly and moving all the way up through her neck and onto her cheeks. For the first time, she knew she wasn't imagining things. There *was* something going on between them. "We can call it a date, if you like," Rose whispered. "I'd like it to be a date."

Akira's face brightened, but then he pulled back, creating some distance between them. In a low voice, he said, "I should tell you some things before… well, before anything else."

He looked so serious Rose almost wished they were talking about the gruesome suicide of Yukio Mishima again. But she nodded to let Akira know to continue.

"You already know that I'm a widower and that I have two children."

"Yes, that I do know." Rose tried to make her words sound like a joke. After all, it was no secret that she'd spent hours and hours with his children the previous week.

But Akira just continued. "My wife's name was Sumiko."

"Sumiko," Rose repeated softly. Hearing her name made her seem even more real.

"Yuka was three and Emi wasn't quite one when she died." Akira's voice was sad, but not full of pain.

"They were so young to lose their mother," whispered Rose.

"It was the hardest thing I've ever had to go through," he said, after telling Rose about the day Sumiko was diagnosed with breast cancer and the difficult weeks that followed. "But somehow, we survived. My daughters and I—we are doing okay now."

Rose stopped herself from reaching across the table for Akira's hands by keeping hers wrapped around her beer mug. "I'd say you're doing more than okay. From what I can tell, you're a good father. And you've got a couple of really great kids." Even though last weekend had been quite the challenge, she meant what she said.

"My daughters are my life. You understand that, don't you?"

Rose nodded.

"But here's the other thing. I know my life is complicated. I never would've been able to manage after Sumiko died without my mother-in-law moving in with us. I'm sure that seems strange to you because it seems kind of strange to everyone. But my daughters weren't even in daycare yet. I couldn't ask my mother for much help because my father had just been diagnosed with Alzheimer's."

As Akira spoke about his unconventional family situation, Rose heard Kazumi's voice in her head, urging her to get out while she could. She'd been in Japan long enough to understand that Japanese family relationships could be very tricky. How many of her students had said they'd *never* marry an oldest son, especially if he lived with his parents? But *this*? Rose knew she should say thanks for the dinner and head straight home. She knew it'd be better to end whatever this thing with Akira might become before it ever got started.

That was what she intended to do. She really did.

Instead, she found herself agreeing to have another beer, and they spent the next three hours talking.

Chapter Eighteen

Rose floated around her apartment the next day, replaying every single thing she and Akira talked about on their *date*. Her body temperature alternated between warmth with anticipatory pleasure and cold fear over what she was getting herself into. She hadn't felt this strongly about a man in a long, long time. And that was good. But this was a *Japanese* man, with a life that was deeply settled in Japan. And not only that, he had a ready-made family. Was she insane to be considering any part of that?

She wanted to talk to someone about her roiling emotions, and that someone was going to have to be Michael. But now that he was in her apartment where they were getting ready to watch the videos his mother had sent this week, she felt hesitant. She knew he'd be all for any sort of progress when it came to her non-existent love life. He'd say she was crazy for worrying about next month, next year, and the rest of her life when nothing had actually happened yet. But she couldn't help thinking that far ahead, even though she herself knew it was kind of crazy.

Rose was getting the evening's snacks ready, and Michael had just slid the video into the player when the phone rang. "I wonder who that is," she said as she reached for it, half hoping it was Akira. "*Moshi-moshi?*"

"And mushy-mushy to you, too."

"Oh, hi, Mom." Rose was surprised that for once, she was calling at a decent hour.

Not wasting a second of her expensive international phone call, her mom got right to the point. "Denise needs your measurements."

"Measurements?"

"For the maid of honor dress, of course."

"Oh." Rose had been trying to forget all about Denise's wedding. "Look, I promise I'll send them to you in a few days. I don't have an American measuring tape. It's only in centimeters." She'd have to ask one of her mathematically minded high school students to convert the measurements for her.

"I don't know why those Japanese people can't count in feet and inches like everybody else," her mother grumbled.

Rose took a breath. "What colors did Denise finally decide on?"

"Lime green and lemon yellow."

"Really?" Rose would've gone with softer colors. Pastels: pinks, violets, and purple. Then she remembered those *were* the colors she had chosen for her own wedding—the wedding that never took place. "Sounds perfect," she said, putting aside those thoughts.

"Oh, yes. We placed the order for the fabric a couple days ago, and Mabel Schwarz's going to make all the dresses. Yours will be lime, and the bridesmaids' dresses will be lemon. Mabel's making matching vests for the groomsmen as well."

The moment her mom's kitchen timer beeped in the background, they said a hurried goodbye and Rose turned around to face Michael. There was no putting it off—she was going to have to convince him to go with her to the wedding.

"Um, Michael," she said, taking the plastic wrap off the brownies she'd made earlier in her tiny toaster oven and sliding the plate toward him. "I have a really big favor to ask."

He reached for one, bit into it, and moaned. "Are you trying to butter me up with sugar? Because if you are, it's totally going to work."

"Maybe," Rose said with a nervous giggle. "You see, there's this wedding in Nebraska. And I was kind of hoping you'd go with me."

"You mean, like a *date* date?"

"Yeah, something like that."

"At a wedding way out in the cornfields?"

"It's not just any wedding," she said. "It's Brad's brother's wedding."

Michael's eyes narrowed in disapproval. "Why in the world would you even consider going to *that*?"

"I don't want to go, but he's marrying my cousin. So I kind of *have* to go." From the way Michael was looking at her, she could tell he understood exactly why going to that wedding would be difficult for her. She pushed another brownie in his direction. "And it's not in the cornfields, either. It's in a church."

"I don't know. I was kind of thinking of going to Thailand during the summer holidays."

Rose couldn't hide the disappointment in her voice. "Never mind, then."

Michael ate his second brownie and shrugged. "But my parents are pressuring me to go to my grandmother's eightieth birthday party this summer. When's the wedding again?"

"August 3. It'd be fun," Rose added hopefully when Michael looked like he was seriously considering it. "You've never been to the Midwest. Think of it as an experiment in life."

"I'll have to double check on things. But if I do go, it'll be on one condition and one condition only. If I ever need to pretend that I'm straight, you've got to be my date. No matter when and no matter where."

Rose threw her arms around him. "It's a deal."

"So tell me, are there any cowboys in the area? I have this fantasy where me and some—"

Rose leaned back and punched him on the shoulder. "Don't forget, you've got to be my straight date."

"A fellow can dream, right?"

With that settled, Michael slipped *Cheers* into the VCR, and as they watched Diane and Sam bicker across the bar counter in the place where everybody knows your name, Rose wondered how to bring up the topic of Akira.

When the tape halted three quarters of the way through one show and began rewinding, Michael chuckled. "I guess we'll never know how that turns out. Good timing, I suppose," he added, checking his watch. "If I don't leave soon, I won't get home at a decent hour."

"Before you go," Rose said with some hesitation, "there's something I've been meaning to tell you. You know my Friday night class at Friendly?"

"The one that threw you the birthday bash?"

"Yeah. Well, there's this guy in it. His name's Akira and—"

Michael stared at her for half a second before letting out a whoop. "Oh! My! God! You've fallen for a student!"

"I didn't say that."

"You don't have to. It's all over your face. Now," he said, leaning forward with an evil grin that took up his entire face, "is it a one-way crush, or have you been having a little hanky-panky on the side you haven't told me about?"

"Oh, shut up about the hanky-panky. It's not like that at all. We've just seen each other a few times. That's it."

"But you'd like it to be more."

"I don't know," Rose said, feeling her cheeks growing pink. "I mean, nothing's happened yet. We're just in the talking stage."

Michael snorted. "The talking stage? What does that even mean?"

"Well, there are issues to consider."

"What issues? If you like him and he likes you, it's simple."

"It's not that simple."

Michael cocked his head quizzically at Rose until a horrified look fell across his face. "Holy crap! Are you telling me he's married?"

"He's—"

"What are you thinking, getting involved with a married man? This isn't like you at all, and—"

"Stop! He's not married!"

"Well, if that's not the problem, what is it, then?"

"He's a widower. And he's got kids."

Michael was silent while he studied Rose's face. "Ah," he finally said. "You like him. You *really* like him."

Rose's voice was full of uncertainty. "Maybe I do."

"What's stopping you from moving forward? It can't be because of his kids because you actually like those little snot noses for some reason," he said, half joking.

"I do like kids. But what if it doesn't work out?"

"Because it might not work out you're scared to give it a go? Coward."

"Go ahead and call me that. But what if this relationship goes any further? What if I start to like them and they start to like me? They could get hurt. I could get hurt." Rose took a breath. "And then there's Japan to consider."

"What about Japan?"

"It's not like it's just about me and Akira and his children. I'd have to decide about Japan. Decide if I want to stay here forever."

"Forever is a long, long time," quipped Michael. "And besides, you like it here."

"True. I do like it here. *Now*. But I need to ask myself if I want to be here in my thirties. My forties. And god forbid, when I'm old and in my fifties."

Michael rolled his eyes. "Don't you think you're jumping ahead of yourself? Like, way, way, way ahead of yourself?"

"Maybe. But then... Well, you see, there's some more stuff that makes it even more complicated."

As Rose told Michael about Akira living with his dead wife's mother, he just stared at her.

Chapter Nineteen

April 29th was Emperor Hirohito's birthday and a national holiday that launched the other holidays that made up Golden Week. Rose dug out the jogging outfit she'd bought at the end of last year, intending to get fit and rid herself of the pesky five pounds that had crept up on top of another pesky five pounds. With Denise's wedding coming up, she couldn't go home looking even more pudgy than before. So she made a plan: she'd become a jogger and join those who use Jingu Park as their running course. Her teaching schedule no longer had her traipsing all over Tokyo, so she had no excuse not to get up early and exercise before work. If she did that every day, that extra weight would magically melt right off!

She slipped the *Thriller* cassette into her Walkman, tucked it into her fanny pack, put the headphones on over her head, and set off at an easy pace. After just one song, she stopped and braced her hands on her thighs to catch her breath. She modified her original plan—brisk walking was also an excellent exercise. After twenty minutes, she reduced her pace to a nice stroll and meandered for a while under the dappled light of the tall trees in the park. She plopped down on a bench and wished she'd thought to bring some money with her so she could get a can of juice from a vending machine. And a book. And maybe some cookies to snack on.

People watching was also a good hobby, she told herself. Educational, too.

Then she noticed Akira and his daughters over by the place where they loan out bicycles of all sizes for free. In the paved area off to the side of the bike path, it looked like he was trying to teach Yuka how to ride one without training wheels. Emi was on a tricycle, peddling in circles next to them. She watched Akira interact with his daughters for a few minutes before heading toward them.

"Hi, everyone."

The girls rushed over to give her a hug, and Rose felt positively giddy when she saw Akira's face light up when he saw her.

"You're out jogging?" he asked.

Rose didn't want to lie. "Mostly walking. And thanks for dinner the other night. It was a nice… um, date." Embarrassed, she turned to Yuka and Emi and said in Japanese, "What's going on here?"

"We're learning to ride bikes!" said Emi. "And I'm next." From her tricycle, she pointed at a bike with training wheels next to what looked like Akira's bike. "Papa's gonna teach me how to ride the big girl's bike next."

"I could help if you like," she offered, glancing over at Akira for confirmation. "You just need someone to hold on from behind, right?"

For the next half an hour, Akira ran with Yuka until she could ride the two-wheeler with confidence and Rose ran with Emi until she was no longer afraid to ride the more wobbly bike with training wheels

"I'm never gonna ride a tricycle again," announced Emi.

"And I'm never gonna use training wheels again," announced Yuka.

"And I'm dying of thirst," announced Akira. He looked down at his watch. "Time's up. We've got to return these bikes and let some other kids have their turns on them."

"Can we take them back by ourselves?" asked Yuka, looking very grownup about it all.

"Sure. Why not?" their father replied, a proud smile spreading across his face.

"Whew," Rose said, mopping her forehead with a handkerchief after they were out of earshot. "I didn't expect to get quite that much exercise today."

"Me either. If you hadn't come along, I would've had to run around twice as much. So, I guess I owe you. Again. How about lunch this time?" Akira smiled and gestured toward the large, insulated picnic bag in his bike's basket. "There's plenty."

"I wouldn't want to intrude on your weekend time with your daughters." A date was one thing, she told herself. This was something else entirely.

"Believe me, they'd love it if you did."

When he asked Emi and Yuka what they thought about Rose joining them, they whooped in approval and set off to find a good shady spot for their picnic. A few minutes later, they were all sitting cross-legged in their stocking feet on a large plastic mat with their shoes neatly lined up next to it. Rose realized this was no simple picnic with peanut butter sandwiches and carrot sticks the moment Akira opened up the bag and began pulling out rice balls, sandwiches, a Japanese-style omelet, fried chicken, sausages cut like octopuses, cherry tomatoes, and sliced apples. There was also a small container with the famous dingledorf, which excited the girls even further.

Rose was now linguistically prepared. "*Kimpira gobo,*" she said, having learned the name after asking the members of the International Thinking Culture Housewives Circle about a dish made with carrots and burdock root.

The girls still insisted on calling it dingledorf.

It was comfortable being with Akira and his daughters, but Rose wasn't sure what to think of the grandmother who had prepared this elaborate lunch for them—the grandmother they all called "Obaachan." She had been more than nice to her last weekend and had even given her a box of cornflakes, of all things. Rose ate a bit of everything laid out in front of her and asked Akira to convey her compliments to the cook when he got back.

Luckily, Emi and Yuka chattered a lot, and it was easy to keep up with their conversations when they revolved around Tokyo Disneyland, fairytale princesses, and whether butterflies were pretty or scary creatures. When Yuka spotted some of their neighborhood friends playing with a ball in a grassy space, the girls ran over to join them.

Now that Rose and Akira were alone, they started talking about their English class, and the topic turned to Kana and Tomo. Rose was a bit hesitant to ask what he thought about Tomo's mother controlling his life, but she did want to know his thoughts on the matter. After all, his mother—correction *mothers*—were an important part of his life, too.

"I guess someone like Kana doesn't fit into her plans for her son," he simply said.

"Even though she's very successful at what she does?" The warm spring breeze blew Rose's hair in her face, and she distractedly swiped it back.

"I imagine she wants him to have the kind of wife who'd support him from behind the scenes."

"And she thinks someone like Kana wouldn't do that?"

"A successful businesswoman might not put priority in getting her husband ahead in the world."

"That's so old-fashioned," Rose said, rolling her eyes.

"I agree." He reached for the last apple slice, bit into it, and chewed thoughtfully. "When I joined my company in 1978, it was pretty much understood by everyone that to get ahead, a man needed a wife. The bosses thought marriage made the men more stable, so they wanted them to get settled as quickly as possible."

"But if one of the women in the company got married—"

Akira sighed. "It's like Naoko said in our class. Women aren't exactly *forced* to quit when they get married, but nearly all of them do."

"Is it true," Rose asked, remembering what Kazumi had told her, "about girls having a better chance of getting hired at a company if they are a two-year college graduate than if they have a four-year degree?"

"Unfortunately, yes," he said. "Companies believe a junior college graduate will work for about five years before getting married. As opposed to two or three for a college graduate. It's seen as a better investment. Especially when the work they are assigned to do isn't all that different. Unfortunately," he added.

"A better investment?" Rose sputtered. "Is that how they view women?"

"All employees are seen as investments for a company," Akira replied. "Men, women. Everyone. And I believe that's not just in Japan. It's the corporate world everywhere."

"I suppose you're right," Rose said with resignation.

"I'm sure my company saw me as an investment when they hired me. I was from a pretty good university. I got married a few years later. Then I had kids." Rose followed his eyes when he paused and glanced over at Emi and Yuka playing a very noisy game of tag with their friends. "I guess you could say I was the whole stability package. After Sumiko died, the company gave me a lot of leeway. They were good about that. They didn't ask me to do too much. They didn't make me go on international business trips or transfer me somewhere. I didn't have to entertain clients at night. They were pretty understanding of my situation."

"As hard as it must've been," Rose said, "at least your company supported you."

"I'm lucky they did. But I'm pretty sure now they want the old Akira Kato back."

"What do *you* want?"

"I'm not sure, but one thing I do know is that I don't want to live for the company. I don't want to be one of those so-called Japanese 'economic animals' you read about in the newspaper. I want to be happy."

Rose had heard plenty about the crushing lifestyles of the salaried men in Japan from the wives she'd been teaching. "I don't really know much about this sort of thing because I'm from a small town. My dad's an insurance agent. Pretty much a nine-to-five job, unless there's an emergency involving crops or livestock," she added with a little laugh. "And everyone else does farm-related work. People back home don't give everything to their work because they feel family's more important."

"Family *is* important," agreed Akira. "The most important thing. And family can be complicated. Like mine."

Rose didn't know how to respond. There was no skirting around the fact that Akira's family situation was not only complicated, it was sticky. The super-glue kind of sticky.

Akira studied Rose's face for a moment before saying, "I have two mothers. My own and Sumiko's. For a lot of women, that's a deal breaker. A lot of women would run off in the opposite direction when they hear that."

"Have you had lots of women running off in the opposite direction?" Rose was attempting to keep the conversation light.

"Actually, you're the first woman I've ever really talked to about this." He swallowed hard and added a little hoarsely, "You're the first woman I've cared enough about to do so."

Even though Akira had two kids and two mothers, Rose couldn't stop her heart from doing all sorts of flip-flops after he'd essentially said that he cared for her.

Chapter Twenty

After the picnic, Akira took Yuka and Emi home and Rose went back to her apartment. She showered and headed to the larger supermarket in the neighborhood to get supplies for the week. It was full of women waiting for prices to be cut for the before-dinner sales. They were easily identifiable as housewives because of the aprons over their clothes—aprons of every style, design, and color. Some of them had babies strapped to their backs, and some were pushing toddlers around in strollers. Not a single man was to be seen, except for those few over in the alcohol section. She hadn't given that much thought to this particular demographic of the Japanese population before, but now she was eyeing them with curiosity. And with a bit of dismay. Under no circumstances whatsoever, could she see herself going around town wearing an apron that looked like it'd been ironed within an inch of its life. She recalled what all her students often said about their Japanese husbands. She remembered Kazumi's determination to never get one. She remembered Keiko hurrying home after every class so her husband and son wouldn't expire from malnutrition caused by a late home-cooked dinner.

When she heard someone speaking English, she turned toward that voice. It was a woman—a *foreign* woman—talking to a toddler. Lots of foreigners lived in Tokyo, but this was the first time she saw someone with a child who looked Japanese. Rose watched them from behind the cabbage display for a moment and then stepped forward.

"Hi," Rose said.

The woman turned, blinked, and then said "Hi" back.

Rose felt embarrassed. What was she thinking, just approaching a total stranger like this? But the woman wasn't just a stranger. She was another *gaijin*. A female *gaijin*. "Sorry, I don't know why I'm talking to you. But 'hi' again."

The woman grinned. "I'm glad you did. I'm Lizzie. And this little gentleman," she said, gesturing to the boy in the stroller, is "Leo. You live around here?"

Rose nodded. "Yeah, about five minutes away. I'm Rose."

"Want to go get something to eat with me at Denny's? I'm killing time until he falls asleep, and then I want to go somewhere with endless coffee and not some tiny half-filled cup for ¥300. And if he goes to sleep, I could actually talk. And talking to a grownup, an *English*-speaking grownup, is not a pleasure I get every day of the week."

"Sure," said Rose, taking an instant like to her.

On the way to Denny's, Rose learned that Lizzie was from California, that she'd been in Japan for about three years, that she ran a little language school out of her apartment, and that she was crazy about her kid.

When they sat down, Rose said, "I hope you don't think it's rude of me to ask, but is your husband Japanese?"

"He is indeed. Why do you ask?"

"Well, there's a guy I kind of like. A Japanese guy. And I saw your son and—"

"So you thought because my kid looks Japanese, you approach me and ask me if I had a Japanese guy, too?"

Rose felt mortified until Lizzie burst out laughing. "That's a famous story in the circle I run in."

"What?"

"Have you ever heard of AFWJ?"

Rose shook her head.

"It's the Association of Foreign Wives of Japanese. It started about fifteen years ago when someone saw another person on a bus with a half Japanese kid and thought maybe she wasn't the only foreign woman in Japan married to a Japanese."

"Oh. Well, yeah. I guess that's why I went up to you. And just because... Well, you seemed nice."

"Tell that to my in-laws."

"Japanese in-laws?"

"Well, that's usually what they are if you marry a Japanese guy," Lizzie teased.

Rose felt tongue-tied. "Me and this guy—it's nothing serious. I mean, nothing's happened. I don't know if it'll go anywhere or not. Probably not. "

"But you like him."

"There're just so many obstacles and—" Rose stopped talking when she realized she was about to tell her life story to a person she'd met ten minutes ago. "So, there's a group of foreign women with Japanese husbands?" she asked, changing the topic slightly.

"Yeah. We try to get together with our kids, have Christmas parties, Easter egg hunts, that sort of thing."

"Sounds nice."

"It's a lifesaver. Listen, if you're serious about this guy, come to one of our gatherings sometime."

"Oh, we're not at that stage yet."

"It's never too early to build a support network. And that's what we are."

Rose sipped at her coffee, thinking that sounded like something she'd need if things with Akira went any further. She thought for about two seconds before telling Lizzie about Akira and his family.

"Well, that sounds pretty complicated all right," Lizzie said. "Maybe even a little odd. But, but believe me, it doesn't even come close to the craziest story I've come across."

"What's the success rate?" Rose asked, as if something like that could be statistically calculated.

Lizzy frowned slightly. "Of foreign women marrying Japanese? Heck, I don't know," she said, shrugging her shoulders. "Some relationships last and some don't."

"Like those everywhere, I suppose," said Rose.

"Yeah. We've got some really old members in our group who were married before the war. One recently celebrated her fiftieth anniversary."

"Wow," said Rose.

"So, I guess you could say those people were successful because they're still here. I can imagine being a foreign woman in Japan back then would've been a heck of a lot more difficult than having a dead wife's mother in the picture."

"I bet you're right about that," Rose said, unable to even begin to imagine the hardships those woman must've endured.

"From what I can see, the unsuccessful ones are when the guy's happy to find a *gaijin* girlfriend because he thinks it makes him look cool. But once he's got the *gaijin* wife, he's pissed off because she's *not* a Japanese wife."

"Seriously?"

"I'm dead serious. Suddenly, she can't do anything right for him. The cooking, the child raising, the interaction with the neighbors. That's when he wants her to be Japanese."

"That's just plain awful," said Rose.

"Right? Well, that kind of relationship never seems to work out. It's the same with foreign guys who think they're getting a demure Japanese maiden, but after they get married, he discovers she's the boss of everything in the house, including every penny he brings home. Or the Japanese girl who thinks she's getting a Hollywood movie character who'll provide her with a charmed and romantic life."

Rose laughed, thinking about Kazumi and her plans for an international marriage.

"And once that knot's tied," Lizzie continued, "she finds he's nothing more than a farting, belching, beer drinking, soon-to-be balding, American football fan."

Rose almost choked on her coffee. "Oh, my god!" You've described some guys I work with perfectly!"

"Marrying a stereotype is never a good idea," Lizzie continued. "Stereotypes exist because there are elements of truth to them, but not everyone is a stereotype. So, if I were you, I'd talk to your guy and find out what kind of person he is and what kind of person he's looking for."

"What do you mean?"

"Does he like you for *you*? Or does he like you because you're a *gaijin*?"

"I think," Rose said, blushing a little, "he likes me for me."

"How'd you meet him?"

"He came to my English class."

"You're his teacher?" Lizzie asked somewhat skeptically. "Does he see you as someone to practice English with? Because honestly speaking, that doesn't seem to work out well in the long run, either."

Rose considered how easy it was to be with Akira. How their time together *never* felt like an English lesson. How being with him felt so easy and right. She shook her head. "I don't think he sees me that way. He's pretty fluent because he lived in California." Then she asked, "What about your husband? How'd you two meet?"

"We met one afternoon in the student cafeteria at Cal State Long Beach. And never looked back. That was about ten years ago."

"How did you know you wanted to commit to Japan?" This was actually more of a concern to Rose than Akira's two kids or two mothers.

Lizzie cocked her head. "What do you mean?"

"How did you know you were willing to give up your life back home completely to live here?"

"I never did that."

Rose was a little confused. "But you're married and you live here now, right?"

"I do live here, but I never gave up my life back home. Not completely." Lizzie leaned down into the stroller and picked up Leo's blanket that had fallen to the floor and tucked it around him. "They've got airplanes, right? So when my husband and I were talking about moving here, I told him I'd only do it on one condition. And that'd be if I could go home every single summer. And I do. For at least a month."

"A month!" Rose exclaimed.

"Yeah. I go home every August. Believe it or not, my parents spend a lot more time with my kid than they do with my brother's kids. And they only live one state away."

Lizzie looked down at her watch and groaned. "I've got to get back. Students are coming in an hour. But listen," she said, scribbling her phone number on a piece of scrap paper from her bag, "call me, and we'll get together again soon. A bunch of us are going to Shinjuku Park next weekend for a picnic, and it'd be nice if you could come."

After they left Denny's, Rose returned to the supermarket to finish her shopping and replayed her conversation with Lizzie. Maybe this thing with Akira wasn't such a dead end after all.

Chapter Twenty-One

Akira and Rose spoke on the telephone every night that week. At first, they talked about small, incidental things, but soon their conversations turned to deeper and more personal matters. Their thoughts, hopes, and dreams. What interested and motivated them. It was on the fourth night of their telephone conversations when Rose told him about her broken engagement and why she came to Japan in the first place. And even though she didn't intend to, she told him about the one-night-stand that resulted in an abortion. In a trembling voice, she confessed that because of *that,* she might never be completely happy. And maybe, she whispered, she didn't deserve to be.

Akira had that kind of effect on her. She felt she could trust him with her secrets.

After a long, compassionate silence, he said, "I know how painful it is to make that decision. From personal experience."

"You do?"

"Yes," he said softly. "Sumiko got pregnant when we were still in college. We'd only been together a few months. We simply weren't ready to be parents."

"I'm so sorry. That must've been a difficult time for both of you." Rose felt her words sounded rather automatic, but she meant them from her heart.

"We could've gotten married, but would it have worked out? Maybe. I don't know. But I would've had to drop out of school, and our lives would've been so different. Maybe we would've ended up resenting each other. The thing is, we'll never know, because we didn't take that path. And here's what I always tell myself. If Sumiko hadn't had that abortion, we might never have had Yuka. Or Emi. Our family would've been completely different. And now, I can't imagine my life without either of them. Not in a million years. This is the life we have now, and not one that could've been or might've been." He paused for a moment to let her take that in. "Don't you see, Rose? We couldn't keep on having regrets about what we did. And neither should you."

Rose pondered his words from the darkness of her room. If she hadn't made the same difficult decision, her life would be completely different now, too. Guilt aside, would it be better? Worse? She had no idea. That wasn't the path she had taken, so she'd never know. "I guess," she said, thinking out loud, "we have to accept that things happen for a reason."

"Have you ever been to the Hase Temple in Kamakura?" Akira asked.

Rose was a little surprised by the sudden change of topic. "Um, no. I haven't."

"That's the temple where the souls of unborn children and babies who died at birth are helped in their journey to paradise. Importantly," he added, "that's where the parents of those souls can find comfort."

"I've never heard of that place."

"Let me take you there."

Although the weather had been fine all week long, the skies opened up the Saturday Rose and Akira made their way to Kamakura, and quite unusual for May, rain came down in sheets. Few tourists were about, but many couples were paying their respects to the *jizo*—the hundreds of tiny statues with knitted red caps and red aprons that were all slightly different in one way or another. They were believed to be the protectors of the little lost souls.

"This temple is for *all* babies' souls?" Rose asked. "Not only just those who were miscarried but also those who were aborted?" It was nearly impossible for her to utter the word in a neutral manner.

"Yes. And for those who were stillborn or who died right after birth. Even though there's no religious taboo with abortion in Japan, people still feel it's a very sad thing. This temple provides relief for the mothers. And," he added, "the fathers as well."

They huddled together under the umbrella in silence. Their shoulders were slightly touching as they looked out at the offerings placed in front of the many *jizo* on the temple grounds.

"The drinks, cookies, and toys are to help the babies with their journey to the other world," Akira explained.

A lump formed in Rose's throat. "I wish I had known about this place before. It would have made things a lot easier."

"You're here now. It's not too late to leave something."

They went to a nearby shop, and she bought a baby rattle, some cookies, and a can of juice. Back at the temple, they wandered around until Rose found a particular *jizo* she liked. "This one," she said. She placed her offerings in front of it and bowed and prayed—not to the Buddhist God, but to the one she grew up with, the one she felt comfortable with.

When she raised her head, Akira nodded at her, and they walked back to the train station in silence. The guilt she'd been carrying for the past couple of years didn't lift away at that moment entirely, but it felt less oppressive. She felt a sense of relief at knowing she wasn't grieving alone. Losing a baby—regardless of how it had happened— was a grief shared by many, and somehow, that made her feel better.

Rose didn't tell Michael about her visit to Hase Temple or its healing effect. Namely, because he never knew how heavily her abortion had weighed on her. He believed her when she said it was behind her. She tried to make herself believe that was true, but it really wasn't.

Until now.

After telling Akira her true feelings, she understood that the hole in her heart had been growing over time, not shrinking. But now, she sensed the grieving period for her lost child was coming to an end. She would never forget her baby, but there was a spring in her step and a lightness in her heart that had been absent for a long, long while.

She smiled at her university students—even the ones who'd fallen asleep in her class or those who constantly chattered in Japanese.

She was patient with her students at Friendly, even that Mr. Honda on Wednesdays, who had the irritating habit of interrupting the women in the group by inserting his own opinions every time they opened their mouths.

Rose felt different. And she acted differently, too. Of course, Michael attributed her behavior to Akira.

He wasn't entirely wrong.

Chapter Twenty-Two

The following Friday, Akira and Rose went to a tiny Italian restaurant just off Yasukuni Avenue. From the moment they left Friendly and headed in that direction, Rose knew tonight was going to be different. It *had* to be. She was ready to take their relationship to the next level, and she hoped Akira was, too. For the past week, all she could think about was what it'd be like to have his hands running over her body. About what he would feel like under her touch. She'd been so distracted by those thoughts, she could barely think about anything else.

She wasn't sure if Akira was on the same page, though. At dinner, he launched into a long discussion of the wine from a particular region in Italy, although it wouldn't have made any difference to her if the wine had come straight from communist Russia. They talked about the new James Bond movie. About Madonna's new number one hit. And the food. They talked an awful *lot* about the food.

"Are you in a hurry to go home?" Akira asked when he paid the bill at nearly eleven.

Rose wasn't.

They went into a deserted café just around the corner from the restaurant called Chanky Coffee. The faded burgundy velveteen wallpaper provided a background for the headshots of 1970s singers—Sawada Kenji, Saijo Hideki, Yamaguchi Momoe, Pink Lady. Not even the stale cigarette smoke masked the dank, musty smell.

"Maybe we should go somewhere else," Akira whispered when their table was unpleasantly sticky.

A woman sitting in the back hoisted herself away from her comic book and shuffled over.

"Two bottles of Coke," Akira said. "And could you wipe the table?"

The woman snapped something to the man who was picking his teeth behind the counter and came back and with a grimy cloth. After giving the table a perfunctory swipe, she returned to her comic book. The man uncapped two bottles of coke and brought them to the table with a couple of glasses. At least the glasses seemed clean.

"So…" said Akira.

"So…" repeated Rose.

Akira reached across the table for Rose's hand, sending powerful bolts of desire through her body.

"I can't stop thinking about you." His hand softened around hers, but he didn't let go. "About you and me. Being together."

His eyes searched hers for agreement, and Rose's heart escalated into a rapid thrum. "I think about that, too," she murmured. It felt like her mouth was stuffed with cotton wool, and she hardly recognized her words.

"I don't know what the future will—"

Rose cut him off. "I don't want to think about the future. I only want to think about what's happening right now."

"If you aren't sure, I'll take you home."

Rose nodded.

"Are you saying no?"

She shook her head, unable to speak. She was *very* sure and her skin tingled.

Akira threw money on the table for their drinks, grabbed her by the hand, and pulled her out of the restaurant. They wove through the late-night drinking crowd and went into the first love hotel they came to.

"Two hours or for the night?" muttered the old woman behind the register. Her eyes were glued to the portable color TV behind the counter, and she seemed to have zero interest in the amorous intents of her customers.

"The night." Akira slipped the woman cash in exchange for a key.

They hadn't spoken since leaving the coffee shop. Rose was afraid she might change her mind, but she was even more afraid he might change his. Akira put the key into the door of Room 406, and they stepped in. The oval-shaped bed covered with a leopard-patterned bedspread had them laughing, and the tension between them disappeared.

"I'm sorry, but I have to call home to let them know I won't be back." Akira picked up Rose's hand and brought it to his lips. In a gravelly voice, he said, "There's a phone next to the elevator. I'll be right back."

Rose studied the room while he was gone, too nervous to sit down. She glanced up and a nervous giggle escaped when she saw the mirrored ceiling.

"Can you hear my heart pounding?" Akira asked when he returned and pulled Rose into his arms.

"I thought it was mine."

Their lips met, and he kissed her gently. It was sweet, slow, and hesitant. As that kiss melted into others, Rose's body was pulsating with desire, so when he slipped his hand under her sweater, she shivered.

"Cold?" he whispered, his breath on her neck.

"No. I'm—" Rose suddenly pushed away from him, ruining the moment.

"What's wrong?" Alarm was all over his face.

"I just realized... We can't... I'm not on the pill."

"Look," Akira said, gesturing toward the box of condoms in plain view on the bedside table. This place was, after all, a love hotel. Rose exhaled in nervous relief but took advantage of the pause to freshen up in the bathroom. She returned wrapped in a fluffy white towel.

While Akira had his turn, she pulled the bedcovers down, exposing crisp, clean white sheets. When he came out, he was naked. Rose dropped her towel and went to him.

Their first time was quick, but memorable.

"I'm sorry," Akira whispered into Rose's hair. "It's been such a long time."

"It was perfect."

And so was the second time. And the third.

"Stop," she said, when Akira reached for her again. "No more tonight. I just can't."

And so, while holding each other, they both drifted off into a deep, dreamless sleep.

Rose opened her eyes and saw Akira's naked back to her, and she flushed with pleasure, thinking of the night they'd just had.

"No, we aren't ready to check out," Akira was saying into the room phone. "What? Yeah. okay. Sure, another day. Full price. What? Oh, no thank you. You don't need to come clean the room."

Akira hung up, leaned over, and kissed her gently. "Good morning, beautiful."

"What's the time?"

"Who cares?" He climbed back into bed and they made love again. Akira's face hovered over hers, and Rose felt his eyes could see all the way to her heart.

They spent the morning talking, cuddling and making more love, but by noon, they were starving.

Rose pointed at the number above the door as they were leaving the room. "I think 406 is going to be my favorite number from now on. My new lucky number."

"Mine, too," said Akira.

They caught a taxi to Harajuku, and passing up the trendy sidewalk cafés with tiny cups of coffee and bite-sized sandwiches, they headed to Sandwich House Bamboo, where they ordered meaty sandwiches with all the works. "You can get more later if this isn't enough," Akira said with a playful grin.

"I'll probably have to," Rose replied as she added potato salad and carrot cake to her order. "I seem to have worked up quite an appetite." With a wink, she whispered, "And I wonder whose fault that is?"

They found a table by the window and sat down, waiting for their order to be served. Rose's eyes were only on Akira, so she didn't notice Kazumi approach the table until she tapped Rose on the shoulder.

"Kazumi! Chris! What're you guys doing here?" Rose glanced behind them, relieved that Chris's friend, Steve, didn't seem to be with them. She introduced Akira just as the couple at the next table were leaving. Chris set his backpack on the chair and turned to Kazumi. "Why don't you have a seat and I'll go order our food?"

"Sure," she said, "but first I need to go to the bathroom. Come with me, Rose." Once they were out of earshot, Kazumi asked excitedly, "Who *is* that? Oh my god! He's hot!"

"He's... uh..."

"Did you sleep with him?"

"Um..." Rose felt her cheeks heating up.

"I knew it," Kazumi said, laughing. "You've got that you-know-what look all over your face."

"Shh," said Rose, hoping no one else could hear. "Keep your voice down. Listen, I don't know what's going to happen between us, so don't make a big deal out of it, okay? I know you don't like Japanese men, but I like this guy. A *lot*. So I want you to promise you'll be nice to him."

When they returned to the table, Chris jumped up to pull Kazumi's chair out for her and Rose slipped into hers before Akira even noticed. Was it possible that against all odds, Kazumi had managed to snag an American gentleman after all?

"I hear you're teaching at Yamanote University now," Chris said to Rose.

"Oh, did Steve tell you that?"

"Who?" Chris looked confused for a moment. "Oh, *that* Steve. No. Kazumi told me. I haven't talked to him in quite a while."

From the way he spoke, Rose could see he wasn't a big fan of the guy, and her opinion of him shot up a few more notches. Her grandmother always said people judge you by the company you keep, and for the first time, Rose understood exactly what that meant.

"I guess you could say we kind of run in different circles," Chris said, making Rose like him even more.

The two couples enjoyed chatting for an hour, but it was beginning to get late. "Call me later in the week," Kazumi said to Rose as they got up to leave. "Let's have lunch."

Rose and Akira caught the bus back to their neighborhood, and as they walked away from the bus stop, Rose began to sense things between them had changed. Akira let go of her hand when a woman with a preschooler on the back of her bike greeted him pleasantly. A moment later, an older woman said hello to Akira, and he mumbled a greeting to her in return. The local grocery store delivery boy, with a large box of heavy groceries balanced on the back of his bike, said hello to both of them as he rode by. With every step they took, Rose felt the distance increase between them. When they got to the corner to go their separate ways, they stopped and looked at each other.

"Well," said Rose.

"Well," said Akira. His hands were in his pocket and hers were clutching her purse to her chest.

"I'd better go," she said.

"I'll telephone you tonight," Akira said as she turned down her street.

Chapter Twenty-Three

After the girls went to bed, Akira and Fumiyo sat in the living room, but their usual amicable silence felt heavy with awkwardness.

"I need to talk to you," Akira began.

Fumiyo jumped up and began fussing with the folded laundry on the sofa.

"Please come back and sit down." Akira pulled a bottle of Kahlúa from the liquor cabinet, filled two glasses, and added a splash of milk. He knew that was her favorite cocktail, and he made regular trips to Kinokuniya Supermarket in Aoyama to keep a bottle in stock for her.

They clicked their glasses together in a silent toast. But frowning with disapproval, she got right to the point. "Are you going to tell me why you didn't come home last night?"

"Don't you know?"

"I guess I do. I am not judging you at all," she said with a sniff. "You are a man. Men do what they do." She took a large gulp and set her glass down rather hard.

Akira spoke gently, knowing this was a sensitive subject for her. "I want you to know I'd never do anything that'd harm our family or anything that'd hurt you."

"So, you *were* with a woman last night?"

"Yes," he answered.

Fumiyo glanced over at Sumiko's portrait on the altar and sighed. "It's not that I don't want you to... It's just that..."

Akira's eyes also moved to the photo. "I know how something like this could be difficult for you. But she's not coming back. No matter how sad we both are that she's gone."

"Is this relationship serious?" Her eyebrows had merged together in a frown.

"I hope it is," Akira replied.

"Is it someone from your office?"

He shook his head. "It's Rose."

"That foreigner."

"Yes."

"So the girls were right," she said with a resigned sigh. Even though she said she had nothing against that foreign girl who had managed things quite adequately when Saburo was hospitalized, she launched into a hundred reasons why a relationship with a foreigner wouldn't work:

She won't want to stay in Japan.

She can't speak Japanese.

She can't understand our ways.

She is so different from us.

Japan is not her home.

What about your future? What about hers? And what kind of impact will this have on Emi and Yuka?

Akira let her speak. But every one of her points, stereotypes and all, was minor. The only thing that mattered was what Rose would decide to do. Because he already knew what he wanted—he wanted Rose.

Several blocks away, Rose was lying on her futon and staring at the ceiling. She tried to read, but she couldn't stop thinking about last night. Her body flushed with remembered pleasure, but she also couldn't shake off the feeling that something was wrong with the awkward way they'd parted.

Had things changed between them now that they'd slept together?

No, she told herself. Akira wasn't like that. But why did he simply walk away from her like they were mere acquaintances?

Rose heard a soft tapping at her door and thought it was her landlady coming over to give her more of the vegetables her relatives out in Chiba were always sending her. When she opened the door and saw it was Akira, she couldn't prevent her heart from doing a little happy dance.

"I was hoping you'd still be awake," he said, holding out a bag from the supermarket. "I brought ice cream."

Rose thought he looked so sweet standing there with such a hopeful look on his face. "You should probably get in here before my landlady gets curious and comes to check."

Akira stepped inside her little apartment, and Rose felt overwhelmed with happiness when he took her into his arms and kissed her. Maybe she had been letting her imagination run wild. Maybe she had been reading more into things than she should have.

"I told Obaachan about us," he said, pulling back and looking into her eyes.

"What'd she say?"

"Who?"

"Your mother-in-law. You were just talking about her."

"Oh, yeah. I was." Akira stroked her cheek and drank in her face as if he hadn't seen her in days. He tucked a loose strand of her hair behind her ear and whispered, "I just got distracted by how beautiful you are."

Rose's hair was messy, she had no makeup on, and she was wearing ragged old sweatpants. That was the perfect thing for him to say, and her heart melted.

"Obaachan had a million reasons why our relationship wouldn't work. Some were the ones I'd been telling myself." He pressed his finger to Rose's lips as she was about to protest. "But for every reason she gave why it couldn't work, I could think of a hundred reasons why it could. We could make it work," he said with growing confidence.

"That's why I came over, even though it's so late. I just couldn't wait until tomorrow to see you."

He cupped her face in his hands and kissed her ever so gently on the lips. "And," he added, "I couldn't help but wonder if you were angry with me when we said goodbye earlier."

Rose felt her neck turning red. "I thought *you* were angry with me."

He seemed genuinely surprised. "Why would you think that?"

Now she felt quite foolish. "Because when we got to Daikyo-cho, you became so quiet. We stopped holding hands. You didn't kiss me goodbye."

Akira looked a little sheepish. "I don't know how to do these things well. And I don't want to use Japan as an excuse but—"

"I get it. Japanese don't fawn all over each other in public," said Rose. "But you were fine until we got back to our neighborhood. I thought you were embarrassed to be with me."

"Do you really believe that?"

"I'm not sure what to believe."

"But maybe you're right. Maybe I did change when we got back here. Because it *is* a bit too close to home. A bit too close to my family…"

Rose couldn't disguise the pain she felt when she asked, "Are you ashamed of being seen with me?"

"What? Of course not. I guess I didn't want word to get back to my family, to my daughters. But not because of what you're thinking," he added quickly. "I didn't want them to get their hopes up. About us. Before we're ready."

"Oh," Rose said, feeling relieved but also a bit embarrassed. "That makes a lot of sense."

"I feel that there's something else bothering you. Something you're not telling me. What is it?"

"I guess," Rose said, not looking at him, "I'm afraid."

"Afraid? Afraid of what?"

"Everything. You. Your family. Your children. Japan. My future." She offered an embarrassed smile to lighten her words. "Call me a coward. You name it, I'm afraid of it."

"I'm afraid, too," said Akira gently. "I'm afraid you won't give my family a chance. I'm afraid my family could get in the way and make you decide not to give us a go. But," he added, "don't you think it'd be foolhardy for us to *not* be at least a little concerned about all these things? Wouldn't having no concern be more of a concern?" He grimaced at his twisted words. "You get what I mean, don't you?"

Rose smiled. She *did* get it. But now that the door had opened for serious discussion, she couldn't move on. Not quite yet. "I know it's too soon for us to talk about love." She tried to keep her tone as neutral as if she was talking about the weather. "The future. That sort of thing. But I can't ignore the fact that you loved Sumiko. Don't get me wrong—that's *good*. But, I guess I'll always wonder if you could ever come to feel for me what you felt for her." There. She said it.

"Sumiko will always be a part of my heart," Akira replied quietly. "But you, my darling Rose—*you* are my second chance."

"But—"

"Don't you think it's possible to love more than one person?"

"In my head, maybe. But in my heart—"

"Look, when my first daughter was born, I loved her a hundred percent. Then Emi came along. I loved her a hundred percent as well. Nothing shrunk in my love for Yuka. It just got bigger. Love can get bigger."

"That's different. They're your children."

"How can it be different?" he said, shaking his head, not understanding. "And besides, Sumiko isn't here. You are. There's no competition."

"Oh Akira, of course there is. When I get old and fat and ugly, Sumiko will always be a perfect and beautiful woman in your memory."

"But I'll be old and fat and ugly, too. And probably bald."

The thought of that made Rose giggle a little. "I doubt it. You'll always be perfect. But..."

"What else is it?" he asked with a frown.

"I'm not Japanese. And," she blurted out, remembering her conversation with Lizzie a few weeks earlier, "I don't even own an apron."

"A what?"

The confusion on Akira's face made her regret bringing such a crazy thing up, but she couldn't stop now. "I could never be like be a Japanese woman, running around and waiting on you hand and foot." Since she was being so honest, she might as well bring up her biggest concern. "And about children..."

Akira's face dropped. "I see. You don't want someone with children."

"No! That's not it. But," she added, "I have to admit I'm not sure if I'm ready for an instant family. The real issue for me is..."

"What is it?" he pressed.

"What if I want to have a baby someday?" She stared down at the floor, knowing it was way too soon to bring up babies since they'd only just started seeing each other. But this, she needed to know. "Having children is something I do think about. And to be honest," she whispered, "for me, this could be a deal breaker."

"You think I won't want any more children because I already have two?"

"It's crossed my mind."

"Rose," he said, directing her face up toward his with his fingertip. "I'll give you as many babies as you want. I love children. In fact, we can start making them right now if you want."

From the way his eyes were twinkling, Rose could tell he was joking. About the timing of baby making, but not about the possibility of having one together someday. "Well, maybe not right this minute," she said. "Let's wait and see how things go."

"I'll give you all the time you need. But," he said, pointing to the bag of ice cream sitting on the counter, "time might be running out for *that*."

"We certainly can't let that happen." Rose got out bowls and spoons and felt overwhelmed with happiness that they'd survived their relationship's first crisis.

Chapter Twenty-Four

Akira and his mother slipped down to the Keio Hospital basement for coffee while his father was undergoing more tests after having another series of strokes that day. While the doctors had been cautiously optimistic about his condition before, they weren't now. His brain scan showed little activity, and recovery was no longer an option. The doctors said it was just a matter of time, but how much time he had left was impossible to know. He could go at any minute or he could linger for a few more weeks. They needed to be prepared for the worst.

"Mom," Akira began, stirring milk and sugar into his paper cup, "maybe this isn't the best time to bring this up, but I've met someone."

Akira's mother looked as impeccable as she always did, but the papery skin under her eyes was tinged purple with exhaustion, making her look every bit her age. "I know," she said. "Fumiyo told me. The foreign girl who babysat when your father had his stroke. Right?" She put her elbows on the table and leaned toward him. "I can't help but be worried about this, though. The foreign way of doing things is different from ours. Remember that family you stayed with in California?"

"Rose isn't like those people," he said, frowning.

"Are you thinking of marrying this foreign girl?"

Akira winced a little at her question. "I don't know. It's too soon to make that sort of decision. But I'll tell you one thing, if she's the right person for me, she could come from the moon for all I care."

"But a Japanese woman would—"

"I don't care about what a Japanese woman would do."

"You say that now, but it could matter later. Do you want a foreigner to raise your daughters?"

"Are you saying only Japanese know how to raise children?"

"Of course not. But don't you think Sumiko would want her children to be raised like Japanese children?"

"Don't try to make me feel guilty by bringing up Sumiko," he snapped, banging one fist on the table. "She's not here. And besides, I know Sumiko would want what's best for me."

"If you say so," she replied curtly.

Akira regretted losing his temper. "I'm sorry, Mom. I didn't mean to snap at you. It's just that—"

She waved her hand to let him know it was okay. "I'm not trying to stop you. I'm just trying to make you see the obstacles you'd likely face. Now if you found someone more like Sumiko—"

"I don't want someone like Sumiko. There'll never be anyone like her. Never. I'm not looking for her replacement. And I'm not looking for someone just to take care of Yuka and Emi. If that was the case, we're fine the way we are."

"But Akira, you need someone."

"For what? Cooking? Cleaning? Babysitting?" He felt bad for saying that, so he added, "Listen, I don't want to make Obaachan sound like she's the maid or anything like that. But I'd rather have her with us than some woman I don't care about."

"Well, of course, a wife is so much more than those things."

"And that's why I'm not about to get involved with someone for the wrong reasons."

"A man in your situation—with children—needs to think about how your actions, your decisions about the future, would affect them as well. You were spoiled by what you had with Sumiko. She was special."

"You're right. I *was* spoiled. And that's why I refuse to settle for anything less. If I can't have the best, then I don't want anything."

"And do you think you're going to get it with that foreign girl?"

"I wish you'd stop calling her that. Her name is Rose."

"All right then. Rose. Do you think Rose is the best person for you?"

"I don't know. But I do know she's the best thing that's happened to me since Sumiko died." Akira's face transformed when he added, "Mom, I never thought I'd find love again, and for the longest time, I was empty inside. I feel like a man again, and I'm happy."

His mother offered a resigned sigh. "I'm glad to hear that, but have you considered the problems that could come up? Things that could dwarf the happiness you feel now?"

"Like what?"

"Rose may want to have children of her own. Have you considered that?"

"Yes. We've talked about that. I'd happily have a dozen more children."

"Could she love Yuka and Emi as much as she would her own child?"

"That'd be a concern no matter who I marry."

"That's true," she agreed. "But how would Yuka and Emi feel if they have siblings that are half foreign? A brother or a sister who'd look so different? Be so different?" She saw Akira bristle at this comment, so she changed the subject. "And what about your company? What would they think if you marry a foreigner?"

"Mom, it's the eighties! I don't care about what anyone in the company thinks."

"You know they're waiting for the man they hired to come back. A Japanese wife would understand that and support you. The way I did with your father. A Japanese woman would—"

"Mom, you've just given me the best reason in the world why I shouldn't marry someone like that. I can't stand the idea of being pushed out the door just so I can bring home a paycheck. The last thing I want is someone who wants me to work as many overtime hours as possible so she could buy more stuff." He narrowed his eyes at his mother. "Would you prefer I marry someone like Yoko?"

"Oh, good heavens, no." She didn't like Sumiko's brother's wife any more than she liked him.

"I want someone who loves me for *me*, and who also loves my kids. Not someone who'd marry a man like me because she's afraid of being an old maid. Someone who'd decide a man with two kids was better than no man at all."

"Do you think you will find happiness with Rose?"

"I don't know. But I do know that if I don't give it a try, I'd regret it for the rest of my life. I'd always wonder if I'd let my second chance for happiness slip through my fingers."

"But you have to be careful of your daughters' feelings."

"I know that. They already like her. I'm sure they'll come to love her."

"That's what I mean. What if Yuka and Emi become crazy about her, but she decides you aren't right for her? Or vice versa? That could hurt the girls."

"Like I said, we're going to take it slow and see what happens."

"Every step that you and that foreigner—I mean Rose—take could seem like giant strides to Yuka and Emi." She looked down at her watch. "We'd better get back upstairs." Before she stood, she added, "I don't want to tell you what to do, but if Rose is the right person for you, I'll stand behind you. And Fumiyo will, too."

Akira nodded gratefully and finished the last drops of his coffee. As he pushed his chair back, his mother touched his arm. She took a deep breath and her face softened as she spoke. "Sumiko has been gone just about as long as your father has. His body may be in that hospital bed upstairs, but he's not the man I married. He's not the man I lived with all those years. So believe me, I know how you feel when you say you want to get on with your life."

Akira didn't trust his voice. His feelings for his father were so mixed, but he knew exactly what his mom was getting at. He loved his father, but the person inhabiting his body was no longer him. What was sure to happen in the next few days was sad, so very sad. But at the same time, if he was being honest with himself, it would bring a kind of relief.

"Because," she continued, "it's time for me to get on with my life as well. It may seem callous to say such things when your father is still alive. But I'm telling you, after he's gone, I'm going to live the best life I can with what time I have left in this world. I don't have as many years as you do, but that's what I'm going to do. And I suppose that means you should live your life the best way you can, too."

Chapter Twenty-Five

"All right," said Rose to her Friday night class after a few minutes of ice-breaking chit-chat. "Tonight's discussion topic, which was chosen by Naoko, is working women. Would you like to start?"

Naoko nodded, opened up her notebook, and began. "I don't know how many of you are aware of this, but the government is working on passing a law forbidding discrimination against women in the workplace, and it is expected to pass sometime next year."

"What kind of discrimination is there?" asked Tomo, as if he really didn't know.

"Well, for one thing, women are rarely hired in career track positions," replied Naoko. "They can never advance at work, even if they stay in the company for twenty years."

"But women quit when they get married," asserted Tomo. "Why would a company invest that much money in a woman if she's only going to work for a couple of years?"

Rose generally tried to stay neutral during the discussions, but Tomo's pronouncement almost had her jumping down his throat. But then she thought about the talk she and Akira'd had on this topic a few weeks earlier and kept her mouth shut.

"What about the women who don't get married? Those who don't quit working?" Naoko was impatiently tapping her pen on the desk when she scanned the room and asked, "Why should they hit the glass ceiling so early in their career when they may have gone to a better university and may be a lot smarter than some man who joined the company the same year they did?"

"Glass ceiling?" asked Daisuke, while checking his dictionary.

"That means women can see the upper levels of a company, but they can never pass through the barrier to get there. That kind of barrier doesn't exist for men," Naoko said.

"Actually," said Akira. "It does. Let's say two men work in a company, and one is a graduate of a prestigious university and the other a graduate from a lower-ranking one. One will advance and the other probably will not. So educational background determines the glass ceiling."

"You aren't wrong about that," conceded Naoko. "However, let's take two graduates from a prestigious university. Say," she added, looking over at Tomo, "Tokyo University. One is a man and one is a woman. Both join a company at the same time. Which person hits the glass ceiling?"

Akira tilted his head in agreement. "I see what you mean."

"This law can fix the problem," Naoko said firmly.

"I'm not so sure," said Akira. "My company is already considering hiring women in career track positions before the law comes into effect. But one concern is if women would be able to work in the same way a man in the same position would be asked to do."

"Why wouldn't they be able to?" pressed Naoko.

"It's difficult to combine a career and a family."

"But you do that."

"Not completely. I can't do everything that's expected of me. I had to turn down an assignment that would've sent me to India for a few months. I couldn't have left my family for so long. And one colleague was transferred to Fukushima for six months on a temporary assignment. His wife and kids stayed in Tokyo and he commuted on the weekends. Would a woman be able to leave her family if they were asked to do that?"

"Men do."

"Yes," agreed Akira. "But not all men. Like I said, I couldn't. Someone needs to be with the kids."

"Japanese companies need to change," said Naoko.

"I certainly agree with you on that," Akira said with a dry laugh. "One hundred percent."

"But most women," said Tomo, getting back into the discussion, "prefer to stay at home, don't they? They want to be with their children. That is the traditional way. Men work and women stay home."

"Are you saying married women shouldn't work?" asked Keiko.

"Why would a housewife want to have a job?" Tomo asked, genuinely perplexed. He seemed to have forgotten that one of Keiko's reasons for attending the English class was to update her skills so she could rejoin the workforce. "There is already so much to do at home."

"Husbands have to do more," said Naoko. "It's simple. Both my parents are lawyers, and they share housework."

"Equally?" asked Rose.

Naoko hesitated. "Not exactly. My mother is home more, so I suppose you could say she does more."

"Does your husband help at home?" Tomo asked, bringing the conversation back to Keiko.

Keiko paused. "I don't have a job yet. But when I do..."

Kana jumped in, showing she was able to follow the discussion. "If he late and you late, who cook? Son?"

Keiko looked uncomfortable and turned to Akira. "What if your wife had wanted to work? Would you have let her?"

"Your question makes it sound like I made all the decisions in my family. I didn't 'let' her do anything," he said with finger quotes. "We discussed things and decided what was right for our family. That's what my parents did, too. So if she'd said she wanted to go back to work, I guess I would've supported her in every way possible. We would've made it work because we were a team."

"I wish my husband was like you," Keiko said, her cheeks turning pink. "Or you," she said, pointing at Daisuke. "Or even you," she said, gesturing toward Tomo.

Silence fell across the room as everyone's eyes turned toward Keiko, who was basically saying that almost any man was better than her husband. Rose'd had her suspicions about that for a long time. After all, Keiko rushed off after every single class, saying she needed to get home before her husband returned. Rose was pretty sure it wasn't because she couldn't wait to see the guy. And even worse, from what she could tell, it looked like Keiko's son was turning into someone just like his father. Rose felt sorry for her, but she couldn't help but think she was partially at fault for babying the men in her family.

"My husband isn't very understanding," Keiko added, looking down at the table. "He isn't young like you, Tomo. He isn't flexible."

Rose found herself nodding solemnly at Keiko's words, but the thought of Tomo being considered flexible almost made her giggle.

"But," Keiko added quickly, as if she didn't want to appear disloyal, "my husband is a very good provider. He works hard for us. He doesn't have time for anything but his job. Maybe when he retires, we can have…" her voice faded and silence fell across the room.

"Women do many things. Family. Work. English class," Kana said, thumping her hand on the desk and making everyone jump a little. "We no like be weak. Money is power."

"That's right!" exclaimed Naoko.

"But what if a woman doesn't want to work?" asked Daisuke. "My mother's a housewife. My father's a teacher. They decide everything together. Well, maybe not *everything* because my mother controls the money. If my father wants something, he has to ask my mother." He uttered a low chuckle when he said, "She's actually quite rich."

"Yes," said Naoko. "A lot of Japanese women do have power in the home. They have a say in what's going on. Sometimes, even *all* the say."

That sounded like some of the housewives Rose had been teaching in the past couple of years. She remembered being shocked to learn they could get bank loans using their husband's salary as collateral but not needing their permission to do so. She was pretty sure that'd be impossible to do in the States. But what Daisuke was saying about his family didn't sound like Keiko's situation at all.

"If your mother's doing what she wants to do," Naoko continued, "and if your family supports each other like you say they do, then it's an ideal situation."

"Yes," agreed Akira. "People need to have the freedom to choose. Men, too. Maybe not every man wants to be the breadwinner."

"Breadwinner?" Kana looked confused, as if the discussion had veered into something else entirely.

"A breadwinner is the person who brings home a salary," explained Rose.

"Oh," said Kana, waving her hand dismissively. "Man be housewife. No problem. Woman get money."

Everyone laughed at the thought of something so radical, and Keiko looked relieved to no longer be the focus of the discussion.

Chapter Twenty-Six

Rose changed her clothes three times before deciding what to wear for dinner. Akira insisted it was going to be just a little get-together at his house, but she knew it was something official—meeting-the-family kind of official. When she called Kazumi for fashion advice, Kazumi pointed out that meeting everyone like this was a half-step behind a formal engagement. A sort of make-or-break situation where Rose would be on inspection. One wrong step, Kazumi warned, could prevent things from going forward.

Rose wasn't actually sure if she wanted things to move forward because everything was just fine the way it was. But she didn't want whatever it was she had going with Akira to end in a puff of smoke, either.

She had already met fifty percent of the matriarchs—the grandmother they all called Obaachan—the day she babysat Yuka and Emi. Today she'd meet his mother, the grandmother the girls called "Baba."

And to complicate things, Akira had just called to tell her their little dinner party had expanded to include Sumiko's brother, his wife, and their kids, who had suddenly decided to go to Tokyo Disneyland and stay with him for the weekend.

Rose pretended to be excited to meet even more of Akira's family, but in reality, she was in a panic. Two mothers were bad enough, but now she's got to deal with the dead wife's brother, too? This simple little dinner was going to be anything but simple. Trial by fire was more likely.

She stepped out of her apartment and got halfway down the lane, but remembering the rainy season had officially started that day, she turned around to go back for her umbrella. She didn't want to get caught out in case it did rain. Every step toward Akira's house brought a sense of dread, but she calmed her nerves by stopping in front of the house on the corner of Akira's street to admire the gorgeous blue hydrangeas.

Well, now or never, she told herself as she finally rang the doorbell.

"I hope you didn't think you had to bring anything," Akira said, opening the door and looking at the bags in her hands.

Rose smiled, knowing that in Japan, you would *never* show up at someone's house empty-handed. She took her shoes off in the *genkan*, turned around and arranged them neatly. She inhaled deeply before stepping into the living room. With five adults and four children, it seemed a lot smaller than it did when she was there a few weeks before.

"Welcome," Obaachan said in English.

"Thank you," Rose replied, also in English.

"Obaachan has been practicing her English all week," whispered Akira.

Rose produced a package with eight individually wrapped early-season peaches and a floral bouquet. In her best textbook Japanese, she said, "Here is a little something for you, but it's really nothing."

What that set expression actually meant was this: Here are some incredibly expensive things nobody in their right mind would ever buy for themselves. I got them to impress you, so here they are.

Rose sensed she must've done something wrong when the older woman looked at the flowers and stammered out a stunned thank you. She glanced over at Akira and saw his lips quirking in amusement.

Had she crossed some kind of cultural boundary? The only explanation she could think of was that the peaches had come from the local supermarket and not from the upmarket Isetan Department Store. She should've splurged and gotten them there for the fancy wrapping paper alone.

"What did I do?" she whispered to Akira after the grandmother had taken everything into the kitchen.

"It's the flowers. You got them at the supermarket, right? It's not a big deal, but those are the kind of flowers used for decorating the family altar."

Rose's face flushed with embarrassment for not knowing that.

Akira's mother came over and extended her hand with ease—like a person who was used to shaking hands with foreigners. In flawless English, she said, "It's very nice to meet you. Thank you so much for helping out with the girls the other day."

"I was glad to be of help," Rose replied, also in English. "And I'm very sorry your husband is ill."

Sumiko's brother Osamu reminded Rose of Tomo from their class—a self-satisfied look was on his face as he looked her up and down. His wife, who had a Pierre Cardin scarf wrapped around her neck and was clutching a Louis Vuitton handbag like it was unsafe to set down in the house, gave her a perfunctory nod. Their sons were laying on the floor reading comic books, but when they saw Rose, they gaped at her as if she was a two-headed alien from outer space. She imagined they didn't have many opportunities to get this close to a *gaijin* down south.

"I'd better warn you," Akira whispered before they all sat down at the table. "These are just the appetizers. Save room for sushi. And dessert."

Akira cracked opened bottles of Kirin beer for the adults and orange soda for the children. Everyone clicked their glasses together, and Obaachan ran back and forth to the kitchen until Akira made her sit down and finish her beer. She drained her glass and hiccuped. Akira chortled and filled her glass again, but this time she set it down. Her face had turned a bright red, and she started giggling.

That was a quick buzz, thought Rose.

"You're the first foreigner Obaachan's ever cooked for," whispered Akira after she went back into the kitchen. "I think she's a bit nervous."

From that moment on, Rose couldn't think of her as anything else but "Obaachan."

They heard the crash of a pot falling onto the floor, and Akira's mother went to investigate, coming back, holding the tipsy Obaachan by the elbow.

"Everything looks very delicious," Rose said in Japanese. She figured the best way to get through the evening would be to praise the food to high heaven, even if it turned out to be something as disgusting as *shiokara*. Luckily, she soon discovered, fermented squid guts didn't seem to be on the night's menu.

Rose couldn't relax because she felt like she was a contestant on a quiz show where she had one chance to provide the correct answer to a stream of unrelated questions. Every person had something to ask, particularly Osamu. It was as if he'd set himself up as the patriarch of the family, and when Akira stepped into the kitchen, he interrogated Rose in a rather aggressive tone, without the typical polite language Japanese used when talking with strangers.

At first, his questions were typical. She smiled when she answered, "No, thank you. I don't need a fork. Chopsticks are fine." And then, "Yes, I can eat Japanese food," contradicting him when he announced she wouldn't be able to eat sushi.

But then his questions turned just plain nosy—almost as if he was performing a background check on her. When she told him her father's work was farm-related, his nose wrinkled in disgust as if she'd said they were sharecroppers. She waited for him to ask where she worked because people usually were pretty impressed by Yamanote University. But he didn't. In fact, she decided not to speak to him any more after he pronounced with his nose in the air, "I can see that you like Japanese men."

Akira and the two grandmothers came back with more platters of food, which stopped her from bopping the guy on the head with his wife's fancy purse. It turned out Osamu wasn't anything like Tomo at all. Tomo may be pretentious, but his eyes weren't cold and calculating. This man, she was thinking while studying his smug face, was not to be trusted.

By the time dinner was over, the coffee was drunk, and the dessert was eaten, Rose was exhausted. As soon as it wouldn't seem rude, she stood and thanked Obaachan for a wonderful meal. Akira offered to walk her home, but she said no. He should stay with his family. Rose was pretty sure they'd discuss her once she was gone, and she wanted Akira to be a part of that discussion in case she needed to be defended.

It turned out she wasn't wrong.

Akira knew his brother-in-law was a bully and a bore. He only put up with him because he was Yuka and Emi's uncle and Obaachan's son. But he'd never liked the guy, not since learning from Sumiko how he'd tried to prevent her from going to university in Tokyo. He and his wife Yoko had insisted a young girl on her own couldn't be trusted. Despite being the top student in her high school, they said she'd end up working as a Ginza bar hostess. But Obaachan, who usually let Osamu believe he was in charge of things, ignored them and encouraged Sumiko to apply anywhere she wanted. The real reason for his opposition, of course, was that he hadn't been smart enough to enter any university in Tokyo when he took his own entrance exams ten years earlier. He went to a second-rate one close to home, and he didn't want his little sister to outshine him on that.

Akira carried a load of dishes to the kitchen and stacked them in the sink. When he returned to the living room, he could tell his mother was angry. Other people might not have noticed because she was as calm and reserved as always. But she had that polite look on her face that could melt steel. Besides, Obaachan's usual jolly demeanor was gone and her lips were tightly pursed.

Osamu was holding a glass of whiskey and tapping a cigarette on the edge of an ashtray, even though he knew Akira didn't like people smoking in his home. "So, Akira, I can see you are quite smitten by this foreign woman. I suppose she's all right—for a little diversion." His smarmy smile insinuated Akira had some kind of itch a foreign woman like Rose would be good at scratching.

Akira's nostrils flared as he asked slowly and deliberately, "What exactly do you mean?"

Osamu didn't hear the ice in Akira's voice, but his mother did. And so did his mother-in-law. Both leaned forward as if they were about to witness a car wreck.

"Clearly that foreigner knows a good thing when she sees it. A fine man with a good job in a good company. A house in a prime location." He glanced at Akira's mother as if to get her agreement, but she just stared straight back at him, expressionless. "And obviously, more money to come. What do you know about her family background? Nothing. They are farmers. Farmers! Our families were samurai."

Akira glowered at the pompous jerk and wanted to tell him that there were samurai and there were samurai and that their families were *not* cut from the same cloth. Instead, he raised his hand. "I'm going to stop you right now. This is none of your concern. And another thing, do not refer to Rose as that foreign woman."

"But what about your daughters?" Osamu inhaled his cigarette, puffed out the smoke, and took another sip of the whiskey. "They are *my* nieces. My poor deceased sister's children. What kind of influence will this foreign...um, what was her name again? Oh yes, *Rose.* What kind of influence would that Rose have upon them?" The way he uttered her name made her sound as if she had a side career as a porn star. "Foreigners are different. They do not understand proper behavior. The way proper women should behave. Look at the ridiculous flowers she brought here tonight."

The look in Akira's eyes as he stared Osamu down was pure menace. "Again, this does not concern you."

"After all these years of my mother working for you, this is how you treat her? By bringing home a *foreigner*?"

Akira was about to let him know he'd gone too far but then realized it wouldn't be worth getting into it with Osamu. That'd just hurt Obaachan. He turned away as if the discussion was over and carried the rest of the dishes, including Osamu's half-filled whiskey glass, into the kitchen.

"Well," Osamu sniffed. "I suppose it could've been a lot worse. She could've been Korean."

Chapter Twenty-Seven

Rose was putting the chairs in her classroom back in order at the end of the day when Kana and Naoko knocked on the door and stepped in.

"What are you guys doing here?" Rose asked. "It's not Friday."

"We're here about Keiko." Naoko's face was full of concern.

"Did something happen to her? Is that why she wasn't in class last week?"

"Her husband divorced her," said Naoko. "She had to move out of the house and leave her son behind."

Rose was shocked into silence. When they'd had that discussion on equality in the workplace and in marriage a few weeks earlier, Keiko hadn't given any indication that things were that bad. "Why?" she managed to get out.

"He discovered she was planning to get a job," said Kana in Japanese. "So, he got his mother to come and stay. And then he filed for divorce and got full custody of their son."

Rose gasped. "How can that happen in this day and age?"

"It is sometimes the Japanese way," Naoko said.

"What about joint custody of their son?"

"There's no joint custody in Japan," said Naoko. "He filed the papers and put her *hanko*—her registered seal—on them, making it legal and official. The thing is, Keiko didn't even know he'd done that.

She only found out yesterday when she went home and found the locks on the door had been changed. She couldn't even get her things."

"That's terrible," said Rose, feeling sick on Keiko's behalf.

"Anyway, she called me," Naoko continued. "My parents are lawyers. In fact, my mother is actually a family court lawyer, so this morning she filed an injunction on her behalf. But it's a difficult case since the papers had already been filed, making the divorce official."

"How could he do such a thing without her knowledge?" sputtered Rose. "Wouldn't that be illegal?"

"She should've kept her registered seal in a secret place. She should've filed a paper at the city office that would've prevented him from divorcing her without her knowledge and consent."

"There's actually a paper for that?" When Naoko nodded, Rose asked, "But what about their son? Isn't it terrible for him to not see his mother? To have her kicked out of the house like that?"

"He's fifteen, so he's old enough to decide which parent to live with. But if he chooses his mother, his father might not have financial obligations to raise him. He could decide not to pay for his education."

"That's blackmail!" Rose said in disbelief. "What kind of man would do that to his child?"

"It seems he is precisely the type of man who *would* do that. If the boy chooses Keiko, she might have to bear the entire financial responsibility of his education. So she must think also what is best for her son. And for her.

"Doesn't he care about what's best for his son?"

Naoko shrugged. "Life has been hard for Keiko for a long time. And that's where Kana comes in. We think Keiko should be the office manager for the new shop she's opening."

"You're opening a new shop?" asked Rose.

"Yes," she said proudly, "in Aoyama. Money man say open new shop and get *gaijin* lady people come."

"Aoyama! Wow, that's impressive Kana! Congratulations! But I thought Keiko wanted to work for a large company."

"She does," said Naoko, "but to be honest, there aren't many opportunities for someone her age in most Japanese companies. It'd be hard for her to fit in, and she'd have to start at the bottom. She'd probably never put her English to good use because all they'd have her do would be to make copies or serve tea to the staff. And that's assuming if she could get a job in the first place. So this idea of Kana's is perfect. That's why we need you."

"Me?"

"You're her English teacher. If you tell her this is an excellent opportunity, she'd listen. You can make it look like she's doing Kana a big favor."

Rose saw the concern Kana and Naoko had for the welfare of an older woman who'd been their classmate for only a few months. A wave of emotion swept over her, and she was proud to call these people friends.

After class on Friday, Rose asked Keiko to stay behind.

"I have something important I'd like to talk to you about." Keiko seemed calm, and interest showed on her face. Rose wondered if Naoko and Kana been wrong about what was going on in her life. After all, she'd just sat through the past ninety minutes as if nothing was wrong. "I don't know if you know this about Kana or not," Rose began, "but she owns a very nice esthetics salon, and it's become quite a successful business."

"Really? I had no idea."

Rose smiled at the surprised look on Keiko's face. "Well, to be honest, neither did I. I found out a while back when I went to her salon for a facial. Anyway, she's opening another branch in Aoyama. In fact, that's why she's been coming to English classes—she's aiming to attract foreign customers."

"How wonderful for her," Keiko said, quite sincerely.

"And well, Kana asked if I knew of anyone who could be the manager of the new salon—someone who speaks English. Not just *speak* it, but who can read and write and deal with customers in English. Naturally, I thought of you. Now, I know you're planning to work for a bigger company. But Kana needs someone she can trust. Would you consider taking the job? At least, until her business gets off the ground? Until you find a better job? Do you think you'd be willing to help Kana out?"

"A tanning salon?"

"It's not only tanning. She offers facials, massages, and whole-body treatments. It's a full experience spa."

"I was thinking of working for a bank or a trading company. But then, at my age…" Keiko's voice trailed off for a moment. "I don't know if you know this or not, but I'm getting divorced. Actually, I'm already divorced. I just didn't know that I was until last week."

"Yes," Rose said. "I do know that. Naoko told me."

"Does Kana know about my situation?"

Rose hoped Keiko wouldn't be upset at everyone for poking their noses into her business. "Yes, she does."

A couple of tears escaped from Keiko's eyes and ran down her cheeks. "Thank you," she whispered with quiet dignity before wiping them away with the back of her hand.

Rose went to open the classroom door, and Kana and Naoko, who were waiting outside, came in.

Kana went straight up to Keiko. "You manager. Speak English everyone. Make money. You and me—we make money."

Rose thought how funny it was that Kana, who had signed up for the advanced English class because she was sick to death of grammar, could get to the heart of the matter in her flawed but eloquent English.

She watched the three women leave together, and she couldn't wait to tell Akira, who was waiting for her at a restaurant down the street, all about it.

Chapter Twenty-Eight

"Well, you certainly are a hard person to pin down," Rose said to Kazumi as she sat across from her at Takano Fruit Parlor in Shinjuku. "Glad I could finally catch you."

"I've been pretty busy," replied Kazumi.

"With Chris, I suppose," Rose said, offering a teasing sort of grin.

"Yeah," Kazumi replied, running her fingers through her hair as if they were a comb. "But not only that. There're all these new classes my mom signed me up for."

"What kind of classes?"

"Cooking. Flower arranging. Tea ceremony. You know, bridal classes," Kazumi explained, rolling her eyes.

Rose barked out a laugh until she realized Kazumi was dead serious. "But I thought you hated that sort of thing."

"I do. I don't know how much longer I can put my mom off. I mean, I'm going to be twenty-four soon. That gives me just one more year, and that's that."

"A year for what?"

"My mom would rather die than let me become a Christmas cake."

"Huh?"

"You know, nobody wants to eat a Christmas cake after the twenty-fifth."

Rose stared blankly at Kazumi, having no idea what she was getting at.

"In Japan, they say a girl who isn't married by the time she's twenty-five isn't any good. Nobody will want her. Just like a Christmas cake. Just like no one wants to eat an expired Christmas cake."

Rose crinkled her nose in disgust. "You don't believe that old-fashioned nonsense, do you?"

"Well, my mom sure does. She thinks she's all modern, letting me live in Tokyo after I graduated from junior college. But only to a certain extent. In her mind, the clock is ticking away."

The server came for their order, and they opened the menu and decided on the deluxe afternoon tea set which came with an assortment of scones and little fruit laden cakes. After the woman walked away, Rose returned to the topic. "If your mother's so old-fashioned, how's she going to take it if you bring a *gaijin* home rather than a Taro or Jiro from a nice trading company?"

"I'll deal with that when the time comes." Kazumi didn't sound quite as confident about her plans to marry a foreigner as she usually did.

"You could always elope," ventured Rose. "Make it a done deal she couldn't say anything about." She pretended her suggestion was serious, but she knew Kazumi would never go along with such a plan because she already had her dream wedding dress picked out—something nearly as fancy as Princess Di's. "Anyway, don't you think she'd be more inclined to accept a *gaijin* if she thinks you're already an old maid? Wouldn't she put up less of a fight?"

"She might. But not my father. He's old school. A foreigner just might give him a heart attack."

Rose couldn't tell if Kazumi was joking or serious. "How are things going between you and Chris, anyway? Is he the Prince Charming of your dreams?"

"Things are all right, I guess."

That took Rose by surprise, because Kazumi was usually overly enthusiastic about her boyfriends. She sensed a huge "but" in that sentence. "Just all right?"

"He's fun and nice."

"Well," said Rose, "he's definitely a lot better than that guy from Australia you were seeing last year. Was it Dan? Or Don? I get all your foreign boyfriends mixed up."

"Don," replied Kazumi, laughing and seeming more like herself again. "Yeah, good thing I only invested a few weeks on that guy. He was a jerk. I guess I'm just going to see where it goes with Chris. Kind of like you and whatshisname. And speaking of *him*," Kazumi asked, skillfully shifting the subject away from her, "how are things going with that?"

Rose felt hesitant to describe her complicated but growing feelings toward Akira. She tried to maintain a neutral tone when she said, "Things are good."

Kazumi tilted her head and frowned. "Only good? You guys were all—what's the word? Oh yeah, 'lovey-dovey' that day in Harajuku. So what happened? Did he show his true colors and become all male chauvinistic about everything after the cow gave away the butter?"

Rose couldn't help but giggle. She never should've shared that pearl of wisdom of her mother's with Kazumi. "It's giving away the milk, not the butter. And no, that's not it at all."

"Well, what then?" Kazumi studied Rose's face for a moment and then let out a big groan. "Did he turn out to be married?"

"No! Well, he *was*. His wife died. But he does have kids."

Kazumi digested that. "How did you find that out?"

"He told me."

"Before or after he got all that milk?"

"Before. He's always been upfront about his daughters." Rose knew it'd be everything else about Akira's situation that would set Kazumi off, and she was right.

"Have you lost your mind?" Kazumi exclaimed. "You've heard about that species known as the 'Japanese mother-in-law'? Let me tell you, no other creature on earth is that evil or that determined to protect their darling sons against their wives."

"I know your grandmother was pretty terrible to your mother. But—"

"You'd have two of them! And one of them's the dead wife's mother!"

"When you put it like that, it does seem rather odd."

"Odd? That's putting it mildly." Kazumi shook her head in disbelief and said, "That's why I'm never marrying a Japanese guy."

"Mother-in-law problems aren't only in Japan, you know. They exist everywhere. But like I said, nothing's decided."

The tea and cakes arrived, and for a while, they forgot about everything else. Both women moaned in culinary ecstasy as they sampled the fruit cakes piled high with freshly whipped cream.

Chapter Twenty-Nine

Wednesday morning, Akira called to let Rose know his father had passed away in the middle of the night. When they hung up, she contacted Kazumi to find out what the funeral protocol would be.

"I don't really know," Kazumi confessed. "I've never been to a funeral in my life."

"Really?" Rose was surprised because back in Felix, funeral attendance was a part of the social fabric, especially with such a large, elderly population.

"What about that new movie? I bet you could get some hints from that."

"What new movie?"

"The one that just won all those awards. *Ososhiki*. You know, *Funeral*."

Rose went to get it from the video shop, but as interesting and as informative as the movie turned out to be, she figured it might be a smart idea to talk to a real person about the do's and don'ts of Japanese funeral etiquette. Her first thought was Mrs. Hayashi from the International Culture Thinking Housewives Circle, but she was out of the country right now. So that left Keiko. Rose arranged to meet her for lunch near Kana's new salon, which was just down the street from Yamanote University.

Rose was hesitant to tell her about Akira, but it turned out their relationship wasn't much of a secret because everyone in the class had already guessed. "That cat," Keiko said, remembering an idiom Rose had taught them several weeks earlier, "is out of the bag."

"Oh."

"Now, let's think of your situation," Keiko continued in a businesslike manner. "Are you engaged?"

Rose's cheeks turned pink while she shook her head.

"All right. So, you aren't a part of the family, then. But even so, you'd better be prepared. Just in case. Now, there used to be strict rules concerning funerals, but things are different nowadays. Especially in Tokyo." Keiko took a dainty sip of the Vienna coffee the server had just set in front of her, without getting so much as a dab of whipped cream around her mouth. Rose, on the other hand, had to fish around in her purse for a tissue to swab some cream off her nose.

"I'll loan you a black dress if you like," Keiko offered. "And you'll also need black stockings and black shoes. No jewelry. Except pearls."

Rose also needed to prepare a special funeral envelope with money. Three thousand yen was sufficient, but it had to be in a black and white envelope, and not a red and white one, which was for wedding money. Keiko also told her she'd have to light incense and bow respectfully to the family. "Basically," she added, "just follow what the people in front of you are doing. Nobody really knows what they're supposed to do at a funeral anyway, so they tend to copy the people ahead of them."

Rose registered all that in her head. Her goal was to get through the ordeal without making a fool of herself.

"Thanks for coming with me," Rose said to Michael on Saturday morning when they met at the station to go to the funeral together. The weather was terribly muggy, but since rain wasn't in the forecast, she left her umbrella at home.

"It'll be an interesting cultural experience." Michael pulled a small cellophane package out of his bag, ripped it open, and removed a black tie and armband. "It's amazing," he said as he leaned into a mirror on the station's platform and put them on, "that you can get this little funeral kit at a station kiosk, right next to cigarettes and chocolate bars."

"Guys are lucky. All *you* need are some bits and pieces to add to your suit." Rose gestured at her dowdy outfit. "But I have to wear this awful thing."

"At least you didn't have to buy it."

"Amen to that."

"Whoever said the little black dress is a sexy number obviously never saw the Japanese little black dress. It's more like a little black tent," Michael said, tsking in disapproval.

"You're not supposed to be sexy at a funeral," Rose retorted. "You're supposed to be funeral-like." And that was exactly how she felt. The dress she was wearing was a few inches too short, but not in a good way at all. The polyester material scratched her neck, and she felt like she was encased in plastic wrap.

When they exited the station, two somberly dressed young men held up black signs with Akira's father's name on them and pointed them in the direction of the temple. It wasn't really necessary because all they had to do was follow all the other similarly clad people who were going to the same place. They waited in line near the temple gates for their turn to sign the guest book and leave their envelopes at a reception table, and in exchange, they received a shopping bag filled with small, wrapped boxes. There were at least a hundred people crammed into the stuffy funeral hall, but more kept filing in. The priests had already begun chanting, and the air weighed heavy with incense.

Rose's feet were killing her. Keiko's shoes, which were a half-size too tight, hadn't seemed problematic when she put them on that morning, but they certainly did now. When it was her turn at the altar, she lit a stick of incense and sent a quick prayer to her Methodist God. She turned and bowed to the Kato family seated to the left of the casket, and they bowed back. She wasn't sure if Akira knew if she was there or not, but Yuka and Emi, who were squirming in their seats, waved at her. Rose offered a hint of a smile back at them.

They followed the other mourners out the side door, making room for the ones who were still arriving. As hot as it was outdoors, the crowd and the incense inside the temple were even more suffocating.

"Akira's father must've been quite the somebody in his day," Michael whispered when a black car pulled up in front of the temple and a driver sprang out of his seat to open the door for a man in his sixties. When the man arrived at the table collecting the funeral offerings, people snapped to attention and bowed deeply. "Who *is* that?" he asked.

Rose gasped. "It's Nakasone!"

"Holy crap! You're right."

Not wanting to seem like *gaijin* gawkers who had never been this close to a head of state before, they stood to the side and tried not to stare at the Prime Minister as he went into the temple.

"Do you think we can leave now?" asked Rose after they stood around for a couple of minutes, unsure of what to do next.

"Yeah, I think the important thing is that you *came*."

"And that I was dressed properly."

"And that you were dressed properly," Michael agreed. "Let's go get something to eat. I'm hungry."

"Are you insane? I'm not going anywhere in public dressed like this. I gotta get out of these clothes. And especially out of these shoes. Let's go back to my place."

Back home, feeling comfortable now that she was wearing shorts and a T-shirt, Rose handed Michael a Domino's Pizza menu. "I found this in my mailbox a few days ago. Want to give it a try?"

"Domino's? You've got a Domino's near you? With *real* pizza?" He cracked up as he read through the offerings, though. "Pizza does sound good, but let's skip the mayonnaise and barbecued chicken one."

"No argument there."

They called in their order for a deluxe combo. Forty minutes later, the doorbell rang and Michael opened the door.

The delivery guy looked like he might have a heart attack when he saw Michael's face. "No speak English," he stammered in panic, even though Michael was speaking to him in Japanese. Somehow the young man managed to hand over their pizza without dropping it and to take their money.

"Hey, it almost looks like the real deal," said Michael, when he peered inside the box.

"Not quite." Rose plucked the corn kernels off her piece and popped them into her mouth. "Now it does."

They were about to start watching the sitcom reruns Michael's mom had sent that week when the phone rang.

It was Keiko. "Was everything okay at the funeral today?"

"Yes, thanks so much for everything. I really appreciate your help." Rose wondered if she was supposed to give her a call as soon as she got home.

"I forgot to tell you about the salt."

"Salt?"

"Yes, you need to throw it over your shoulder when you go into your house. It's for warding off bad luck, or evil spirits. To keep them out of your house."

"Oh, *that* salt."

She and Michael had gone through the funeral goody bags as soon as they got back. Green tea, a large bath towel, and oddly enough, packages of salt. Those she just emptied into her saltshaker.

Keiko's shocked silence after Rose confessed that made her feel like she might've made a huge mistake. "Is it poisonous?"

"Oh no. It's just an old Japanese custom. It's um, what do you say? Superstition. It should be okay."

After hanging up, Rose told Michael evil spirits might come to plague her because of her mishandling the funeral salt.

"You don't really believe that, do you?"

"No. But I need all the help I can get. What if it makes Akira's father's spirit unhappy?"

"Seriously?"

"Nah. But still. I kind of wish I had known about that."

Chapter Thirty

Later that night, Akira called. "Thanks for coming today."

"I wasn't sure if you saw me there or not."

"Oh, I saw you, all right. The entire hall lit up when you came in."

Rose smiled into the phone. "Your father was a lucky man to have many people who wanted to say farewell to him. He must've had a *lot* of friends."

"I suppose some people at the funeral were his friends—especially the old guys. But a lot came to pay respects on behalf of their companies."

"I also saw the prime minister."

"His father and my father went way back. It was nice he could take the time to come."

"What was your father like? Before he got sick?"

She cradled the receiver in her neck as she stretched the phone cord toward the fridge to pour a glass of cold barley tea. The advantage of having such a tiny apartment was it was never necessary to take more than three steps in any direction. She sat back down and listened to Akira talk about his father's career in the Foreign Ministry. About the book he wrote on foreign policy. And about his post-retirement career as a television commentator.

"What about the war?" As this might be a taboo topic, Rose added, "My father was in China—not as a soldier exactly, but as an airplane mechanic."

"It's a little complicated. My dad grew up with a lot of opportunities, you know, because of his family background. His father and grandfather were influential people in the Meiji and Taisho Eras. So my father went to the best high school in Tokyo. Then to the University of Tokyo where he studied economics. But," he added, "none of that would've gotten him out of military service. It would have made him an officer, and he would have probably gotten killed like many of his friends were. But unfortunately—or I guess you could say, fortunately—he got tuberculosis. That kept him out of the army and kept him alive. So, in a way, he was lucky."

"I guess that *was* lucky. And he must've fully recovered from TB, considering he lived on for so many years."

Hesitation was in Akira's voice when he said, "I don't know if you know much about the fire bombings of Tokyo."

"Fire bombings?"

"The Americans dropped fire bombs on Tokyo in the spring of 1945, destroying about half of the city."

"I didn't know that." Basically, she only knew about Hiroshima and Nagasaki.

"About 100,000 people died—mostly civilians. Some consider it to be one of the worst war crimes in history, but—" Akira stopped. "Anyway, I'm getting off the point. The thing is, before the fire bombings, there was hardly any food in Tokyo. People were basically starving. So my grandfather sent his family to Karuizawa. They had a house there, and he figured they'd be able to get food from the local farmers or grow their own. And besides, the mountain air was better for someone with TB. So, my father, his sister, and my grandmother went to Karuizawa." He paused for a moment, before saying, "My grandfather was supposed to join them but got caught in those raids. His body was never found."

Rose gasped. "Oh, how terrible!"

"War *is* terrible," Akira agreed. "And just a generation later, the children of the enemies can be like us."

"It makes you wonder what war is all about in the first place."

"That's for sure."

Rose wanted to talk about something less dismal. "Tell me, how did your parents meet each other?"

"Well, I guess you could say it was an *omiai*."

"An arranged marriage?"

"Not exactly an arranged marriage in the traditional sense. After the war, my father worked with the occupation army, and one of his superiors was my mother's uncle. He thought they'd make a good match, so he introduced them. And I guess they liked each other well enough to go on a few dates, and a couple of months later, they decided to get engaged.

"It sounds more like a blind date to me."

"That's probably a better way to put it. But no matter what it was called, it worked out well for them. I guess you could say my parents were kind of unusual for their generation. They took vacations together, and my mom even went with him on some of his business trips abroad. She's not what you'd call your average kind of Japanese woman, especially for someone her age. She was certainly different from my friends' mothers. In a *good* way," he added.

Rose listened carefully, knowing that people generally modeled their own lives by how their parents had lived theirs.

"My mother's father," Akira continued, "was a pretty liberal thinker for back then, especially when it came to women. Because if it'd been up to my grandmother, my mother probably wouldn't have gone to university. She was very old-fashioned, and she thought if her daughter was too educated she wouldn't be able to find a husband."

"I guess it was a different world back then for women." Rose didn't mention that her own mother had tried to dissuade her from getting a master's degree because she thought it didn't make Brad, who barely squeaked through college, look good.

"Anyway," he continued, "my grandfather taught at a women's university, and he argued that his daughter needed to be just as educated as his students. And because of her education, she was a great help to my dad."

"I wish I could've met your father. He sounds like he was quite a man."

"I wish you could've met him, too." Akira's voice was tinged with sadness. "Especially before... Well, before he got sick."

"What about Sumiko's parents? Did they have an *omiai*?"

"Yeah. Theirs was very traditional. Obaachan's husband was a lot older than her—about twelve years. I don't think they knew each other at all beforehand. And after they got married, she moved in with her mother-in-law, who I gather was a real piece of work. And her husband? Well, he was never home because it turned out he had a whole string of mistresses."

Rose made a face into the phone. "That's just awful. How terrible for her."

"Yeah, but you could say that she got the last laugh on that one."

He went on to tell her how she had ended up with all her husband's money. About how she had outsmarted her son and his uncles by not turning over the control of it to them. Akira chuckled when he said, "They all believed she'd be putty in their hands, but she hired the same lawyer who'd handled her husband's will, and he made sure her future was secure. As a result, she's got complete freedom."

"That's amazing," Rose said, unsure if she should admire Obaachan or pity her. She was pretty certain her own grandmother wouldn't have moved in with any of her own kids, let alone their spouses, to clean and babysit if she had become financially independent. Her grandmother would've probably gone on one cruise after another, imagining herself to be living in her favorite TV show, *The Love Boat*.

Chapter Thirty-One

Rose was in the part time teacher's room at Yamanote University, marking papers and killing time before she needed to head off to her night classes at Friendly. Lunch was over, and the other teachers had either left for the day or had gone to their afternoon classes. It was raining miserably—the kind of rain that seems to come from every direction, rendering an umbrella completely useless. She knew she'd be drenched by the time she got to the station and was putting off that particular torture for as long as she could.

"Rose-sensei?" called a voice from the door.

Rose glanced up and saw Professor Hayashi, the husband of the leader of the International Culture Thinking Housewives Circle, striding toward her.

"Oh, Hayashi-sensei. Good afternoon," she said formally as she stood up.

"May I have a few words with you?" he said as he sat down across from her.

"Yes, of course." Rose's stomach twisted into a knot, but she kept a smile on her face. Whenever Kenny wanted to talk to someone at Friendly, it almost never meant good news.

"How is everything? Are you happy here?"

"Uh, yes. Very much so. It's different from what I'm used to doing, so it's a challenge. But yes, I really enjoy teaching here." When he didn't reply, Rose added, a slight tremor in her voice, "Is everything okay? Have there been any complaints?"

"Absolutely not. I didn't know you could speak Japanese. The office staff has informed me that you generally speak to the administrators in Japanese."

"Well, I try to speak it as much as I can. I'm taking lessons." Rose wondered if she was supposed to have talked to them in English, to provide them with some sort of language practice.

"What do you think is your level? Advanced? Intermediate?"

"I don't know," she said. "I'm going to take the Japanese proficiency test at the end of the year. My teacher says I should try for Level 3. So intermediate, I guess. I'm pretty sure I don't know enough Chinese characters for Level 2."

"Mm. Level 3. Jolly good." He sucked air through his teeth and scratched his head. "The staff in the office like you. They say you are easy to get along with."

Easy to get along with? Did that mean she just behaved like a normal and decent person? Compared to the British woman Angela, who came in on Tuesdays, Rose figured that yeah, she *was* easy to get along with. At first, Rose thought they could be friends because, after all, they were the only foreign women there. But Angela was barely civil to anyone and treated the administrators like they were her servants by always making demands on them. Rose now made sure she sat on the opposite side of the teachers' room. Even Steve was better than her.

"If you have time," Professor Hayashi said, pushing back his chair, "would you mind terribly stopping by my office? Shall we say in about thirty minutes? I would like to have a little meeting with you."

Rose tentatively rapped her hand on his office door at precisely four o'clock. When he let her in, the three men who were sitting at a seminar table stubbed out their cigarettes and stood to greet her. Professor Hayashi introduced her to one of the university's vice presidents, the English faculty dean, and a Charles Dickens specialist. They motioned her into the empty seat across from them. She folded her hands and placed them on her lap to keep from fidgeting. The afternoon was becoming more and more bizarre.

Hayashi-sensei spoke first. He informed her that her classes had become so popular among students there was a waiting list for the fall semester. He said the office staff liked her because she spoke with them in Japanese. Furthermore, one of the associate professors of the English department, who had stopped in the part-time teachers' room to ask for help with the English in his paper dealing with the semantic differences between *this* and *that*, had also found Rose to be very agreeable.

When the department's research assistant came in with tea and cakes, Rose's fear of being fired from what had turned into her favorite job dissipated. They probably wouldn't be feeding her if they were trying to get rid of her.

After the assistant closed the door behind her, the dean spoke for the first time. In fluent English, he said, "We'd like you to apply for a full-time position."

"Excuse me?" Rose wasn't sure she had heard correctly.

"We need a tenured native English-speaking professor in our department, not only to teach but also to help with confidential matters throughout the year. The professor we've had for many years, a man from New Zealand, will be retiring early due to poor health. We'd like you to replace him. Starting from the fall semester. That is, if you plan to stay in Japan."

Their offer stunned Rose, and she needed a moment to think. She did plan to stay in Japan at least until next March, maybe even another year. She didn't want to admit it, even to herself, but a lot depended on how things went with Akira. But this job offer changed *everything*. She could quit Friendly, move forward with her career, and take things slowly with Akira. "Y-yes," she said, her voice trembling a little. "I'm planning to stay." As soon as she spoke, she realized her words were true. She liked working with young adults. She knew she'd never be content teaching elementary school children again, which would be her likely fate if she returned to Nebraska.

"We'd like to know a little more about your research interests," continued the dean. "Your graduate degree, Hayashi-sensei has told us, is in child development and education. But would you be able to combine that with the interests of our English Department?"

Rose nodded, not entirely sure what he was talking about.

"And," he asked, "have you published any papers?"

Professor Hayashi spoke up. "This is the book Rose-sensei co-authored with me." He pulled out a slim volume Rose had never seen before, though it had her name on the cover, and handed it to the dean. Was that from some proofreading he'd asked her to do a few months back—the one she refused to take any payment for?

The dean examined it and nodded. "This will do for now."

The head of the department then asked Rose what her current area of research was.

Feeling a bit cornered, she said, "I'm sorry, I haven't had much time for research these days because I'm studying Japanese."

From the way the men were looking at her, that had been the right response. But truthfully? It'd never occurred to her to do any research on any topic. Her graduate study focused more on the practical aspects of education than on the theoretical ones. She had a feeling that was going to have to change pretty quickly.

Over the next hour, the professors explained the application procedure, which would have to be completed within the next three weeks. Then, the documents would require approval at a higher-up level. However, they were optimistic her appointment would be confirmed by the end of July. If all went well, she should submit her letter of resignation to her current academic establishment then and start in mid-September when the fall semester began.

Current academic establishment? Rose forced herself not to snicker.

After the others left, Professor Hayashi described the job in greater detail. Knowing she'd be late for work, she borrowed his office phone to let her current academic establishment know. She also phoned for a taxi, thinking today, of all days, that particular luxury was well-deserved.

By the time she sailed through the door at FECC, the staff room was empty.

Before Kenny could get after her for being more than an hour late, she jumped in with an excuse she'd been saving for just the right occasion. "Oh Kenny! I'm so sorry I'm late. I couldn't tell you this on the phone, but I was almost here and suddenly I got my period. Blood was everywhere!"

Kenny snapped his mouth shut. Clearly, he didn't want to hear any more.

"It was just awful," she continued, thoroughly enjoying his discomfort. "Like a slaughterhouse. An absolute bloodbath. I had to go all the way back home to change my clothes. You should've seen it, blood everywhere and—"

Kenny held up his hand. "Don't let it happen again. But pay still goes down."

Rose nodded and hid her glee. If that university career thing didn't work out, maybe she could go into acting.

She forced the job offer out of her head or else she'd never be able to get through the next three classes. But it took great restraint to not do a little happy dance as she headed toward her classroom. In just a month or so, she'd be free of this place. She couldn't wait to see the look on Akira's face when she told him tonight. She'd wait until it was a done deal before telling anyone else—even Michael. No sense in jinxing anything.

Several weeks later, Rose was in the university's part-time teachers' room on the last day of the semester, struggling over whether to give a B or a C to a student who had received a decent score on the final exam but had been absent from the class five times. The British woman, Angela, had finished her grading ten minutes after her class ended and zipped out the door without even a see-you-next-fall *sayonara* to anyone. The other foreigners, John, Peter, and Steve, were sitting at a large table, joking around while filling out their grades.

Surprisingly, she was getting kind of used to Steve being such a buffoon, and the other two guys were actually pretty nice. It turned out John, the British guy from Lancaster, was working on his master's degree at Temple University and was taking classes with both Michael and Kazumi's boyfriend, Chris. Peter, the other Brit, and Steve always poked fun at John, saying graduate school was a big waste of time and money since there was so much work to be found without one. As usual, Rose pretty much kept her mouth shut and watched from the sidelines.

"Hey Rose," John called out. "Want to come with us to Old Irish to celebrate the end of the semester?"

She looked up from her papers. "I wish I could go have a beer with you guys, but I've got to get to my other job. Thanks for asking, though."

When Professor Hayashi came in a few minutes later and headed straight to Rose, the good-natured bantering came to a halt. Everyone knew he was a powerful man. When he asked Rose to come to his office, she stood and followed him. She couldn't hear what the guys were whispering as she walked out the door, but she figured they were discussing the doom of her extremely short-lived university career.

"We have an appointment with the president in ten minutes," the professor said as they got into the elevator.

"The president?"

"He will present you with your certificate of appointment."

"It's official?"

"Yes. It's official."

Rose grinned at Hayashi-sensei and let out a happy sigh of relief. Until that exact moment, she was half afraid the whole thing was some sort of hoax, that the job offer would evaporate into thin air.

Twenty minutes later, she returned to the part-time teachers' room.

Steve offered her a gentle and condescending smile. "So, how did it go? What happened?"

Rose wanted to tell this big news to Akira first. Or maybe even to Michael. But Steve looked like he'd been waiting for her to say she'd been fired for falsifying her qualifications and for sneaking into a world she didn't belong.

"Oh, it was fine. I went to meet the university president. For my letter of appointment and to see my new office."

"Your new office?" The smirk on Steve's face had rapidly slipped away.

"Yes. I'll be full time in September."

"They gave you a contract? As a *gaikokujin kyoshi*?" He sounded as shocked as if she'd told him she was President Reagan's love child.

"Not a contract. It's for tenure." The *gaikokujin kyoshi* position was generally as high as a foreigner could go in Japanese academia, but Rose had actually gone even higher.

"T-tenure! But how did you—"

The look of disbelief on Steve's face aggravated her. "Well, I *do* have a master's degree. And I've also co-authored a book." If she was going to toss in that fib, she might as well go whole hog. "And of course, there's my research in education. So don't underestimate me just because I don't brag about myself all the time, like some people."

John let out an enormous belly laugh and came over to slap Rose on the back as if she was one of the guys. "Touché! Well done. And congratulations on the job."

"Thanks," she said, beaming up at him. "I appreciate that."

"Are you sure you don't want to go out for a drink with us? To celebrate the end of the semester *and* your promotion."

"You know what?" Rose said. "That sounds like a great idea. Let me go make a phone call."

She had never used any of her sick days at Friendly, and what better time to start than right now? The sour look on Steve's face when she came back after making her call suggested he wanted to spend the next couple of hours trash talking her rather than drinking to her success. Well, too bad for him.

"You guys ready?" she said, gathering up her things.

As a tenured associate professor, one of her jobs would be to oversee the foreign part-timers, and she relished the fact that she was going to be Steve's boss.

Chapter Thirty-Two

"Kampai!" Michael raised his glass in a toast after Rose finished her last day at Friendly English Conversation College. By the time she'd signed all the paperwork and turned over all her teaching materials that were considered the property of the school, it was nearly ten. "Congratulations on being the first of us to escape from the friendly place of insanity. How does it feel?"

"To be honest, a little sad. It's the end of an era, so to speak. And I did like the students." Rose was surprised to find her voice shaking a little.

"Even Creepy Kaneda?"

Well, that certainly cured her momentary melancholy. "Maybe not him."

"Anyway," said Michael. "I have some good news of my own. It turns out there's a sudden opening at this women's college in Kanagawa from September and I snagged it. The professor in my materials development class introduced me. So you aren't the only one moving up in the world."

"That's fantastic!" Rose was thrilled for him.

"Granted," he said, putting on a fake serious face, "some people get to ride their bikes to their cushy new university jobs, while others have to commute for three hours. But that's the way the good-luck cookie crumbles, I suppose."

"Oh, quit complaining," she scolded. "You've got your foot in the door, and that's what counts. At least, that's what you've always told me. What are you going to do about Friendly?"

"I've renewed my contract for another year, so it's still in control of my visa. But I made it perfectly clear I'd be taking off two weeks to go to the States. So, lucky you. I can definitely be your date at that cornfield wedding."

Rose wanted to climb across the table to give Michael a hug. Until that moment, she was unsure if she'd have to endure her cousin's wedding alone or not. "I owe you big time."

"You most certainly do. I'll be sure to let you know when payback time comes, though. With tons of interest, of course."

"I wouldn't expect it any other way," she deadpanned.

The server came with their antipasto course, and as they started to eat, Rose said, "You know Akira's class at Friendly? Their contract is ending, but they want to keep on studying English with me. So from September, we're going to have the class at Kana's salon."

"You're stealing Friendly's clients away from them?"

"If you put it that way, well, then yes."

"Good for you," he said with hearty approval. He tore off a piece of the crusty bread in the basket and dipped it into a little bowl of olive oil. "That's an interesting new take on the *eikaiwa* industry. Tanning and talking. Who knew? I can just see the slogan: People who tan together talk together."

"You know, I'd tell Kana that," she said with amusement, "except knowing that little entrepreneur, she'd do exactly that: start a tanning/language school."

"Is Akira going to join the class?"

"Why wouldn't he?"

"Well, besides the fact he sees you all the time anyway, wouldn't it feel awkward taking money from him? It's kind of different when he gave money to the school, don't you think? Rather than directly to you?"

"That's why I told him to bring wine to the class instead."

"Wine?"

"Hey," she said, shrugging her shoulders, "we can do whatever we want. Drink. Tan. Talk."

Michael chortled and said, "It could become a whole new type of industry." He paused when the server removed their antipasto plates and set down tiny bowls of minestrone soup. He spooned a little into his mouth before saying, "Changing the subject, how're things going between you and Akira, anyway?"

Rose wanted to say how great things were. About when she was with him, everything felt perfect. She wanted to tell Michael she'd never felt so comfortable with a man before. Or so loved and protected. But instead, all she could say was, "Things are good."

Michael squinted at her. "Only good?"

Rose produced a guilty little laugh. "I didn't mean that the way it sounded. Things are *really* good."

"Are you having doubts?" Michael asked.

"Of course, I'm having doubts. Who wouldn't? It'd be crazy not to." Rose dipped a corner of her bread into the soup, and ate it before continuing. "The thing is this. When we're together, it's great. His daughters are great, too. And when I see him and his daughters together, I think that maybe I could be a part of that. In fact, I *want* to be a part of that."

"I sense a big *but* here," he said quietly.

"I can't help having so many mixed feelings. It's such a big decision to take things any further. So I kind of think it's best to keep things the way they are. For a while, anyway."

"You don't have to jump into anything, right?"

"No, I don't," answered Rose.

Michael studied her face for a moment. "You're not telling me everything, are you? What's really bothering you?"

Rose looked down at the table. "I guess I'm kind of scared to tell my parents about Akira."

"That's crazy," he said with a snort. "Are you afraid they'll be like Tomo's mother and forbid you to see him or something?"

"No, they wouldn't do that. But I know they won't be happy. They'll say he's from a different country, a different culture, a different race. I guess you can say they still have a lot of that World War II mentality in them."

"Are you telling me they're bigots?"

"Yes. Well, no." Rose dragged her hand through her hair. "I don't know, really. I just don't know how to tell them that I might end up staying in Japan for the rest of my life."

"That's a load of crap," he said, somewhat harshly. "Why don't you try telling your parents you're gay and see how that goes?"

"When you put it that way," Rose said, "I guess things could be a lot worse."

Michael blinked at her for a moment and then hooted at her comment. "You're too funny." He reached across the table and patted her arm. "Trust me. You'll be fine. Your parents will be fine. But if I were you, I'd tell them in person. Not in a letter. Don't be a coward about it."

"I know. I'll tell them when I'm back for the wedding."

"By then, you'll have a better idea about where you and Akira are going. No sense in telling them now," he said as the server came to remove their soup bowls. "Believe me, it's all in the timing."

"Did you wait to tell your parents until you were sure you were gay?" Rose asked as she pulled off a chunk of the bread and ate it.

"Honey, I knew I was gay when I was in preschool. But I waited to tell them until they finished paying for my education."

That really surprised Rose. "Would they have actually cut you off?"

Michael shrugged a little. "If you're in a position like mine, you've got to be careful. Some of my friends got disowned by their families. I decided to stay on the safe side and not take a chance. I wanted to be sure I could earn a living before telling them." He finished up the wine in his glass before adding, "Just in case."

"So, what happened when you did tell them?"

"Well, my mom cried, thinking she'd turned me gay by letting me help her put on makeup when I was about six. As if," he said with a snort. "And my father wanted me to go to a psychiatrist."

"A psychiatrist?" Michael was the most level-headed person Rose knew, and hearing this for the first time was quite disturbing.

"But," he continued, "they got used to the idea. Eventually. Some relatives won't have anything to do with me at all now. Especially my Aunt Shirley. I wonder," he mused, "how she's feeling now after her Hollywood dreamboat Rock Hudson announced today he's got AIDS. Will she have to burn all her fan paraphernalia in protest now that she knows he's gay, too?"

That bit of information sidetracked Rose. "What? Are you kidding me? Rock Hudson's *gay*? Did you know that?"

"No," he said with a sad smile, "but now the whole world certainly does. Poor man. No one deserves that."

Even though Michael was full of jokes, Rose could tell he'd been hurt by what he went through with his family. "You never told me about any of this before."

He waved his hand like it wasn't a big deal. "Yeah, well, my parents are cool with everything now. But the others? I figure it's their loss, not mine." He shrugged and added, "But now you know why I like living in Japan. When you're already an oddball *gaijin*, being gay doesn't matter so much."

The server brought Michael's spaghetti carbonara and her salmon cream pasta, and they ordered two more glasses of the house wine and another bread basket.

"Anyway," Michael continued, winding the creamy spaghetti around his fork, "the only thing you have to worry about is doing what's right for you. You either take a chance or you don't. Life's full of opportunities, but you've got to grab them when they come."

"I know, but—"

He leaned forward in his seat. "Listen to me, Rose. You can't just sit around and wait for some sort of sign. That's just an excuse to not do anything at all. And unlike you," he said in a surprisingly defiant tone, "who could marry your partner in a flash with no one blinking an eye, I would *never* be able to do that."

It took a moment before Rose got what he was really saying. "You've met someone, haven't you?" she asked, studying his face.

"Maybe," Michael replied, trying to be all calm about it.

"Oh my god!" Rose exclaimed. "Tell me about him."

"Nope."

"Nope?"

"I don't want to jinx it."

"Jinx it? Now who's talking crazy?"

Michael's mysterious smile could have rivaled the Mona Lisa's. "We've been keeping our relationship on the down low right now. Not for any reason other than we just want to see if we're right for each other. We're...dating."

"Dating?"

"Yes, in the sense of wining and dining each other. And," he added after a pause, "We decided to get tested."

Rose frowned and shook her head.

"For HIV."

"Oh."

"Because we're going to be completely exclusive."

Excitement was rising in Rose's voice and the person at the next table tossed her a dirty look when she asked, "Are you telling me you found Mr. Right?"

Michael couldn't stop beaming from ear to ear. "I found Mr. Right."

"And you've been keeping him a secret from me?" she said in a lower voice with a pretend scowl. "For exactly how long?"

"A couple of months. I didn't tell you because I wanted to be sure. Maybe after we get back to Japan, you can meet him."

"We can double date!"

Michael groaned and rolled his eyes, but he looked awfully happy.

Chapter Thirty-Three

Akira had taken a day off from work to help Rose get things done before her ten-day trip to Nebraska. "So, what's the plan?" he asked as they went down the subway steps of Yotsuya San-chome Station.

"First, I've got to get some traveler's checks. And then, I've got to go to the immigration office in Ikebukuro to submit the documents to change my working visa status and get a re-entry permit, so they let me back into Japan. After that, I need to get souvenirs for people and a wedding present for my cousin."

"I guess Isetan Department Store's a good place for the shopping."

Rose shook her head. "Everyone at Friendly goes to the Oriental Bazaar in Harajuku for that sort of thing. It's aimed at tourists, but that's what people back home like. And it's cheap."

"Okay. So, bank, immigration, and shopping. And then, I'd really, *really* like to make sure we have enough time to go somewhere and...uh, you know, take a nap."

Rose giggled a little. "I suppose I'll be ready for a nap after all that. I'll be totally exhausted by then, for sure."

"Hopefully, not *too* exhausted," Akira said meaningfully.

After going to the bank, they headed to immigration in the Sunshine Sixty building. Their faces dropped when they saw all the people lined up.

"Maybe we should've come here first," Rose said with a groan.

But things proceeded rather smoothly after she submitted her documents, probably because the President of Yamanote University had called the immigration office himself to inform them of her impending application for a status change. Friends in high places, she was quickly beginning to understand, were not to be underestimated.

With her reentry permit stamped in her passport, they got on the Yamanote train line and headed to Harajuku. They bumped shoulders as they walked down the tree-lined street in Omotesando, and Akira took her hand and intertwined her fingers with his. She squeezed his hand back in appreciation.

"It's nice to play hooky together," he said. "Too bad we can't do this every day."

At the Oriental Bazaar, she loaded up with lots of little gifts to give people in her hometown. And as for Denise's wedding present, she chose a ceramic Lazy Susan platter with a pretty Asian pattern on it.

"But that doesn't look Japanese at all," protested Akira. "How about these?" He held up a beautiful set of lacquered miso soup bowls.

Rose shook her head. "They wouldn't hold up in the dishwasher. And besides, my cousin wouldn't know what to do with them. Believe me, this is perfect for holding snacks while watching Cornhusker games."

Akira looked puzzled. "Cornhusker?"

"You have a *lot* to learn if you want to be with me," she said, laughing. "The Cornhuskers are the Nebraska football team and they're a super big deal. People get together and have parties to watch the games. So trust me, she'll like this."

With the shopping taken care of, they had lunch at a conveyor belt sushi restaurant, flagged down a taxi to go back to Shinjuku, and checked into a love hotel called the Loyal Rest.

An hour later, they were soaking in the bath. Rose was leaning against Akira, and he was gently caressing her breasts. She couldn't imagine any other place on earth she'd rather be than right there, right then. But she knew couldn't hold onto this moment forever. She'd been telling herself to take things one day at a time, but every day went by so quickly. She was beginning to understand that a thousand perfect days meant nothing if they led to nothing.

Emotional tears formed in the corner of Rose's eyes. Her mouth felt dry as she took a deep breath and whispered, "I love you," for the first time. When Akira whispered the same words back to her, she was pulsating with happiness. "Maybe," she said, "when I come back from Nebraska, I could spend some more time with your daughters. Maybe we could do some fun stuff together and see how that goes."

"That'd be great!"

"But that doesn't mean—"

"I know," Akira said, toning down his enthusiasm a few hundred notches.

"It's just a baby step."

"Getting the astronauts to the moon and back involved baby steps. All great endeavors do," said Akira philosophically.

Chapter Thirty-Four

"Papa," asked Yuka as they were eating breakfast the morning Rose flew to Nebraska. "Are you going to marry Rose?"

Obaachan nearly dropped the plate of eggs she was carrying over to the table.

"I don't know," he answered honestly.

"Will she become our new mother?" asked Emi.

"Let your father eat his breakfast in peace." Obaachan poured coffee into his cup. "It's not any of your business."

"It *is* their business," Akira corrected. "It's all our business. Mine. The girls. And yours."

Obaachan harrumphed and turned away. "You men always do whatever it is you want to do. It's part of being a man. My husband did that. Osamu does that, too."

"Do you think I'm like them?"

She turned around. "Actually, no. I don't."

"Obaachan, what is it men always do?" asked Emi, looking at her with interest.

Akira raised his eyebrows at Obaachan, wanting to see how she'd pull herself out of that tight spot.

"Well," she said, "men have to make decisions. Sometimes they decide things other people don't feel comfortable with. Sometimes it might not be in the best interests of the whole family. But once a decision is made, the family has no choice but to go along with it."

Akira hadn't expected her to produce such a detailed and honest explanation. At least, it was honest from her perspective. "A good man," he countered, "does what he thinks is right, and not just for his sake, but for the people he loves. A good man will not hurt the people he loves. But sometimes they don't understand the reasons for his actions."

"Sometimes," Obaachan added, "the people who care about a man can think more clearly than he can. Especially when it comes to practical matters. And especially when a man is not thinking with his head."

"Sometimes," Akira said softly, "it is the heart that speaks the loudest."

Obaachan harrumphed again, but with a little less force.

Then, Emi asked. "Papa, did you know an ostrich has three stomachs?"

"No," he said, laughing. "I did not know that."

The subject moved away from his marital future and to what the girls had learned at daycare the previous day. Obaachan had been right about one thing, he was thinking as the girls filled the room with their chatter. He was going to do what he was going to do, regardless of what anyone else thought. On this, he would not, could not, compromise.

That afternoon, Fumiyo and Michie were in a traditional Japanese restaurant at the top of Mitsukoshi Department Store in Ginza. They had just visited the French impressionistic exhibition in the department store's gallery and were hungry. A kimono-clad woman gave them *oshibori* towels and cold barley tea and left them with the menu.

Michie wiped her hands on the towel and let out a contented sigh. "You have no idea how good this feels—to be able to go out whenever I want. To not have to worry about what's going on at home. Or if Saburo's causing a disturbance at the daycare."

Fumiyo nodded, knowing *exactly* how good it felt to be rid of a troublesome husband. At least Michie's troubles with Saburo were fairly recent. Hers began the moment she drank the sacred sake at her wedding ceremony.

As if Michie could read Fumiyo's mind, she said, "I am grateful for the good years I did have with my husband. But I can't help but be glad that the bad years are over. Saburo would've hated what he'd become. And," she said as she opened the menu, "I'm going to enjoy every minute I have left in this world. That's why you and I are having the deluxe lunch today."

Fumiyo looked down at the menu and gasped a little at the price. She'd never spent so much before on a lunch and rarely that much on a dinner. But she could afford such a treat if she wanted. "Why not live dangerously and order a bottle of Kirin beer to go with it?"

"I like the way you think." Michie signaled the server and placed their order. The beer arrived immediately, and Michie filled their small, chilled glasses. "*Kampai.*"

"*Kampai,*" replied Fumiyo, feeling downright giddy over this lunchtime rebellion as they clinked their glasses together in a toast. Remembering she had to pick up the girls in just three hours, she set her glass down after taking a few sips. She couldn't arrive at the daycare center smelling like a boozing granny.

"I suppose," Michie said, getting right to the point, "sooner or later, we'll have to discuss Akira's future. Well, what I mean is, *our* role in Akira's future."

"You mean if he marries that American girl?"

"If he marries anyone."

Fumiyo sighed, picked up her beer, and took another sip. "I know."

"Have you thought about what you're going to do when that happens?"

The beer gave Fumiyo the courage to say aloud what had been on her mind the past few weeks. "I've been thinking of buying an apartment."

"In Tokyo?"

"That way, I could still be close to the girls. And besides, I *like* living in here."

"So you have no plans to return to Kyushu?"

Fumiyo shook her head. "I-I don't want to. I don't think I could live with my son's family again. Well, they aren't as easy to be around as Akira."

"Have you started looking for a place?"

"No, but I suppose the time has come for me to do so." Fumiyo described the breakfast conversation they'd had that morning and added, "Akira wants that American girl for sure, but whether he's thinking with his head or his man parts, I don't know. He said he's waiting for her to decide. Imagine that. What's there to think about? Yes or no. Nothing in between. I don't know what those Americans—"

"Can you blame the poor girl for her hesitation? My son's life is not without complications."

"And I suppose I'm the biggest complication of all."

"You've been an extraordinary help," Michie said kindly. "For all of us."

"I know it's time for Akira and his daughters to move on to the next stage of their lives," Fumiyo said reluctantly. "And time for me to move on to mine."

"I do believe you are right. It *is* the right time for you to do that."

Fumiyo hid the shock she felt when she heard Michie's words. "Well," she said with a lot more cheer than she actually felt, "I guess I'll stop by that real estate company in the neighborhood to see if I can find somewhere around here. I've heard buying something can take time, and it's quite complicated. Maybe it's good to start now."

Fumiyo's gut twisted as she spoke. Was she really going to take that step? Become independent at her age?

"You could do that." Michie paused as two servers came to the table and set down two enormous trays holding an array of exquisite little dishes of food for each of them. She smiled up at them in thanks, and after they walked away, she continued. "Like I said, you could buy an apartment. But I have an idea I'd like you to consider."

Fumiyo leaned in and listened to what Michie had to say.

Chapter Thirty-Five

Bringing Michael to Nebraska was the best idea Rose had ever had. With him by her side, no one saw her as the jilted bride in one of the town's most memorable scandals. She introduced him around, and he shook hands and chatted as easily as if he were a politician out collecting votes. Her mother began fawning over him the moment they'd arrived, and later said to Rose, "He must come from a good family. I bet they're moneyed people, with such nice manners like that."

Rose hoped she wasn't already ordering the wedding invitations.

"How about stopping in for a beer?" Michael pointed at the Corner Saloon as they were taking a stroll around the town in the early evening.

"We can't go in there," Rose said, grabbing Michael's arm as he headed toward the doors.

"Why not?" he asked with surprise.

"Because the 'nice' people of Felix don't go there. According to my grandma, that's for the local riffraff, and she'd kill me if she knew I went in there."

"Oh, come on. Please? Let me live out my fantasy—you know, the stranger in town walks into a bar. Everyone falls silent and—"

"Not here. We can drive over to Riley later, and you can be the stranger in the bar over there. The only person from around here who goes into the Corner Saloon is Old Man Jones. He's there every afternoon and stays until one of his sons carries him home."

Michael looked hopeful when he asked, "Will there be cowboys in Riley?"

Rose snorted. "Probably not. You'd have to go out west for that. Maybe to Ogalala or Sidney. But, the fact is, we can't drink here. Not in Felix."

"How can the bar stay in business if they don't have any customers?"

"I didn't say no one goes there. Just no one from *Felix*. People from Riley come here to drink and people from Felix go to Riley to drink."

"You've got to be kidding me," Michael said, shaking his head in disbelief. "So, if we can't get a drink, what else is there to do around here for excitement?"

Ten minutes later, they were sitting on a picnic bench at the Dairy Palace up on the highway and shooing away the flies who wanted to share their chocolate dipped soft cream cones. "I can't believe you haven't noticed."

"Notice what?" said Michael, licking the melting ice cream off the side of his.

"How nice my mom is to you."

"Well, she *is* nice. I don't know why you were so worried about coming here."

Rose snorted. "You really don't see it, do you?"

"See what?"

"I bet she's hoping to announce our engagement at Denise's wedding reception."

Michael looked so horrified he almost dropped his ice cream. "Listen, I'll go along with being your fake wedding date. And you owe me big time for that. But I draw the line at being the fake fiancé or the fake husband. Even for you, my dear. And besides, you know you're going to have to tell them about Akira sooner or later, because you and I both know exactly where that's heading."

"But it'll break their poor little hearts when they find out the man of my dreams isn't *you*."

"Coward."

"With a big capital C tattooed right across my forehead." She finished her cone and wiped her sticky lips with the back of her hand. "I know I have to tell them. But I guess I don't want to hear all their reasons why my relationship with him is wrong. I mean, we haven't decided anything definite, so why make my family upset if there's nothing to tell? I can always write them a letter later."

"Believe me. I do understand where you're coming from. But it's better to be honest, no matter how hard it is. Trust me. Just tell them."

Rose let out a long sigh. "You're right. I will. Just let me get through the wedding first." She chuckled a little when she added, "You know, thanks to you being here, my mom hasn't mentioned how I let Brad Billford slip through my fingers even once. And her usual criticisms of my weight, makeup, hair, posture, and clothes are also down to practically a zero. It's all because of you."

"Admit it. I'm your knight in shining armor."

"You're my knight in shining armor," she echoed. "But listen, when you go to that bachelor party, don't tell anyone you're gay. And don't flirt with the bartender. Or burst into any gay pride songs. Stop laughing. I mean it!"

"All right. I promise I won't do any of those things. I'll just be a complete and utter fake."

"And, um, Michael?"

"What?"

"I wouldn't mind it at all if Brad or his cow of a wife got the wrong idea about us. After what they did to me."

"Out for some revenge, are we?"

"Can you blame me?"

"I'm nothing if I'm not a great actor," he said, slinging his arm around Rose's shoulder as if secret cameras were filming them.

Michael's enthusiasm over his role as the ardent boyfriend could become problematic if they didn't watch out. "Let's not overdo it, though," she said, laughing and scooting a little bit away. "Let's just keep them guessing about us, okay?"

Because Brad was the groom's best man, there was no avoiding him or his fiancé-snatching wife at the wedding festivities. But at least Kimberly, who was enormously pregnant, wasn't going to be a bridesmaid. Rose wouldn't have to walk down the church aisle with her, pretending there were no hard feelings. Her plan was to remain civil but ignore them as much as possible, which was fairly easy to do with Michael by her side.

The church's Ladies Association wedding shower was a nightmare of déjà vu for Rose because it was almost identical to her own bridal shower. She remembered being just as excited as Denise was acting now when she unwrapped her own bridal shower gifts, having no idea that by nightfall, everything would fall apart. That was the night Brad told her he had been cheating on her with Kimberly. And since Kimberly was pregnant, he'd be marrying her instead.

Rose felt the women's eyes on her as she helped Denise unwrap the household gadgets and wrote down who gave what so Denise could send out thank-you notes later. Good thing Michael had insisted she get her hair cut and highlighted at a fancy salon in Harajuku before they left Japan. He was right. Appearances were everything, and she knew she looked damn good.

That evening, Denise's high school friends hosted a lingerie shower/bachelorette party. Kimberly, as the best man's wife, was invited, but she couldn't come, making it unnecessary for Rose to fake a sudden bout of the stomach flu. No way was she going to spend an entire evening making pleasant small talk with that woman. Tonight, Rose could sit back and relax with people she hadn't seen in ages, people she'd known her entire life. She was prepared to have some fun.

The first round of margaritas was passed around, and as Denise unwrapped all the presents, Rose realized that if she did stay with

Akira, sexy nightwear could never be a part of her life. Not with small children running around. And certainly not if the grandma was in the house, too. As she was mulling that over, she didn't realize Erica, one of the other bridesmaids who'd been a few years behind her in high school, was talking to her.

"Oh, she's just all dreamy over that boyfriend of hers," said Denise. Everyone tittered.

"He's not my boyfriend," said Rose.

"You can't fool us," said Denise. "You're in love, and it's all over your face. I can't tell you how many times in the past few days you've had a far-away, lustful look in your eyes."

Rose smiled as she scooped up a good tablespoon of onion dip onto a Ruffle's potato chip and popped it into her mouth. Denise wasn't entirely wrong. She was beginning to miss Akira something terrible.

"Come on, tell us," said Erica. "When do you think you and Michael will get married?"

"I already told you, he's just a friend."

"She doesn't want to talk about it. Yet." Denise offered a theatrical wink, making everyone laugh some more.

Rose joined in on all the good natured bantering about Denise's upcoming wedding night, her honeymoon in the Ozarks, and the tiny, but charming, house she and Brian had rented over on Oak Street. At the back of her mind, she was hoping Michael wasn't doing anything at the bachelor party in Lincoln to blow their cover.

By the time they left the party after midnight to go back to Rose's parents' house, where Denise was spending the night, Rose was mostly sober and Denise was completely smashed.

"Shhh. You'll wake up Gladys Hawking," Rose warned after Denise started singing "I'm getting married in the morning," from *My Fair Lady* as they took a shortcut through the old lady's backyard.

"I don't care." Denise let out a long belch.

"Anyway, you're not getting married tomorrow. It's the day after tomorrow. So you'll have to change your song."

"But I love that song. I want to sing that song. And I want to have another drink. I want—" Without warning, Denise leaned over and vomited into ninety-four-year-old Hilda Hoffenbrow's hedge. She wiped her face and let out a weak giggle. "I can't believe I just did that."

Rose inwardly groaned. Hilda was a notorious gossip, and she'd probably be at the Uptown Café at the crack of dawn tomorrow telling anyone who'd listen that the Wilson girl had thrown up in her bushes. That the Wilson girl sure was a wild one. That she hoped Brian knew what he was getting into because Denise probably had a bun in her oven. And if she did, how could the poor man even know for sure that the baby was his? Because back in her day, girls never gave out the milk for free.

"Don't worry," said Rose. "I'll fix it." She found the garden hose and sprayed the bushes, flushing all the evidence into the gutter.

Back at the house, Denise plopped down on the porch swing next to Rose. "I'm going to be happy," she slurred. "You know, really, really happy." Denise's breath smelled sour and her hair was a mess.

"I'm sure you will be. I'm really, really happy for you."

"You're not just saying that?" Denise asked, suddenly sounding a bit more sober. "Erica said that you might be jealous of me because of what happened between you and Brad."

"That's a bunch of nonsense," Rose insisted, an edge to her voice.

"Erica also said I should comfort you. She said that this whole wedding is painful for you and that Michael is just a front. That you brought him here to disguise your feelings for Brad."

That Erica should just mind her own business, thought Rose, honestly piqued. "Listen, Denise. If that was true, don't you think I would've told everyone that Michael *was* my boyfriend? We're just friends. Period. Friends. And besides, I'm a million percent over Brad. I'm way better off without him."

"Maybe I shouldn't have had all those margaritas," Denise said as she pulled herself out of the swing and wobbled toward the guest bedroom at the back of the house where she'd be sleeping. "They've made me feel jittery."

Rose remained on the porch and contentedly watched the stars—so many more than could ever be seen in the Tokyo sky. When the clock struck two, she gave up waiting for Michael and tiptoed upstairs to her old bedroom, which had been converted into her mother's craft room. It felt strange, but at the same time, familiar and comforting. Especially with her father snoring on the other side of the wall.

The next morning, Rose pulled back the drapes of the upstairs guest room a little after eleven, letting the sunshine in. Everyone had gone to Lincoln for an all-you-can-eat spread before the four o'clock wedding rehearsal, but Rose got them out of that by saying they were just too jet lagged. Denise, despite her evil hangover, winked at her, suggesting Rose's real goal was to finagle some alone time with Michael. That was true—she did want to be alone with Michael. But not for the reasons Denise was imagining.

"I'm dying," Michael moaned.

"You aren't dying. Get up." Rose shook a couple of Tylenol tablets out of a bottle, handed them to him, and set a large glass of water on the bedside table.

He swallowed the pills, drank the water, and flopped back down. "The last thing I remember was the tequila shooters. After that, things are rather vague."

"What possessed you to drink so much?"

"It was a night out with the guys. I did guy stuff. Manly stuff. I can hold my liquor like the rest of them. But darling, I draw the line at peppermint schnapps." He rubbed his head. "I guess I could be in even worse shape if big glasses of sweet liqueur were my thing."

"Yeah, you gotta watch out for that around here. One of the biggest mistakes I've ever made was stealing my grandmother's crème de menthe from under her kitchen sink when I was in the ninth grade and drinking the whole thing with a friend. Cured me forever of binge drinking anything that sweet," she said, shuddering at the memory of the hangover. "Anyway, what did you think of Brian?"

"He's not my type. I prefer men who are—"

"You know what I mean."

"Well, I guess he's all right. That is, if you like the type who thinks beer pouring out of one's nose is a sign of great talent."

Rose groaned a little. "I guess he hasn't changed all that much since high school. And what about Brad? What did you think of him?"

"You have no idea how lucky you are. Trust me on that."

"What do you mean?"

"Well, you know I'm not one for gossip."

Rose snorted out a laugh.

"Okay, well, maybe I am. I do love some juicy gossip. Okay. Well, where I come from, guys with pregnant wives aren't supposed to go out to the parking lot with an underage girl and come back twenty minutes later zipping up their pants."

"Seriously?"

"I'm not so sure about the underage part. But yeah. Your ex definitely had a good time at the party."

Chapter Thirty-Six

Denise, like brides-to-be everywhere, spent the morning of her wedding in a nervous state of panic. And Rose, like maids of honor everywhere, spent her morning calming the bride-to-be down. There was a particularly bad moment when Denise discovered a nearly invisible zit on the tip of her nose as she was putting on her dress. But Rose managed to save the day by covering it with a dab of foundation and giving Denise a large glass of white wine before they headed off for the church.

Rose, in a high-necked lime-green satiny dress with puffed sleeves, held her head up high as she walked down the aisle holding a bouquet of sunflowers. She stood on the other side of the pulpit from Brad, the best man. She hardly spared him a glance, but with dark circles under his eyes, a messy stubble on his chin, and somewhat greasy hair, he looked bad. *Real* bad. He looked like he had continued the bachelor party debauchery all the way up until an hour ago. Even from ten feet away, Rose could smell the booze. She held herself up even taller and maintained a serene look on her face.

When the music for the bridal procession began, the congregation stood and faced the entryway where the bride and her father were standing, ready to walk down the aisle. Rose caught Michael's eye and winked at him.

Shortly after the ceremony began, it became obvious the church's air conditioning was failing. The overhead fans weren't really doing much of anything except stirring the hot and humid air around. Rose felt sweat trickling down her back and she heard the rustle of the programs being used as fans while she tried to focus on the ceremony. Despite the heat, Denise looked like a perfect, beautiful bride as she gave her vows. And from the way Brian was grinning from ear to ear at his wife-to-be, Rose was beginning to think perhaps her cousin had made a good choice. Maybe Brian wasn't like his brother, who looked like he was about to spew his guts all over the altar at any moment. The heat wasn't doing him any good at all, but at least he didn't drop the ring as he fumbled around for it in his pocket when it was time to give it to the groom.

When the ceremony was finally over, the congregation practically chased the wedding party down the aisle, eager to get inside the fellowship hall next to the sanctuary where they knew the air conditioning hadn't gone kerplunk.

Considering all the meltdowns Denise had that morning, Rose was worried she might add the failed air conditioning to the list. But Denise smiled happily, receiving congratulations from the guests as they filed past, heading toward the cake and Hawaiian punch provided by the Ladies Auxiliary. Rose, being the perfect the maid of honor, stood with the wedding party and smiled until her teeth hurt. When the newlyweds finally headed for their table, Rose followed, making sure the bride's long train didn't get tangled among the chairs, and she helped Denise settle into her seat and arranged everything so the skirt and veil fell attractively about her. Then she went over to Michael, who, despite the roasting temperature in the church, had barely broken a sweat. In fact, he looked downright dapper in his simple, dark gray suit and blue tie.

"Well, that's done and dusted," he said, pulling out a chair for Rose in a gentlemanly manner. "And you survived."

"I survived," Rose said, slipping off her high-heeled shoes under the table where no one could see. "Actually, better than that. I'm doing really well."

"I'll say. Just think. That could've been you." He nodded at a table across the room, where Brad was slumped over in a half-conscious state. Kimberly was hissing in his ear and trying to get him to take their squirming toddler. Neither looked like they were having much fun at this wedding at all.

"Do you think I should go over and thank her for having done me such a big favor?" whispered Rose. She was pretty certain that from this day forward, she wouldn't give Brad or Kimberly a second thought. She was done with all that.

"Go on. I dare you."

"Nah. I'll just leave them to bask in their marital bliss," she said with a completely straight face.

"Speaking of bliss," Michael asked. "What's next on today's agenda?

"Well, thank goodness the photographer took the formal wedding pictures before the ceremony, so there's no need to go back into that oven of a sanctuary. We can chill out here for a while. Literally," she added, with a chuckle. "But at five, we'll head over to the steakhouse on the highway for the banquet."

"At *five*?" Michael pushed his half-eaten slice of cake away from him.

"Well, that *is* supper time for a lot of people around here. But don't worry. They'll have plenty of booze. And after all the old ladies leave, there'll be a DJ from St. Louis to play music. The party'll probably go on all the way to midnight."

"Imagine that," Michael said.

"Hey, Rose," called out Erica. "Come on! Denise wants you."

Rose inwardly groaned. She hadn't even had a chance to take a bite of the cake yet. "What's going on?"

"Denise is leaving soon to go get ready for the banquet, and she's going to toss her bouquet. Don't you want a chance to catch it? To be the next person to get married?" Erica looked over at Michael and raised her eyebrows meaningfully.

"Oh, I don't—"

"Go on," urged Michael. "Give it a try."

"You heard the guy!" Erica said, giving Michael an all-knowing smile. "Let's go."

Rose, with all the other single women, ranging in age from about twelve to fifty, gathered outside at the bottom of the church's steps. From the way Denise was scanning the crowd, Rose could tell her cousin was planning to chuck the bouquet right at her. And she might have caught it if it hadn't been for that Dixie Donahue, elbowing her in the ribs as she leaped into the air, grabbing the ultimate prize of the day.

Chapter Thirty-Seven

The day after the wedding, Michael flew to Boston to see his family. Rose spent the rest of her week in Felix seeing old friends, visiting elderly relatives, and shopping. But if she was going to tell her parents about Akira, it was going to have to be tonight because she was going back to Japan in the morning. And she'd have to do it before the *Tonight Show* came on because no one and nothing was allowed to interfere with Johnny Carson in her parents' household. Apparently tonight's guest was going to be Betty White, and her mother had been looking forward to that all day.

Rose sat down on the brown Naugahyde couch her parents had bought when she was in elementary school. Other than having a new RCA console colored television, the room had hardly changed. Framed photographs covered the walls—not only every school picture Rose had ever had taken of her but also those of her parents and other relatives. The bookshelves were full of condensed Reader's Digest volumes and a table holding the bits and pieces of her mother's crafts in progress was against one wall. Her father, who always had a 1000-piece jigsaw puzzle going, had pushed the card table in front of his recliner chair so he could work on his latest one in comfort.

"Mom. Dad," Rose said when she finally got up the courage. "I want to tell you that I've met someone."

Her mother looked up from the macrame wall hanging she was working on and took off her reading glasses. "I can't say I'm surprised. I knew something was going on between you two. That Michael's a nice boy, and I suppose you could do a lot worse, even if he's not from around here."

"But, Mom—"

"I guess you could wear the wedding dress you already have. I don't think there's anything wrong with that, right? After all, it cost a fortune, and you never walked down the aisle in it. And besides, I don't think you've put *that* much weight. It should still fit, but even if it doesn't, Mabel Schwartz could alter it. Now, Michael's about the same size as Dustin, so he could wear his tux. Don't you think he'd look downright spiffy in it?"

Rose was thrown off by the image of Michael in what she thought of as her cousin's *Saturday Night Fever* tuxedo.

"Owen, do you think we should fly out east to meet his people?"

Her father nodded. "That wouldn't be a bad idea."

Rose blinked at him in surprise because the last time he'd left the state was when he went off to war.

"And then, what about—"

"Mom! Stop! I didn't say I'm getting married. I just said I met someone. And it's *not* Michael!"

"Well, my goodness, dear." Her mother sat back, crossed her arms, and pursed her lips. "There you go again, getting all worked up over nothing."

"I'm not all worked up," Rose said with complete exasperation. "I'm—"

"Well, if it's not Michael, who is it?"

"It's not anyone you know. It's someone I met in Japan. I've been telling you ever since I got here that Michael's just a friend."

"What does your young man think about you traveling with a different young man?" A whole new type of disapproval was in her mother's voice when she added sarcastically, "A *friend*?"

"He doesn't—"

"I didn't bring you up that way at all. This sort of behavior is something I'd expect of a Hardy," she said, shaking her head and naming the town's riffraff. "But not a Millstone."

"He knows Michael and I are just friends from work."

The scathing look on her mother's face showed disbelief that members of the opposite sex could ever merely be friends.

"And that's not even the point," continued Rose. "The person I like is Akira Sato, and he's one of my students."

Her mother's expression immediately shifted from disapproval to horror. "Do you mean to tell me he's *Japanese*?"

"Yes," Rose said, with more bravado than she felt. She recalled what Michael had said about telling his parents he was gay to garner up more courage for herself.

"Oh, dear lord!" her mother cried, wringing her hands. "I knew something like this would happen. Owen, didn't I tell you something like this would happen? We never should've let the girl run wild halfway around the world. I've said time and time again—"

"Now, Doris, let's just listen to what the girl's got to say."

Rose couldn't believe how calmly her father was taking this.

"But an Oriental? It's unnatural! You don't see crows mating with sparrows, do you? Or cats with dogs? The good lord—"

"Now, Doris—"

"Oh, Rose! What will people say now? First you went and lost Brad and now you do *this* to us?"

"Rose isn't doing anything to us. She's a big girl. She can—"

"But Owen, this is about—"

"Now, Doris. Why don't we just—"

"How will I ever hold my head up in town when people get wind of this? It was bad enough when your wedding—"

"Doris!" shouted her father. "I said, shut up and let the girl talk!"

Rose had never, not even once, heard her father speak to her mother that way. Judging by the shocked look on her mother's face, she hadn't either.

"Tell us about your young man," her father said to Rose, bringing calmness back into the room.

Rose took a deep breath. "Well, he's really nice, and—"

"They all are," her mother interrupted. "At first. But Japanese men beat their wives. I read something about that in *Reader's Digest*."

Rose ignored that last piece of nonsense and described Akira as positively as possible. But she did leave out a lot of the important details. Let Michael call her a coward, but one step at a time was all she could manage. She'd tell them about Akira's kids and the mother-in-law stuff later. Maybe in a letter when she was five thousand miles away.

"Rose," her dad said, leaning forward in his chair and speaking with quiet determination. "If you marry this man, you might live in Japan for the rest of your life. Are you ready for that? It's good you have a job you like, but are you prepared to stay in Japan forever and ever? How can you know for sure if this'd be the right thing for you to do?"

Her dad, in his calm way, recognized the Achilles' heel of everything. Could she stay in Japan forever? Did she really want to do that? And for the first time, she understood what such a decision could mean to her parents. She was, after all, their only child. What would happen to them when they got old? Who would take care of them if she made a life for herself on the other side of the world?

"Dad," Rose said softly. "Like I said, I'm not sure what's going to happen. I just wanted to let you know that I'm involved with someone. That's all."

Her mother harrumphed, and muttering something under her breath about marrying in haste and repenting at leisure, she went over to the television and switched it on.

Thank goodness for Johnny Carson.

Chapter Thirty-Eight

Rose returned to Japan with her bags full of things she couldn't get there—shoes her size, bras without unnecessary padding, slacks that weren't too short. Lots of American food and presents for Akira's family. It was amazing what could fit into two duffle bags and still be under the seventy-pound weight limit for each one. She'd have to send everything home from the airport because there was no way she could lug it all back on the train.

"Rose!" she heard as she wheeled her luggage cart out of the customs exit.

"Akira!" She threw her arms around him, expecting an I-haven't-seen-you-in-nearly-two-weeks kiss, but he stiffened a little and patted her back. "Maybe we should let the other people get out the door first."

Rose turned and saw the line right behind her. They moved to the side to let the others pass, and she said, a little tearfully, "I didn't know you were coming to meet me."

"I figured you'd be tired and would have a lot of stuff to carry."

"You're my hero."

Maybe there was no passionate greeting at the airport, but here he was, taking control of the luggage and leading her to his car. He loaded the trunk and once inside the car, he reached for her and kissed her. "I've missed you so much."

"I've missed you, too."

"Are you in a hurry to get back to your apartment? Because if you aren't, we could go to one of those places they have near the airport for... um, you know, resting?"

Rose felt giddy at the prospect of some *resting*. "I wouldn't mind a nice comfortable rest."

Akira kissed her again, deeply this time. "But we can't stay all night, though. Is that okay?"

Fifteen minutes later, Akira pulled into a parking lot in front of a love hotel shaped like a spaceship. Leaving Rose's bags in the car, they checked in, showered together, and fell onto the bed. It was as if they'd been separated for years, and not just for ten days.

Later, in the car heading into Tokyo, Rose said, "I told my parents about you."

"What'd they say?"

She skipped over the drama. "They were mainly concerned about me staying in Japan forever." Then she added, "But I also told them things weren't that serious yet."

"I see." Akira gripped the steering wheel and looked straight ahead.

When she heard the hurt tone in his voice, she said softly, "We've only been together a few months. I don't want them to think I'm rushing into anything."

"Did you tell them about my family?"

"I should've, but I didn't. I have to let them get used to things little by little. They'd find a man with children hard to accept, regardless of where he came from."

"I know."

"Listen. I *do* love you, Akira. It's just that I'm just not a hundred percent sure that—"

"What we have is permanent?"

"That's not it. Can't we just see where it takes us for a little while longer?"

A few days later, Rose and Akira were under the sheets in the cool, air-conditioned room of what had become their favorite love hotel in

Shinjuku. It was easier than tiptoeing through Rose's backyard, trying to avoid her landlady. And, of course, staying over at Akira's place was out of the question. Rose couldn't imagine anything worse than coming face to face with the grandmother in the kitchen or in the bathroom.

This was supposed to be a lunch date, but lunch could wait. In between their lovemaking, they talked. And every conversation they had brought them closer. Rose couldn't deny the fact that she could no longer see a future for herself without Akira in it. Her head was beginning to accept what her heart had been telling her all along.

But not one hundred percent. Not yet.

"You know," she said, stroking his smooth, hairless chest. "I could never be like a typical Japanese housewife. And even if I wasn't starting this new full-time job in September, I'm pretty sure I wouldn't want to."

"I know you're worried I can't do anything in the house. But I can. And what I don't know, I could learn."

"I'm sure you *could* learn, but would you? Japanese men don't have the best reputation when it comes to this sort of thing, you know. You should hear the way my students talk about their husbands, their fathers, their brothers. Sometimes it seems like a competition to see who's got the laziest and worst man around."

Akira chortled. "Let me tell you a secret. When Sumiko was alive, I washed the dishes sometimes. And hung out the laundry. I'm not totally incompetent when it comes to such things."

Talking about Sumiko when they were naked in bed together no longer seemed completely strange to Rose. She knew that just because Akira had loved Sumiko once, and still did in a way, didn't mean he loved her any less.

"I wouldn't want you to be a Japanese wife. All I want is for you to be *you*. The beautiful rose I fell in love with."

His voice faded, and Rose sensed some hesitation in his words. "But what?"

"If things go the way that I truly hope they do," he said thoughtfully, "I want you to be Yuka and Emi's mother. Not just my wife. They *need* a mother. Someone for them to love, like a mother. And someone who'd love them back like a mother."

Rose blinked back emotional tears at the thought of becoming a family. "If it goes that far, I'd want that, too."

"I see how you are with them and how they are with you. I hope someday you'll be the one they'd consider their mother. They don't remember Sumiko now at all," he said sadly. "But at the same time, I don't want them not knowing who she is. Because she is a part of them. Can you understand what I'm saying?"

Rose nodded.

"And if we have children together, I want you to love all the children equally. I don't want a biological child of your own to replace my daughters in your heart."

Rose sat up in bed, and said stiffly, with a touch of anger in her voice, "Look, Akira. Let's get one thing straight. If I do agree to this, I never, ever want to hear you say those words."

Akira sat up as well and stared at Rose. "Wh-what words?"

"*Your* daughters. *Your* daughters. You always say that. But if I say yes to you, you are to *never* say that again."

"B-but, what do you want me to say?"

"*Our* daughters, you idiot. I want you to say our daughters. If you want me to be their mother and if you want me to love them like my own children, then you can't say *my daughters* whenever the mood strikes." Rose's anger faded when she saw Akira understand what she was getting at.

"Oh, Rose," he whispered. "I love you so much."

Chapter Thirty-Nine

Akira needed to take a quick business trip to Osaka, but before his flight, they had lunch at Moti's in Roppongi, one of the few Indian restaurants in Tokyo. Having never eaten Indian food even once in her life before coming to Japan, she had become quite a fan and wanted Akira to give it a try. He certainly liked the naan, the bread that was practically the size of the table. And the salad. And the grilled tandoori chicken. But the mutton curry and the vegetable curry were too spicy, and he needed to drink a half dozen glasses of water to put out the fire.

"I could get used to this," he said, wiping tears out of his eyes. "If you really wanted me to."

Rose laughed. "You shouldn't have asked for the spiciest level. Mine's level three, and it's spicy enough. But no," she said, mocking him, "you had to be all macho about it and get level five. And then you finished everything!"

"Something I may regret until the day I die," he said, rubbing his stomach but still smiling. "I may never recover from this."

The waiter brought over yogurt desserts and glasses of iced chai.

"I wish you didn't have to go to Osaka this afternoon," Rose said, not for the first time that day. "I thought you were having the whole *Obon* holiday week off."

"I know, but it's just for one night. The company forgot to send some documents, and the only way we'll have them when we open after the holiday is if someone goes and gets them now. And that someone turned out to be me because I'm the only one who didn't leave town this week. But," he said, reaching across the table and taking her hand, "I'll be back tomorrow."

"Well, I hope you get something in return for giving up one of your days off." Rose tried to sound supportive and not whiney.

"Hey, I have an idea," he said with sudden enthusiasm. "Why don't you come with me? All I have to do is go pick up the papers. We could eat Osaka-style *okonomiyaki*—and you can stay in my hotel room. You don't even have to go home right now to get anything. You can pick up whatever you need for the night in Osaka."

Rose's eyes shot up. "I love that idea!"

Akira went to call the travel agency from the pink pay phone by the cash register, but when he returned to the table, she could see she was in for a big disappointment.

"There's not a ticket to be had. I should've realized that before I got your hopes all up. All three travel agencies I called said the only way to get on that flight would be if there was a last-minute cancelation, but with the holiday prices, it'd cost a fortune. They said it was a miracle I got a seat on my flight. The company reserved it for me, so I have no idea what that cost."

"Well," Rose sighed, "it's just for one night, like you said. I guess I'll see if Michael wants to come over tonight and watch videos."

Michael met her at the video shop at Yotsuya San-chome so they could pick through whatever was left before the shop closed for the holidays. They settled on *Ghostbusters* and *Terminator,* even though they both had already seen them. Then they stopped at Marusho supermarket to stock up on beer and snacks to enjoy with the movies.

"You're a goddess," Michael said when he stepped into her apartment and met a cool blast of air.

"I am, aren't I? I'm sure I'll regret leaving the AC on when they send me the electric bill, though."

"It's official," he announced. "I'm moving in with you. This is much more civilized than my place." Then he popped opened two cans of Kirin beer and handed one to Rose. Half a can disappeared in a couple of gulps.

"So my big news," he said, with a happy face showing there was no need for concern, "is that we got the HIV tests back."

"And?"

"All clear. I'm meeting Kentaro's parents next week."

Rose was surprised. "It's that serious?"

"No point in wasting time."

"They know about him being—"

"They've always known. And they've always been okay with it. Probably because he's got an older brother and an older sister. The family line is intact no matter what he does," he said with a grin. "So, Rose, my dear, any advice for meeting the parents?"

"Well, one thing I know for sure—don't show up with flowers designated for the ancestral shrine. That's a big no-no." Michael snorted, and she added, "Otherwise, just be your usual charming self." Rose could tell he was actually nervous about meeting Kentaro's family, so she patted him on the shoulder. "You'll be fine. If he loves you, they will, too."

"I hope so. I mean, this takes our relationship to a whole different level. Kind of like when you met Akira's family." Michael finished his beer and popped open another can. "What?" he said when Rose gave him a look. "I'm dehydrated."

"Maybe a glass of water?" she suggested. "I don't want to have to go make a beer run in the middle of the movies just because you're thirsty now."

"Nag, nag, nag." He set the beer can down and opened a bag of seaweed-flavored potato chips. "If necessary, I'll go get us more beer from that new vending machine they've got over by the dry cleaners.

"You're lucky you know what you want," Rose said, returning to their earlier topic. She reached into the chip bag for a handful. "Sorry to make this all about me again, but I wish I was as confident about my where relationship with Akira is going as you are with your relationship with Kentaro."

"I can't understand what's holding you back," said Michael. "I don't know why you're so afraid. Either you love him or you don't."

Rose sighed. "My heart says yes, but my brain says whoa! Slow down." She glanced at the empty beer can in her hand and realized she'd completely finished hers as well. Now Michael raised *his* eyebrows, and she gave a guilty little laugh. "I guess I'll know when I know."

"Like when you're ninety?"

Rose moaned. "I hope I can make a decision before then."

"I wouldn't worry too much if I were you," he said with a practical voice. "It's better not to rush into anything if you have any doubts. And you don't have any pressure. Your biological clock, no matter what you may think, isn't forcing you to decide right this second. With your fancy new job, you won't ever have to get married just to get a visa to stay in Japan."

"Who'd do such a thing?"

"Lots of people do," said Michael. "Well, heterosexuals, that is. Not people like me who can't get married. The thing is, if you have a spouse visa, you can do just about anything. And then after that, it's a lot easier to get permanent residency."

"Well, I think it'd be crazy to marry someone just to get a visa. Especially if you didn't love the person."

"Totally agree. I just heard about some guy who paid a Japanese bar hostess a million yen to marry him so he could get a visa."

"That's preposterous."

"But I also heard that when the authorities found out, they deported him."

"People do all sorts of crazy things," Rose said, shaking her head, "but it's best not to break the law."

"Good citizen, Rose." Michael patted her on the head like she was a good dog.

She swatted his hand away. "Why don't you get things started and I'll fix some cheese and crackers."

"Hey," Michael said as soon as he turned on the television. "It looks like there's been a plane crash."

"Do they say where?"

"It's some flight out of Haneda."

Rose swiveled around. "Haneda! Akira flew out of Haneda this afternoon." She wrung her hands as she tried to catch what the newscaster was saying, and when the flight number was announced, she felt like she had been punched right in the gut. "That's Akira's flight! He told me at lunch, and I thought it was funny. Flight One Two Three."

"Listen," said Michael, trying to put his arms around Rose to calm her down. "They said they didn't have all the details. Before we begin to panic, let's just wait and see what—"

She shoved him away from her with such force he almost fell over backwards. "I've got to get over to Akira's house right now!"

Michael switched off the TV and the air conditioning and ran out the door after Rose.

Chapter Forty

Akira's mother was the one to let her in. Her face was tense, and she clutched a handkerchief in her hand.

"I-I saw the news." Rose kicked off her sandals and stepped up into the house, not bothering with the niceties of arranging them properly. There was no need to clarify which news she was referring to.

"I know Akira was going to Osaka today," his mother said with a shaky voice that somehow still managed to sound calm, "but there's more than one flight to Osaka, you know." She looked over at Obaachan. Hope was in both of their eyes.

Rose grabbed Akira's mother's hand. "But he *was* on that flight. We talked about it at lunch today. We both thought being on flight one, two, three, was pretty funny. We even joked about it. We joked about it! Oh my god! Oh my god!" she moaned. An even more strangled noise came out of her mouth when she realized that she would have been on that same flight if she had been able to get a seat.

Michael, who came into the house right behind Rose, pushed her down onto the sofa and forced her head down between her legs. "Breathe," he said, crouching in front of her. "Breathe."

He looked up at the two older women and bowed a silent greeting. The blood drained from their faces when they took in what Rose had just told them, and they collapsed into each other's arms. Emi and Yuka, who didn't quite understand what was happening, began to wail. Rose rubbed away tears with the back of her hands, but they continued pouring out of her eyes as if they contained an infinite supply.

Michael moved onto the sofa and encircled his arms tightly around Rose. Yuka and Emi inserted themselves into that embrace, and Rose pulled them to her. The poor things were terrified. And rightfully so.

Michael then took charge. Even though he'd never been in Akira's house before, he searched the cabinets until he found what he was looking for. Well, almost. It was a bottle of Kahlúa. "This'll do," he said aloud before pouring a good two inches into three small glasses. "Here," he said, handing one to each of the women. "Drink this."

They followed his instructions as if he was a doctor prescribing cold medicine. He couldn't very well give alcohol to the children, so he went into the kitchen, opened the fridge, and poured glasses of milk. "Drink this," he said to Yuka and Emi. And they did.

An eerie silence, peppered by a few choked sobs, fell over the room while everyone's eyes stayed glued to the television. Akira's mother kept getting up to change the channel, but all the networks reported the same thing over and over and over.

Some kind of explosion had occurred right after the plane took off from Haneda Airport.

The flight, with five hundred and twenty passengers and crew, crashed into the mountains in Gumma thirty minutes later.

There was no news on survivors.

Rescue operations were suspended because it was getting dark.

"How can they suspend the rescue operations?" Rose cried as she paced back and forth. Adrenaline and fear surged through her body. "Just give up like that? People could be injured. They need to get up there. Right now! What's wrong with them?"

"Rose," warned Michael. "You're scaring the children."

She clamped her mouth shut. He was right. But that was when she knew for sure Akira was dead. That was the only plausible explanation for why they weren't searching for survivors. There simply weren't any.

She shivered in shock, and twisting and untwisting her hands, she stared blankly at the television through her tears. Akira had been with her just a few hours earlier, and now he's gone. Gone!

Why, oh why, she moaned to herself, had she been so reluctant to commit to their relationship? Now she'll *never* be able to tell him how much she loved him. How much he meant to her. How she wished she could tell him that being with *him* was what she wanted more than anything else in the world.

Michael picked up a deck of cards on the bookshelf and shuffling them as smoothly as if he had a part-time job in a casino, he called to the girls, "Do you know how to play Go Fish?" He lured them away from the television and to the dining table. He sat facing the TV, so they'd have their backs to it.

Through her tears, Rose gave Michael a nod of thanks. Those poor girls. First, they lose their mother, and now they lose their father. Rose felt a stabbing pain for the loss of a family that would never have the chance to be. Her chest felt like a hammer was chiseling away at her heart—working at it until it would shatter into a million pieces. And once that happened, she knew she'd lose any semblance of control.

For now, she inhaled and exhaled.

Brushed away tears.

And repeated over and over to herself: He's dead. He's dead.

No one heard the key turning in the lock on the front door or that someone had come into the house. No one realized when the wooden door to the living room had slid open. So when Akira stepped into the middle of the room and softly called out, *"Tadaima,"* everyone, including Michael, let out a scream of shock.

Rose's breath lodged somewhere halfway between her chest and her mouth. She couldn't remember how to operate her lungs, let alone expel the air.

Was she seeing a ghost?

But a ghost wouldn't be grabbing his children and swinging them in the air.

A ghost wouldn't be hugging the girls' two grandmothers.

A ghost wouldn't come over to her, wrap his arms tightly around her, and say how much he loved her.

"Is it you?" Rose said, pulling back and looking into his face. "Really, really *you*?"

"I missed the flight."

After the shock of seeing Akira lifted, it was utter pandemonium. Everyone spoke at once. Buckets of tears were shed, but now they were tears of relief, tears of joy.

"The curry we had for lunch must've upset my stomach," Akira explained in a mixture of English and Japanese, so everyone could understand. The children were nestled in his lap. Everyone else had pulled up chairs to be close enough to be able to keep touching him, to make sure he really was right in front of them.

"I don't know what was in it," he said, "but I had to get off the train twice to go to the bathroom before getting to Haneda. I was only five minutes late, but they'd already closed the gates and wouldn't let me though."

"It was a miracle," blubbered Rose. "A miracle."

"A miracle," he repeated, his face also soaked in tears. "I can't think of what else to call it. But the only thing that was on my mind was how angry my section chief was going to be if I didn't get those documents. I tried booking a later flight, thinking I'd even pay the difference out of my own pocket. But seats on every single flight to Osaka were sold out. So I decided to go by train. I knew there wouldn't be any seats on the Shinkansen either because of the holiday, but I figured I could just stand for a few hours. I went to Tokyo Station and had about twenty minutes to kill before departure. I went into the waiting room, and that," he said with a shaking voice, "was when I saw the news on the television. I wanted to call, but the lines for the phones went on forever. I figured coming straight home would be quicker."

With enough death and destruction for one night, they turned off the television. Akira was alive, and that was all that mattered. Michael brought out the Kahlúa again, and the adults polished it off while the girls drank the little bottles of Coca-Cola he'd also found in the cabinet. The girls eventually fell asleep on the floor, and Akira and Michael carried them up to their room. Close to midnight, Akira's mother and Michael left. The other grandmother went to bed, and Akira and Rose were finally alone.

She clutched his hand as if it had been super-glued to hers for life, feeling so emotional she could barely speak. "I thought you were dead," she managed to choke out.

"But I'm not." Akira stroked her face and looked into her eyes. "I'm here."

"You're here," Rose said, stroking his face in return. "When I thought I'd never see you again, I knew without a doubt I loved you. That I wanted to be with you. Now I know that more than *anything*."

"Does this mean—"

"Yes," she said with trembling lips. "I'm in. I'm *all* in."

Chapter Forty-One

For the next week, every TV station focused on the crash of Flight 123 that killed nearly all the 520 people on board—its causes and how the delay in rescue operations resulted in even more fatalities. Blame was tossed in every corner. And when it was announced that the singer Kyu Sakamoto was one of the people killed in the crash, his worldwide 1963 hit "*Ue o Muite Arukou*" (known as the "Sukiyaki" song in English) was played repeatedly, even on the American military radio channel.

Rose felt guilty for feeling so relieved Akira's life had been spared. She felt guilty for being so happy when so many other people were suffering.

Akira came over every night after his daughters went to sleep. They made love in Rose's futon, and afterward, they talked about their hopes, their dreams, their futures. They'd become a new family—the four of them. And, eventually, there could be five, maybe six. Two little brothers, they both agreed, would round things out nicely. They discussed rebuilding Akira's house, making it bigger and putting in a little granny flat on the first floor for Obaachan. Rose said Sumiko's mother would always be a welcome part of their new lives, but this was a compromise that made her happy.

On Saturday morning, Akira's mother called. "Please come to dinner tonight at six o'clock. There are many things to discuss."

This invitation, which felt something like a command, took Rose by surprise. The only thing she could do was to accept.

Moments later, Akira telephoned.

"What's up?" Rose asked cautiously.

"I gather I'm not the first person to call you so early."

"It looks like I'm having dinner at your mother's place tonight. Please say you're coming, too. And please tell me your snarky brother-in-law isn't."

"I'll definitely be there, but I doubt Osamu will, since my mother can't stand him."

"Do you know what it's about?"

"I think she just wants to get to know you better."

"Did you say anything about us?"

"Of course not." They'd both agreed they wanted to get used to the idea of a future for themselves without pressure from others to decide anything specific.

That evening, Rose rang the doorbell at Akira's mother's house at six. This time she came with a box of expensive little pastries straight from one of Isetan Department Store's exclusive cake shops and skipped the flowers entirely, just in case she made another floral social blunder.

She hadn't seen either of the two older women since the night of the airplane crash, and she hadn't realized how raw her feelings still were. When she stepped into the living room, the memory of those horrible hours of believing Akira was dead returned. She blinked back tears, but when she saw the two grandmothers doing the same, there was no holding back. Akira's mother patted Rose's arm as she swallowed her own sobs. But Rose wanted to hug her, and so she did. After what they'd all been through, Rose wasn't about to worry about something so minor as hugging protocol. And then she hugged Obaachan, who surprisingly hung onto Rose with equal force. The girls also wanted their fair share of Rose, so she grabbed them and swung them around a little. A sort of hug, a sort of horseplay. And everyone laughed.

"I've already given the girls their dinner so they can watch cartoons in the other room," said Akira's mother, shooing them in that direction. "There's much to discuss, and it's best not to do that in front of them. Some things are not for their ears. At least, not yet."

Rose looked questioningly at Akira. He shook his head. He didn't seem to know what was going on, either.

"We want to talk to you," Akira's mother said in English. "To you both."

Rose watched Akira's eyes go over to the other grandmother, whose head was nodding up and down. Whatever was happening, these two were clearly in cahoots.

"All right," Akira said, his voice wary. "What is it?"

"Don't just stand there. Sit down."

Rose and Akira positioned themselves on one side of the table, and the two women sat on the other.

Akira's mother's face was unreadable when she came right out and said, "We think you two should get married." Then she repeated herself in Japanese. "Fumiyo and I have discussed this at length, and we think this is for the best."

"*You* discussed this?" Akira sputtered. "I'm sorry, but this really isn't any of your—"

His mother cut him off. "Oh, calm down. Isn't this what you want?"

"Well, yes. But—"

"But what?"

Words shot back and forth in Japanese like they were the ball in a Wimbledon tennis final, but Rose understood the gist of what they were saying.

They thought it was time for Akira to get married again.

They thought Akira and Rose liked each other well enough, and Rose, they had determined, was a good person. Look at how she was with the girls and how much the girls liked her. Look at how handled herself last week when they all thought Akira had perished in the airplane crash.

So, the two of them announced, it was time for Akira and Rose to get married.

"I'm moving out." Obaachan said, addressing Rose in simplified Japanese. "So you won't have me under your feet."

Akira turned to Obaachan with surprise. "But I thought you didn't want to go back to Kyushu."

"Who said anything about her going back to Kyushu?" interjected his mother. "She's staying right here in Tokyo. With me. This place is plenty big enough for the two of us."

"And just to let you know," added Obaachan, "I'm giving Osamu and Yoko their inheritance now. I've talked to my lawyer, and we calculated what everything is worth. I'm signing my house over to them, and a portion of the cash, which is earmarked for my grandsons' education." She frowned when she added, "Who knows what they'll actually do with it, though? But the thing is, I'll live on the rest of my money. And if anything is left over, it'll belong to Emi and Yuka someday."

"Are you sure you want to just give them your house?" asked Akira.

"I never liked it to begin with. Too many unpleasant memories associated with that piece of land. Even after rebuilding, it feels like my husband's mother is still around, waiting to torment me again." With an assertive nod of her head, she said, "What I want to do is to stay here in Tokyo."

"And what I want is for Fumiyo to stay with me," said Akira's mother. Her entire face softened when she said, "Don't you see Akira? This is the best solution for everyone." Then she turned to Rose. "So, what will it be? Yes?"

"Mom! Stop!" To Rose, he said, "I'm sorry for this ambush. We can leave right now if you like."

Rose stood. But instead of heading toward the door, she turned and faced Akira square on. "Yes," she said.

"What?" he asked.

"My answer to them is yes."

"You don't have to say anything now—"

Rose mustered up her best Japanese. "Last week, I thought you were dead. *We,*" she added, turning toward the two women, "thought you were dead. It's a miracle you missed that plane. It's a miracle you're here tonight. Life is short. You already know my answer is yes, but now it's time to let everyone else know that, too. I want to marry you. And soon."

"Are you sure?" he whispered.

"More than anything." She had never been so certain of anything in her life, and her voice echoed that.

"Akira wrapped his arms around Rose and kissed her as if they were the only two people on the planet.

Obaachan frowned and muttered, "I suppose we'll just have to get used to this sort of thing from now on, since she's a foreigner and all."

Rose and Akira pulled apart in embarrassment. Rose's cheeks felt like they were on fire. Only engaged for thirty seconds, and she had already crossed some sort of cultural boundary.

It was impossible to read the look on Akira's mother's face when she stood and said, "I'll be right back." She returned holding a small box. "Your father gave this to me many years ago," she said to Akira. "I've never really liked jewelry, so I've hardly ever worn it. Please give it to Rose."

He opened it and immediately snapped it shut.

"What's wrong now? Isn't this what—"

Holding up a finger to silence her, Akira called into the other room. "Emi! Yuka! Come here!"

The girls seemed to sense something exciting was happening, and they trotted into the room. Akira winked at them before getting down on one knee. They had read enough fairy tales to know what was coming and began to squeal excitedly.

"Rose," he said dramatically. "Will you marry me?"

Rose smiled over at the girls, before turning back and looking straight into Akira's eyes. "Yes," she said in a strong and determined voice. "I will marry you."

When Akira slipped the ring on her finger, she nearly fainted. The diamond had to have been at least three carats.

"Are you going to be our new mama?" asked Emi.

Rose tore her eyes away from the ring. "I'll be your mom," she said in Japanese. She looked over at Sumiko's mother before adding, "But I'll never be your mama. You only have one mama and she'll always be with you. I'll be your mom."

"Mom," said Yuka.

"Mom," said Emi.

"Darling," said Akira, as he pulled Rose into his arms and kissed her again.

Chapter Forty-Two

Tokyo, May 2015

Rose was sitting in her living room, looking at a magazine that mentioned the singer Kyu Sakamoto, and her mind couldn't help but return to the airplane crash that killed him and so many others. In just a few months, it would be the thirtieth anniversary, but no matter how many years had passed, she remembered that day like it was yesterday. She could never forget how she felt when she believed Akira had been killed in the crash and how she felt when she discovered he wasn't. Life, she had come to understand, could be taken away in an instant. Life, she now knew, was precious. And never to be taken for granted.

She frowned at a couple of age spots that had recently appeared on her hands and mused that sometimes the past thirty years felt like thirty days. The floor creaked overhead, indicating her husband, the birthday boy, was finally awake. She took the pancake batter out of the fridge, set it on the counter, and finished setting the table. When she heard the upstairs shower turn on, she knew he'd be down in fifteen minutes. He was nothing if not regular with his morning routine.

She got out her laptop and logged into Facebook. She had resisted joining for the longest time but got such pleasure from it now she wondered why she had put up such a fight in the first place. Sure, it sucked up time, but it was a great way to keep in touch with people.

Some people. When she received a friend request from her ex-fiancé a few years back, she ignored it. She didn't hate him. In fact, she hardly ever even thought about him. But she didn't need him in her life, either. So when she bumped into Brad and Kimberly Billford at the Lincoln Walmart last summer, she almost didn't recognize either of them. Brad was recovering from knee surgery and rode a motorized shopping cart filled with processed food and so many snacks it looked like he was stocking an underground bunker for the end of days. Kimberly, with stringy gray hair and a triple chin, didn't look a thing like the woman who had stolen her fiancé in the early '80s. After exchanging a few pleasantries and going on her way, Rose felt giddy with satisfaction. She may not have the figure she'd had in her twenties, but she felt positively svelte next to those two. Sure, it was petty, but it was sweet knowing that she and her husband had held up a hell of a lot better than those two.

The computer dinged with an incoming message from Emi: *Sorry, Mom. I promise I'll be home tonight.*

That's what you said yesterday, Rose messaged back. *And the day before.*

I know. But it couldn't be avoided.

Rose replied: *I worry about you.* She wanted to tell the girl to stop treating home as a place to shower and get clean clothes, but she didn't.

I'll be fine. I promise I'll be home tonight for Dad's birthday. Seven o'clock for sure. Gotta go. And Emi signed off.

Rose was worried that if Emi wasn't careful, she'd end up being too busy to go to her own wedding. Rose and Akira's wedding album on the bottom shelf of the bookcase caught her eye, and with weddings on the brain, she took it out and opened it. She shook her head, smiling at the happiness on their youthful faces. But no wonder neither of her girls wanted to wear that awful dress when it was their turn to walk down the aisle. So eighties! And her hair! She must've used an entire can of hairspray to make it that puffy.

That wedding took place just four months after the plane crash. Life was too short and Rose insisted she didn't want to wait. Michael had been so right when he advised her to step back and let her mother handle everything. Even though she had put up quite a squawk about Rose marrying a Japanese man, she was determined to make her daughter's winter wedding outshine her niece's summer one. At least, she and Michael had joked, there'd be no worries about the air conditioning in the church conking out at the end of December.

Basically, all Rose had to do was show up in Felix with her Japanese entourage, who filled up every room in the town's motel. There were the two Japanese grandmas and Akira's two daughters. Her friend Kazumi didn't want to miss the chance for her first trip abroad, so of course she was there, too. And Daisuke, Kana, and Naoko from her Friday night class at Friendly. Keiko and Tomo couldn't swing the trip, but they sent a gigantic flower arrangement instead. Hayashi-sensei and his wife, the leader of the International Thinking Culture Housewives Circle, flew in and out so quickly their flight time was far longer than the time they had spent on the ground. And Michael, bless his heart, was willing to go to Felix *again*, but this time, he brought Kentaro. Everyone assumed they were just friends, so all the girls in town flirted with them outrageously. And good sports that they were, they flirted outrageously back.

That ring of Akira's mother worked wonders because the moment she got off the airplane waving a three-carat diamond around, her mom did a complete about-face. That, and the fact that Akira's mother was wearing a full-length mink coat, made her convinced that her daughter was marrying into a moneyed family. All her objections vanished because as far as she was concerned, wealth trumped marrying someone from a different country, a different race, and a complicated family structure. Rose glanced down at the more sensible ring she'd been wearing for quite a while now and smiled. The original one was at the jeweler's, being reset and resized.

Back on Facebook, she saw Michael had just posted pictures of his weekend trip to Hakone with his seminar students. His hair may be gray, but he looked pretty much the same as he did when they first met. Back then, neither imagined they'd both still be in Japan well into the twenty-first century. Michael had even become a Japanese citizen, although he hadn't been able to talk her into going down that path as easily as he had convinced her to join him in the doctoral program at Temple University.

It had taken her nearly ten years to complete her Ph.D. With work and family and all—she just couldn't finish any quicker. Those were the hardest years for her, and every day was a struggle. At times, she wanted to murder Michael for dragging her through all that torture. After all, she already had tenure and didn't need to put herself through that. But later, when it was over and done with, she was glad she did. That wasn't the first time she learned life was full of opportunities that came by being in the right place at the right time.

Her computer dinged again, and Rose clicked "Liked" in the pictures Kazumi had just posted of her newborn granddaughter. Since the wedding album was still out, she opened it again and studied Kazumi's and Daisuke's faces. She saw no hint in their pictures of it being love at first sight for those two, but it must've been. Because the minute they returned to Japan, Kazumi broke up with Chris.

"What about your lifelong dream of marrying an American?" Rose had asked, dumbfounded, when Kazumi told her she'd fallen in love with Daisuke.

"He's an English teacher. That's almost the same thing."

Rose didn't quite agree with that logic, but she did think Kazumi and Daisuke were suited for each other. Three daughters and four grandchildren later, their marriage was certainly a success. It was an enormous coincidence that Kazumi's old boyfriend Chris reappeared in Rose's life a full decade later when he started working at Yamanote University in a tenured position for the International Relations Department. His hair had thinned a bit on top and his belly was a bit more pronounced, but he was still the same nice guy he always was. They occasionally talked about the old days, but they were mostly too busy with the here and now of faculty meetings, committee work, and research projects. And, of course, with their own families.

Rose had lost touch with a lot of the people she used to know back in the eighties, but Facebook had been a great way to reconnect. How else would she have ever found out that everyone's nemesis back at Friendly was spotted checking receipts at a Costco exit in Chiba? A former Friendly English Conversation College teacher had taken a picture of Little Kenny on the sly and posted it on his wall, getting at least a hundred comments from people who used to work there.

And as for that awful Steve? He hit the news big time a few years back when he got caught mailing weed to himself in a peanut butter jar. After a lengthy stint in a Japanese jail, he was deported. Thank goodness he'd quit Yamanote University years earlier because the media also discovered he only had a high school diploma and had been working in higher education with a falsified degree. He eventually confessed that when he came to Japan back in the seventies, he photocopied someone else's diploma, whited out their name, and typed in his. Three of the seven universities he'd been teaching for ended up holding press conferences to disassociate themselves from him. The jerk was probably now working at some gas station in the middle of nowhere and still bragging about himself.

Suddenly Rose remembered she was supposed to make reservations for the works at Kana's Omotesando salon. It was going to be a fun mother-daughters spa day. Of course, it would take quite a bit of persuasion to get Emi to set aside the time for that, but Rose would force her to go, even if she had to blindfold her and tie her up to get her there. She typed an email to Keiko, who, as the retired managing director of Beauty Japan Inc, no longer handled reservations. But for old times' sake, she always took care of Rose.

Rose never could figure out how Kana had managed to pry Tomo away from his mother and marry him. Or to be perfectly honest, why she had ever wanted to in the first place. In fact, no one could understand what that stunning CEO of a nationwide chain of esthetic salons, who was now fairly fluent at English, was doing with a bald, pudgy career bureaucrat. But as Michael liked to say, there's just no accounting for true love, and for those two, that was the damn truth. Their wedding followed Rose and Akira's by about a year and was attended by everyone, except, of course, Tomo's mother.

Rose had just sent off her email to Keiko when a Skype call from Yuka came in.

"Howdy, Yuka," she said when their computers connected. "How're things in the Lone Star State?"

"Oh, Mom, you say that every time I call."

"Of course I do. I'm a broken record. How are things? How're the kids?"

"They're fine. Zach's giving them a bath right now, so I thought I'd call while it's quiet enough to think. I can't wait to get back to Japan. I have a whole list of things I want you to cook! I'm really hankering for some dingledorf."

"So the main reason you're coming back is just to eat my food?" Rose asked, laughing. Her girls never forgot the time she babysat and didn't know what the food in the fridge was.

"Of course, that's not the main reason! I miss you and I miss Japan so much. I bet Dad's all excited about the wedding."

"Well, you know him. He pretends not to be excited, but of course he is. Between you and me, I think he's a little disappointed there won't be a father-daughter dance like there was at your wedding. This is going to be typically Japanese—the kimono, the wig, and all that stuff."

Yuka turned serious. "Emi told me Uncle Osamu's coming. Are you *really* okay with that?"

"I can't say that I am," Rose sighed, "but I'm not really against it either. Having him come is more for Obaachan's sake than anything else. She's forgotten everything that happened, so I'll pretend I've forgotten as well. It'll make her happy, and that's important. If she even recognizes him."

"You're a far better person than I am, Mom. Because I'll never forgive him for what he did. Ever."

"You were only ten when all that happened."

"I know. But I'll never forget. Don't expect me to be nice to him and that nasty wife of his."

Rose didn't want to waste time discussing those two people. Aiden and Sophia had finished their baths, and she wanted to say goodnight to her grandchildren before they went to bed.

"If we don't Skype before then," said Yuka as they signed off, "I'll see you next week."

After the video call ended, Rose looked around the room. She was going to have to get busy and childproof the house before the kids descended upon them. Then she remembered she needed to call Obaachan's caregiver at the nursing home to make sure Obaachan had her hair done the morning of the wedding. She might be in a wheelchair and she might be in diapers. She might have forgotten what she'd eaten, or even if she *had* eaten. But she'd know for sure if her hair hadn't been colored and permed for an important event.

The sound of footsteps on the staircase prompted Rose to pour two mugs of coffee and turn on the gas to heat up the pan for the pancakes. It was time to get her husband's birthday celebrations started.

Julian stepped into the kitchen, looking every bit as handsome now at sixty-five as he did when Rose met him twenty-three years ago in the university library.

"Happy birthday!" she said, throwing her arms around his neck. "It's pancake day!"

"What a surprise!" Julian said, even though she always made pancakes on his birthday.

"You can get the rest of your birthday present tonight," she whispered into his hair, even though they were the only people in the house. "After everyone else goes home."

"I look forward to unwrapping it," he said reaching down and squeezing her butt affectionately. This was the same conversation they had on every occasion that involved gift giving.

"So, are you going to the university today?" he asked.

"No. I don't have any meetings and I don't have any classes. I'm glad because there's so much to do here."

"Did Emi stay out all night again?"

"She's only been home three times this week." Rose sighed as she flipped the pancakes over. "Well, she was here on Tuesday for dinner, but she went out right afterwards. She just comes home to take a shower or get a change of clothing. But what can you do? She won't listen to a thing I say."

"But Rose, that's the way things are in a science lab."

"I could see her working like a dog when she was still writing her dissertation, but now the PhD is behind her." Rose slid a stack of pancakes onto Julian's plate. "To be honest, I worry a lot more about her now than when she flirted with delinquency as a teenager."

"Yeah, those were pretty hard times, all right. But we survived, didn't we?" Julian slathered his pancakes with butter and Canadian maple syrup, knowing today of all days, Rose wouldn't make a face and remind him of his blood pressure. Then he reached for the coffee pot and topped up their cups. "Admit it. You're super proud of our daughter, the physicist."

"Of course I'm proud! I'm so proud I can hardly stand it. But I swear, if she misses her own wedding next week because she's tied up in the lab with Haruto doing some stupid experiment, I'll kill them!"

"Don't worry. I'll do the killing for both of us if it comes down to that. But Haruto promised me they'd wind everything down this week. Next week they'll concentrate on the wedding. And of course, he said nothing would interfere with their honeymoon in Bali."

After Julian's sixth pancake, he groaned a little and patted his stomach. Then he stood, gathered his lecture notes from the counter next to the kitchen table, and slipped them into his backpack, along with his MacBook Air and iPad. "Unlike you, Ms. Professor of Leisure, I don't have a free day. Two classes, a curriculum committee meeting, and a Skype meeting with that Oxford University Press editor."

"Don't be late though," Rose said, following Julian to the *genkan*. "Because Michael and Kentaro are coming around 6:00."

"With Taiga?"

"No," replied Rose. "He's got cram school tonight. You know what it's like aiming for a medical university. No time for anything but study."

Michael and Kentaro were in their forties when they adopted the hyperactive three-year-old child of one of Kentaro's distant cousins, who just couldn't handle the stress of being a young single mother any longer. It turned out Taiga wasn't hyperactive after all—he was just off-the-charts smart.

As Julian went out the door, Rose added, "Be careful. You know how much I worry about you on that damn motor scooter. I wish you'd just ride a bike like me. It's so much safer to be on the sidewalks."

"That's for wimps," he said, grinning. He pecked her on the lips, put on his helmet, and wheeled the scooter out of the garden.

Rose listened to the sound of the engine until it faded into the distance and then went back into the kitchen. She'd had enough coffee, so she poured the rest of hers down the drain.

What should she do now? Mark essays? Prepare for her presentation coming up in Hong Kong? Revise the manuscript of her new book?

With a to-do list a mile long, she had the overwhelming urge to sort out the kitchen cabinets, to weed through the closets, or to clean out her cosmetics drawer. The house always became spotless whenever deadlines loomed overhead. She knew she should get all that university stuff out of the way before Yuka and Zach arrived with the kids next week, but she just wasn't in the mood to work. Instead, she went into the living room, and tried to decide which parts of it needed altering to accommodate two overactive preschoolers.

When she and Julian rebuilt the house in 2005, they decided, after discussing it with the girls and Obaachan, not to keep the cumbersome family altar where the wood had rotted away in the back. Instead, she had a Buddhist temple remove the ancestral spirits from the old altar, and then, in another ceremony, they had them rehoused into a mini-altar that fit neatly into the newly built-in bookcases. Rose and Julian didn't really believe in any of that, but the ceremonies at the temple did make Obaachan happy.

Rose knew that visitors to their home thought it was strange to have an ancestral altar and photos of Akira, her first husband, and Sumiko, Akira's first wife, on prominent display in their living room. But that never bothered her or Julian.

"Without them," Julian would say to anyone who'd listen, "our family wouldn't be here. Without them, where would I be? Everything that happened before—all those people—they were the making of *us*. The making of our family." Julian always looked full of pride whenever he talked about his family.

And, of course, Rose agreed with him. Because without Sumiko, without Akira, and even without Akira's entire family ahead of him, the life Rose was leading now wouldn't exist.

She took Akira's picture down from the shelf and dusted it off with the corner of her shirt. If he were still alive, he'd be in his late sixties. Would he have a middle-aged paunch? A balding head? False teeth? Impossible to imagine! He lived forever in her mind as a smiling, handsome thirty-eight-year-old.

The age he was when he died in that awful accident.

Chapter Forty-Three

Thursday, March 22, 1990. Most of what had happened that day was a blur, but of all the bizarre things Rose could remember—that was the day George Bush had announced to the world that he didn't like broccoli. And as President of the United States, no one could force him to eat it. They all had a good laugh over that at the breakfast table, especially since Yuka and Emi were arguing over who'd get the last broccoli floret in their breakfast salad.

Akira had taken the morning off to go with his mother to Keio Hospital. Because she'd been experiencing an increasing amount of chest pain and shortness of breath, her doctors were recommending coronary bypass surgery. Before making any concrete decisions, she wanted Akira to speak to her doctor as well. The meeting was productive, and it turned out she wouldn't need to decide anything right away. To celebrate, they were going to go have lunch at a popular Italian restaurant that had just opened up in Aoyama.

They stepped into the intersection when the light changed to cross the street to get a taxi going in that direction. But a small truck ran through the red light at full speed and plowed into four pedestrians. Two of those pedestrians were Akira Kato and his mother Michie Kato.

Rose was at her desk in their tiny upstairs study, preparing to start her fifth year as a tenured associate professor at Yamanote University, when the phone rang a little before noon. At first, she couldn't catch what the caller was saying. The woman spoke so fast, and after becoming frustrated by Rose's incomprehension, she began shouting. As if *that* would help.

Eventually, though, Rose understood. And in that moment, her life changed forever.

A fifty-five-year-old driver from Fuchu had suffered a massive and fatal stroke while driving and lost control of his car. Emergency staff from Keio Hospital rushed to the intersection to administer first aid. Akira's mother and a forty-year-old father of three elementary school children died within minutes of the accident. A college student from Kyoto had both legs and her left arm broken, but she suffered no other serious injuries. Akira was alive when Rose reached the emergency room, but his body was as shattered as if he'd been a porcelain doll thrown against a concrete wall. Rose hardly recognized him. But when he opened his eyes, she could see he was still there under all the bandages.

It was obvious he wouldn't be for long, though.

Obaachan, who was visiting Osamu and Yoko in Kyushu, flew back to Tokyo immediately. In shock, the two of them arranged the funeral for Akira's mother. And then, just a week later, a funeral for Akira. The funeral company handled the details—the Buddhist services, the wakes, and the banquets. Akira's friends and colleagues at Tominaga Corporation took care of the condolence tables and recorded the contents of the cash envelopes at both funerals. Rose could scarcely remember to breathe, let alone eat. In black formal wear, holding Yuka and Emi's hands and trying to stop her tears, she bowed to the mourners as they paid their respects. Behind the scenes, though, her friends held her while she sobbed. They fixed meals for her and the girls. They tried to take away some of the burden of her having to put on a stoic public face to the world.

The same people who celebrated with her at her wedding were with her again when she needed them most. And there were her new friends from AFWJ, the foreign wives' club she'd joined before she'd married Akira. They rallied behind her in practical and emotional matters.

For weeks, Rose felt numb. It was all she could do to put one foot ahead of the other. For the first time since high school, she had a slim figure, but the bags under her eyes just made her look old. She got out of bed and took care of routine matters because of the girls. She wanted to seem normal in front of them.

But inside, she was dead.

One month after Akira died, Rose was reborn as a tiger.

No one, but *no one,* was going to take her daughters away from her.

She had always planned to adopt Yuka and Emi, but she and Akira imagined they had all the time in the world. They never dreamed their lives would shatter the way it did. They never dreamed Sumiko's brother would sue for his nieces' custody. That he would publicly announce Rose was an unfit foreign mother.

What was at stake, of course, and everybody knew it, was their inheritance. Akira had inherited his mother's estate, and when Akira died a week later, the estate was divided according to Japanese inheritance law: fifty percent for Rose and fifty percent for the children. Unknown to her, Osamu and Yoko had already gone through the money Obaachan had given them a few years earlier. And now that his nieces were quite wealthy, he saw an opportunity too good to ignore. Behind a phony veil of concern for their physical and emotional welfare, he went to court.

Akira's bank accounts were frozen when he died, but that wasn't a problem since Rose had plenty of her own money in her own bank accounts. She could pay for both of the funerals and take care of all their household bills. She knew Akira's family wasn't poor, but she never imagined how much money there was. From the family lawyer, she learned the value of the two residential properties in the heart of Tokyo, a resort home in Karuizawa, a small apartment building in Shinagawa (which she had known nothing about) and cash and investments. Even the book her father-in-law had written decades earlier was still bringing in royalties. Rose gasped when the lawyer informed her the inheritance tax was going to be hundreds of thousands of dollars. But then he advised her to sell the apartment building in Shinagawa. That was why it had been bought in the first place—it was a hedge for the inheritance taxes.

Osamu couldn't touch Rose's share of the inheritance, but he did his damnedest to get hold of Yuka's and Emi's. And he might have been able to win that fight because there were plenty of people who agreed with him. How could a foreigner raise Japanese daughters in the proper Japanese way?

But Akira, as broken as he was after the accident, made a hand-written document, naming Rose as his daughters' legal guardian. Osamu's lawyer pointed out loopholes in the document and even insinuated Rose must have pressured a dying man to sign things over to her instead of to his Japanese relatives. But the nurses, who had given Akira the pen and paper and who had acted as signature witnesses, testified he was completely lucid when he wrote down his last wishes. Rose, they told the court, wasn't even in the room at the time.

Thank goodness Japan protected the privacy of minors, and the girls' names weren't dragged through the media in a court case that caught the attention of the tabloids. Luckily, her university was sympathetic when she had to take weeks off to go to court, where she had to listen to Osamu's lawyer paint her as a flighty foreigner with multiple sexual partners (a lie!) who planned to return to the USA with all that Japanese money she'd gotten her hands on (another lie!).

"That foreign woman is not a blood relative to those children like my client, and she is not Japanese. Therefore," the shady lawyer had basically argued, "there is nothing more to say."

True, Rose wasn't the girls' biological mother. But she was the only mother they knew. She loved them and they loved her. The judge ruled in her favor, probably because of her excellent lawyer, who also happened to be Naoko's mother. Once again, her students from her favorite class when she taught at Friendly had come through for her. They certainly were the Super Six!

It also didn't hurt that Rose was permanently employed by one of the most prestigious universities in Japan—one Osamu would never have been able to step foot in as a student.

It was Obaachan's testimony that did the trick, though. And that Osamu hadn't expected. He never imagined his own mother would stand up in court and say that no one but Rose would be the best mother and guardian for her grandchildren, the daughters of her dearly beloved deceased daughter. Certainly not her son or his wife. She went on to list so many reasons why, the judge finally had to stop her.

All the petty grievances between Rose and Obaachan were no longer important. It didn't matter that Rose didn't do the laundry properly. It didn't matter that Obaachan gave the girls candy right before dinner, even though Rose always asked her not to. Rose felt a love for Obaachan as strong as if she were her own mother. Stronger, in fact, because she could never imagine her mom standing up in her defense the way Obaachan had done. In fact, she'd come right out and said Rose was crazy for fighting so hard for children she had no biological obligation to raise. She thought Rose should cut her losses and come home with her share of the inheritance.

As if that were an option!

Rose won the court case, and the girls were safe with her. The judge ordered Osamu to cover all the hefty court fees as well. She'd never forgive that man or his wife for what they had put her through when all she wanted to do was mourn the loss of her husband. It was difficult to put a price tag on her suffering, but it was sweet knowing that he had been hit where it hurt him the most.

Obaachan made an irrevocable choice when she aligned herself with Rose, and there'd be no going back. Rose became the daughter she had lost. She owed her that. Some people may have thought she had been saddled with a giant ball and chain, but she didn't see it that way. It was love, pure and simple. She legally adopted her daughters, and she informally adopted a new mother as well.

Rose rented Akira's mother's house to an expat family who wanted to live in a Japanese neighborhood more than one where foreigners tended to live. Obaachan moved back to her old room in Akira's house, and she took up pretty much where she had left off five years earlier. Spry as ever, she managed all the household details.

Rose's job kept her busy, but she attended every PTA meeting and volunteered when she could at the girls' schools. Everyone became accustomed to the blond foreign woman with her Japanese daughters. Newcomers—teachers or students or their parents—gawked at them in surprise, reminding her how unusual her family was. But people quickly learned to never ever call the Kato girls *hafu*. They weren't half Japanese and half American. They were *Japanese* children, Rose said once, pounding her fist on the desk of a hardheaded junior high school teacher. They were bicultural. Bilingual. But they were not half.

She was also grateful Michael had persuaded her to start her PhD. Work, family, and study had stretched her so thin she thought at times she might snap in two. But it also kept her focused and her mind clear. She'd have dinner with her family in the evenings, and while the girls and Obaachan watched silly shows on TV, Rose went upstairs to study or to mark papers. Sometimes she read novels, usually mysteries. Never love stories.

She was content. Life was good, and she loved her family. But she was lonely.

Until she met Julian.

Chapter Forty-Four

"Akira," Rose said, looking over and speaking to the photo on the bookcase again. "You were right way back when you said it was possible to love two people. Remember when I was worried if you could love both me and Sumiko?"

She never imagined she'd find love again after Akira died, but she did. Akira'd had his second chance, and then she'd had hers.

She met Julian in the Temple University library on a Saturday afternoon when she was working on the discussion chapter of her dissertation. Julian, who specialized in pragmatics and was a professor at Waseda University, was teaching a graduate course at Temple University that semester. The library was nearly empty, and the two of them started talking. They ended up going to a café and staying for three hours. The next night, they went to an Italian restaurant in Shibuya. Rose had been upfront about her complicated family from the get-go, but that didn't faze Julian one bit.

After several months of seeing each other, Rose brought him home to meet everyone. Obaachan and the girls adored him right from the very beginning. He could make everyone laugh with his silly antics. He was a good listener. A good talker, with plenty of stories. He also spoke fluent Japanese—far better than Rose.

Julian also believed in second chances. His own marriage to a Japanese woman broke up when she decided, after ten years, that she simply no longer wanted to be married to him. Later, he came to believe that was because he was destined to be with Rose. By the time they got married in 1994 in a small ceremony in Hawaii, they already felt like a family. With no children of his own, he was happy for Yuka and Emi, fourteen and twelve, to call him "Dad." And not willing to leave anything up to chance, they became his legal daughters as well. Of course, Akira would always be their papa and Sumiko would always be their mama. Their parents were now simply Mom and Dad.

Later that summer, Yuka and Emi went to a language camp in Australia, and Rose and Julian went to Karuizawa. They needed to take care of some of the structural problems in the old Kato house, but they also wanted to spend some time alone together, like honeymooners. Rose rarely visited that house, because it was too cold in the winter, and in the summer, she usually took the girls to Nebraska.

The place was old and musty, but it was sprawling and solidly built. It was filled to the brim with things the Kato family had brought from Tokyo, things that had escaped the wartime firebombing: old furniture, old kimonos, old pottery, and old books. Julian joked that if their day jobs ever fell through, they could open up a chain of antique stores. Rose was tempted to just shut the doors and pretend none of it existed.

When Rose first heard Julian shouting from one of the storage rooms on the second day of their visit, she thought he was having a stroke or a heart attack.

"Are you okay?" she asked, rushing to the room.

"Look what I found!" Julian sputtered, holding out a small cedar box.

Rose sat down on a creaky wooden stool and opened it. After studying the contents for a moment, she looked up at him, disbelief all over her face. "Is this what I think it is?"

"I think so," he replied.

"How come no one in the family ever said Isabella Bird was a family connection?" Rose gently lifted out bundles of letters that were tied together with a faded blue satin cord.

"Maybe we should look at them more carefully in a different place," suggested Julian. "Somewhere less dusty. You wouldn't want to damage any of them."

"You're right." But a perfunctory glance showed the famous British explorer's name was clearly written on the envelopes, all of which were addressed to the same person: Gonbei Kato. Rose had never heard of him, but he had to have been one of Akira's ancestors.

That night, in the clean and dust-free room they slept in, they poured over everything and discovered that somehow Isabella Bird had struck up a friendship with Akira's great-great-great-grandfather, whom they'd learned from the letters, had studied law in the UK as a part of the Iwakura Mission in the 1870s.

"How come no one in the family knew about this?" Rose asked for the hundredth time that night. "How come this important bit of history was never mentioned?"

This was big. Very big.

"Maybe the two of them were more than just friends," suggested Julian. "She wrote to him for years. Look, here's a letter postmarked from her travels in Korea. And another from China. This one's from Egypt."

"Do you think I could do something with any of this?" Rose asked. "I mean, in terms of research? You know how sick to death I am of child language acquisition."

Julian laughed, knowing that Rose had only gone in that research direction because of her MA in Child Development. Everyone in her university had expected her to combine that with language, but she'd never been all that crazy about linguistics. "Why not? With your Ph.D. behind you, you can do whatever you want. I'm pretty sure no one has *anything* like this. When we get home, you can check online and see what's out there."

And Rose did exactly that.

Her seminal book on the famous Victorian explorer, Isabella Bird, was published by Oxford University Press in 2003, and as a result, she was invited to speak at conferences all over the world. But even better, inspiration hit, and she turned her knowledge of that remarkable woman into children's stories. Her series featuring Isabella Bird and the children she met while traveling around the world was both a critical and a commercial success. Every one of those fifteen books was dedicated to Akira.

Rose always marveled that she had been on the brink of leaving Japan in 1985 and going back to Nebraska. But she followed her heart, took a great leap of faith, and stayed. She couldn't imagine having any other life but the one she had now. She had been so lucky—she found her way to this world, where she not only had two great loves but also two great daughters.

Sometimes she felt sad thinking of her only pregnancy. Because no matter how hard she and Akira (and later she and Julian) had tried, she never got pregnant again. But she believed someday she'd meet the little spirit she had to release into the cosmos. Meanwhile, she liked to imagine he or she was spending time with Akira and Sumiko until that day came.

Rose was jolted out of her thoughts when her phone vibrated in her pocket. It was Emi.

"Mom! The jeweler just called. Grandma Kato's ring is ready. Do you want to come with me to go pick it up? We could have lunch afterwards. Just you and me."

"I'd love to, sweetie. I can't think of anything else I'd rather do today."

Glossary of Selected Japanese Terms

Baba	Informal/ friendly term for grandmother
-chan	A friendly form of "san" (often for children), attached to a person's given name
Eikaiwa	English conversation class. Sometimes referring to an English conversation school
Futon	Padded bedding for sleeping on the floor, generally in a *tatami* room
Gaijin	Foreigner
Gaikokujin kyoshi	Foreign instructor (a university appointment often given to foreigners in Japan from the 1950-1990s)
Genkan	Front entryway where people take off their shoes
Irashaimase	Said by staff in shops and restaurants to welcome customers. "Welcome"
Itadakimasu	Polite words, commonly said before eating something. Literally translated to mean "I'm going to eat"

Izakaya	An eating/drinking establishment
Jiji	Grandpa
Jizo	Small Buddhist statue found in some temples
Kaachan	Informal form of "*Okaasan*" (mother)
Kampai	Said when raising glasses for a toast. "Cheers!"
Karaoke	Singing with recorded music. Sometimes in bars but often in *karaoke* businesses where friends can rent a room for singing and drinking
Konnichiwa	A greeting. "Good day" or "Good afternoon"
Kotatsu	A low table used in winter with a built-in heater under the tabletop and covered with a quilt
Love Hotel	A hotel, often quite nice, frequented by couples where rooms can be rented by the hour and/or overnight
Moshi-moshi	Said when answering the phone. "Hello"
Obaachan	Informal/friendly term for grandmother (*Obaasan*). Can be used

for one's own grandmother or for an elderly woman

Obento

A boxed lunch

Obon

Summer holiday in the middle of August where families pay respect to their ancestors

Ochazuke

Hot tea poured over rice. Often eaten at the end of the meal

Ohayo gozaimasu

Good morning

Okonomiyaki

Japanese style savory pancake

Omiai

A formal introduction for couples that could lead to marriage

Oshibori

A hot or cold towel (depending on the season) given to customers at the beginning of a meal

Ososhiki

Funeral

-san

An honorific attached to a family or first name, with the meaning of Mr., Mrs., or Ms. For example: Rose-san

Sensei

Teacher

Shichimi

A seasoning made of seven spices.

Shiokara	A pickled dish, generally made with fermented squid innards and commonly served as a first course in an *izakaya* when one orders an alcoholic drink
Shochu	A Japanese distilled spirit made from sweet potatoes, barley, or rice
Tatami	A matted flooring made of straw for Japanese rooms. An average sized room is generally made up of six *tatami* mats
Yakisoba	Fried noodles
Yakitori	Grilled chicken on a stick
Yakuza	Japanese gangster

Acknowledgements

I am truly grateful for the many people in the vibrant writing community in Japan who have encouraged and helped me polish my craft over the years, especially the members of the Tokyo Writers Workshop and the organizers and attendees of the annual Japan Writers Conference.

I would also like to say thank you to friends who have read and commented on various versions of *The Making of Us*, including Stephanie Tanimura (who came up with the idea for the book's title), Melissa Noguchi, and Louise George Kittaka. Thank you so much!

Special thanks must also go to Japan-based authors Suzanne Kamata and Lea O'Harra for their incredible feedback on an early version of this book. You both are truly are my inspiration!

Thank you to my publisher Reagan Rothe and the incredible publishing team at Black Rose Writing for believing in me. I'm proud to be a member of the supportive and talented Black Rose Writing family, where I have made many friends.

I would also like to say a special thank you to the members of AFWJ (formerly known as the Association of Foreign Wives of Japanese) for not only being my lifeline ever since I became a member in 1982, but also for being my sisters in Japan. Without all of you, I don't think I could have survived the ups and downs of living in Japan for almost five decades.

Finally, thank you to my family and friends who have always supported me in all of my dreams, and especially my grandchildren for always making me laugh: Tory, Narushi, Luca, Elio, Yukiya, and Serena. And, of course, I'm sending a million hugs for my very special angel in heaven, Kaho Margaret.

About the Author

Diane Hawley Nagatomo was born in the UK and lived in Nebraska, Spain, Massachusetts, New Mexico, and California before coming to Japan in 1979. She is a semi-retired professor from Ochanomizu University and has written extensively on issues concerning gender, culture, and education. She is also the author of two other novels: *The Butterfly Cafe* and *Finding Naomi*. While not teaching or writing, she and her Japanese husband of more than 40 years spend time with their six grandchildren.

Other Titles by Diane Hawley Nagatomo

Note from
Diane Hawley Nagatomo

Word-of-mouth is crucial for any author to succeed. If you enjoyed *The Making of Us*, please leave a review online—anywhere you are able. Even if it's just a sentence or two. It would make all the difference and would be very much appreciated.

Thanks!
Diane Hawley Nagatomo

We hope you enjoyed reading this title from:

www.blackrosewriting.com

Subscribe to our mailing list – *The Rosevine* – and receive **FREE** books, daily deals, and stay current with news about upcoming releases and our hottest authors.
Scan the QR code below to sign up.

Already a subscriber? Please accept a sincere thank you for being a fan of Black Rose Writing authors.

View other Black Rose Writing titles at www.blackrosewriting.com/books and use promo code **PRINT** to receive a **20% discount** when purchasing.